MURPHY

SATAN'S FURY MEMPHIS

L. WILDER

D1558666

Murphy

Satan's Fury MC Memphis
Copyright 2019 L. Wilder
All rights reserved.

*BookBub- https://www.bookbub.com/authors/l-wilder

L. Wilder's Newsletter (sign up for giveaways and news about upcoming releases) http://eepurl.com/dvSpW5

*Special acknowledgement- The quote, *Murphy's Law- Anything that* *can go wrong, will go wrong,* was written by Edward A. Murphy, an engineer who was working on Air Force Project MX981.

Cover Details:

Cover Model: Josh Mario

Photographer: Wander Aguiar

Cover Design: Mayhem Cover Creations
www.facebook.com/MayhemCoverCreations

Editor: Lisa Cullinan

Proofreader- Rose Holub www.facebook.com/ReadbyRose/

Teasers & Banners: Gel Ytayz at Tempting Illustrations

Personal Assistant: Natalie Weston PA

Catch up with the entire Satan's Fury MC Series today!

All books are FREE with Kindle Unlimited!

Summer Storm (Satan's Fury MC Novella)

Maverick (Satan's Fury MC #1)

Stitch (Satan's Fury MC #2)

Cotton (Satan's Fury MC #3)

Clutch (Satan's Fury MC #4)

Smokey (Satan's Fury MC #5)

Big (Satan's Fury #6)

Two Bit (Satan's Fury #7)

Diesel (Satan's Fury #8)

Blaze (Satan's Fury Memphis Chapter)

Shadow (Satan's Fury Memphis Chapter)

Riggs (Satan's Fury Memphis Chapter)

Murphy (Satan's Fury Memphis Chapter)

Damaged Goods- (The Redemption Series Book 1- Nitro)

Max's Redemption (The Redemption Series Book 2- Max)

Inferno (Devil Chasers #1)

Smolder (Devil Chaser #2)

Ignite (Devil Chasers #3)

Consumed (Devil Chasers #4)

Combust (Devil Chasers #5)

The Long Road Home (Devil Chasers #6)

My Temptation (The Happy Endings Collection #1)

Bring the Heat (The Happy Endings Collection #2)

His Promise (The Happy Endings Collection #3)

❀ Created with Vellum

QUOTE ACKNOWLEDGEMENT-

Murphy's Law- Anything that can go wrong, will go wrong.
-Captain Edward A. Murphy

PROLOGUE

Whether it's been a mishap, a heartbreak, or an unexpected turn of events, we've all had at least one of those defining moments that have marked us in one way or another, changing us forever. I'd like to say that I'd only had one of those moments in my life, but sadly, there'd been more than I could count. Each time it had taken a piece of me, scarring me right down to my soul—the first one was the day my old man packed up all his shit and walked out on my mom and me.

My father was a lowlife asshole who took advantage of my mother and anyone else who'd let him, so I figured we were better off without him. My mother didn't agree. His leaving had gotten to her in ways I'll never understand. She started going out at night, partying and sleeping around like a fucking teenager. By the time I was sixteen, I'd stopped keeping track of the men who my mother moved in and out of our house—all of them had bolted as soon as she mentioned the word marriage.

I figured she'd give up on men altogether, but she never stopped trying. She was continuously on the hunt for her Mr. Right, leaving me to my own vices—which suited me just fine. I'd have rather been with Amy, my best friend and future fiancé, than anyone else in the world anyway.

Amy lived next door, so she knew things at my place weren't exactly the greatest, but she understood, especially since her home life wasn't much better. There were times when things got pretty rough for both of us, but together we'd find a way to pick up the pieces. Thankfully, things weren't always bad. In fact, we had a lot of good times together, no matter what we were doing or where we were, so it was no surprise that as we grew older, our friendship turned into something more.

We were both seventeen, naive and full of hope, sitting on her window ledge with our feet dangling out onto the roof. After several minutes of comfortable silence, I glanced over at Amy. It was clear from her expression that she had something on her mind, so I asked, "You okay?"

"Do you think your mom is happy?"

"I don't know. I guess. Why?"

"I just think it's sad that she hasn't found someone who genuinely loves her. I would think that would really hurt."

"Maybe ... but she seems to think that Joe is 'the one.' He supposedly loves her," I scoffed.

"Yeah, well ... she said the same thing about Danny, Rick, and John, but all those jerks ended up breaking her heart."

"I suppose, but you have to give her credit. She hasn't stopped trying."

"Give her credit? Are you kidding me?" Her eyes skirted over to me. "She's all but forgotten that she has a son who she should be taking care of."

"I can take care of myself."

"That's not the point, Linc. You shouldn't have to take care of yourself. That's what moms are for," she argued.

"I guess both of our moms missed that whole *good-parenting* lesson."

"You can say that again."

She looked up at the stars above, and after several moments, she asked, "Do you ever think about the future?"

It wasn't a question I expected her to ask, and I certainly had no idea what kind of answer she was hoping for, so I hesitated with my response. "Um ... *yeah*. Sometimes."

"When you think about it"—her blue eyes locked on mine—"what do you see?"

"I don't know. What do you see?"

"Oh, no you don't." She leaned towards me, nudging me with her shoulder. "You can't answer a question with a question, Lincoln."

"All right, then." I gave her a quick shrug as I answered, "When I think about the future, I see *you*."

A soft smile crossed her face. "You do?"

"Well, yeah. It's always been you and me. I can't imagine my life without you in it." I inched my arm around her waist and asked, "What about you? What do you see when you think about the future?"

"I see us in a little white house with a front porch swing and flowers along the walkway." Her voice was low, almost a whisper, as she continued, "It's a thousand miles from here, and our parents have no idea where we are. There's no yelling ... no fighting ... and there's food on the table every night. Things are good. Things are the way they're supposed to be."

"Sounds pretty damn good to me."

"Yeah, it sure does."

I pulled her close to me and said, "I'll do whatever it takes to give you all that and more, Amy. Just wait and see."

With no means to go to college, I decided to join the military. Amy wasn't exactly thrilled with the idea about me leaving, especially for such long increments of time, but I assured her that it was the quickest way for us to get that little white house with the front porch swing. Our time apart was hard on both of us, but with each day that passed, it got a little easier. I'd only been gone a few months when Amy started nursing school. Even though she was busy, she still found time to write me every day, and we talked on the phone as often as possible. Without even knowing it, Amy had gotten me through some pretty rough spots. I'd close my eyes, think about her crystal-blue eyes and adorable smile, and I would get a temporary reprieve from the death and destruction that surrounded me. She gave me something to live for, so when I returned from training, I asked her to marry me. By then, she'd gotten a taste of the military life. She had an idea of what it would be like to be a soldier's wife, and even though she knew it wouldn't be easy, she accepted my proposal, assuring me that she loved me enough to put our life together on hold for a little longer.

While there were many things that marked me during my four years in the Army, it wasn't until the end of my tour in Afghanistan that I encountered my second defining moment. After spending over nine months overseas, I was finally heading home. I'd never been gone that long before and was eager to get back to Amy. She had no idea I was coming, so it was going to be one hell of a surprise. I couldn't wait to see the look on her face when she opened the door and found me standing on the other side, so as soon as the plane landed in Memphis, I got my rental car and headed over to our place. As soon as I pulled up to the house, I grabbed my bag out of the car and rushed up the front porch steps. I knocked on the door, and my heart started racing when I heard rumbling inside the house. Moments later, the door flew open and Amy appeared with a startled look on her face.

Instead of jumping into my arms, she cinched her bathrobe tightly around her waist as she gasped. "Linc? What are you doing here?"

Paying no regard to her odd behavior, I stepped forward and wrapped my arms around her waist, lifting her in the air as I hugged her tightly. "I'm on leave for the next two weeks, baby."

With a half-hearted hug, she asked, "Why didn't you tell me?"

"I wanted to surprise you."

"Well, you definitely did that," she mumbled under her breath. "I wish you would've told me you were coming. I would've met you at the airport."

"I know, but like I said, I wanted to surprise you." I lowered my mouth to her neck, and as I started to trail kisses along the curve of her jaw, I whispered, "Damn, I've missed you. I can't tell you how good it is to see you."

"It's good to see you too."

When she started to pull away from me, I quickly lowered her feet to the ground and said, "I've got another surprise for you."

I reached into my back pocket and pulled out an envelope. As I handed it over to her, she said, "I don't know if I can handle any more surprises right now, Linc."

"Well, this is one that can't wait." I watched her expression as she opened the envelope. "I've wanted to do this for a long time but just didn't have the means to make it happen. That all changed this summer when I was promoted to corporal."

A look of confusion crossed her face as she stared at the two tickets to Cancun. "What is this?"

"We're eloping, baby. It's time for us to make things official."

I'd barely gotten the words out of my mouth when a man came walking down the hall. He was a tall guy with dark hair. I don't remember much more than that, other than the fact that he was only wearing a pair of boxers as he asked, "Amy ... is everything okay?"

"Who the fuck are you?" I roared.

"I'm, uh ... umm," he stammered.

He was too freaked out to answer, but it didn't matter. I knew by the look on his face that he'd been screwing around with Amy, and that's all I needed to know. Rage washed over me as I lunged towards him and growled, "You goddamn motherfucker!"

"Wait." Amy reached for me as she shrieked, "Linc ... Don't."

As soon as the asshole realized I was about to beat the hell out of him, he held up his hands at his sides and pleaded, "Look, man. I don't want any trouble."

"You should've thought about that before you started fucking my girl!"

I reared my fist back and then punched him in the face, nearly knocking him out. His head flew back as blood spewed from his mouth. Before he had a chance to recover, I slammed my fist into his gut. He toppled forward as he wrapped his arms around his stomach, but it did little to protect him from my continuous blows to his abdomen and face. I hit him again and again, and in a matter of seconds, he was a puddled mess on the floor. Worried that I might actually kill him, Amy scurried in front of me and pushed me back as she shouted, "Stop, Linc!"

When I saw the panicked look on her face, I froze. With my heart pounding rapidly in my chest, I inhaled a deep breath and tried to rein in my anger. I grit my teeth as I snarled, "What the fuck is this guy doing in my house, Amy?"

"I'll explain everything, but you're gonna have to stop and listen to me."

"Just tell me!"

She cradled his face in her hands, and with complete adoration in her voice, she said, "This is Kevin. He's one of the doctors from the hospital. We've been seeing each other for the past few months, and—"

"What?" I motioned my hand towards the douchebag on the floor. "You've been seeing him for months, and you didn't fucking tell me!"

"I wanted to, but I just didn't know how." She looked up at me with sad eyes and said, "You have to know that I loved you, Lincoln. I wanted a life with you ... the life we dreamed about, but you just kept putting me off. It was always, just a few more months .... First it was training, and then, you headed off to Afghanistan and I had no idea if you were ever coming back! I couldn't take it."

"So, you go and spread your legs for some asshole doctor you've been working with?"

"It's not like that, Linc." She stood up and looked me right in the eye. "We started out as friends ... He listened to me. He was there for me, and—"

"He listened to you? Are you fucking kidding me?"

"He's a good man, Lincoln."

"I'm sure he's a goddamn prince!"

"You're not being fair!" She reached for my arm, clinging to me as she said, "You knew how I felt about you leaving. I tried to get you to stay. I begged you, but you just wouldn't listen."

"So, you decided to act like a fucking whore and shack up with someone else?"

"Look, you can put all of this on me if that makes you feel better, but we both know that's not true!"

"I'm done listening to this bullshit, Amy." As I started for the door, I noticed several boxes and bags of luggage stacked in the doorway. I'd busted my ass to get her that

8

house with the fucking swing on the front porch, but it was all for nothing. I turned and glared at her with disgust. "I want you out by morning. Leave the key in the mailbox."

With that, I grabbed my bag and stormed out of the house, slamming the door behind me. From there, I don't even know how I made it back to my rental car. I was totally consumed with emotion—rage, heartbreak, and absolute disbelief. I looked back at the house, and a feeling of anguish washed over me when I saw Amy standing there with tears in her eyes. I could've gone back and tried to talk it out with her, but I knew that wasn't gonna change a damn thing. We could never go back to the way things were. My heart would still be broken. *I would still be broken*. I glanced down at the plane tickets to Cancun and ripped them to shreds before tossing them out the window. I was done. Love was just some fucked up illusion. Unlike my mother, I wouldn't spend my life looking for something that simply didn't exist.

1

MURPHY

While we'd won battle after battle, Satan's Fury was always at war. It was the price we paid for reigning supreme over the Memphis territory. With the Mississippi River at our fingertips, everyone knew it was a sweet spot and wanted to claim it as their own. Unfortunately for them, that meant going head-to-head with the most notorious MC in the south. While we always managed to come out on top, we'd never faced an enemy like Josue Navarro—a Mexican cartel boss with an unrelenting thirst for revenge. His brother, Rodrigo, had come to Memphis looking to score big, but he'd gotten himself killed in the process, leaving his brother clueless as to who was to blame. Even though we weren't the ones who actually pulled the trigger, the blame still fell on our shoulders, and Navarro set his sights on ending us all. We knew he had the means to destroy everything we'd worked for, but we'd never cowered down from a fight. We'd been preparing to take him head on when he was arrested for killing Jason Brazzle, his niece's best friend. We all knew he'd try to get the charges dropped, but there was no way that was gonna happen with an eyewitness and photographic evidence. Our problem was solved, but there was a catch.

The eyewitness—the person who was willing to put her life on the line to put him behind bars—was Reece Winters, my brother Riggs's old lady. She was a reporter for the *Memphis Metro* and had been working on a piece about the cartel. Hoping to get information on Navarro's brother, Reece had gone to question Jason. When she arrived at his apartment that day, she was surprised to find Navarro and his men were there. From the fire escape window, Reece had watched Navarro kill Jason and reported it to the police. Shortly after, she became their prime witness, and they asked her to testify at his trial. Knowing that she and her son were in serious danger, Gus, Fury's president, had arranged for us to get her to safety. T-Bone, Gunner, and I, along with Riggs and two of our prospects, Crow and Rider, packed up Reece and her son and headed up to Jed's cabin in the Appalachian Mountains—a place where we could protect her from Navarro's watchful eye. While we'd felt certain that Reece and her son would be safe there, I wasn't taking any chances. As the club's sergeant-at-arms, it was my responsibility to ensure everyone's safety. It was a job that I took very seriously, so I'd left no stone unturned as I set up a list of strict surveillance procedures for each of us to follow. The brothers and I would take shifts monitoring the grounds with every precaution to make sure that no one came snooping around.

After living there for over a month, we'd all settled into our routines, and while everything seemed to be going as planned, I wasn't about to let my guard down. The trial was quickly approaching, which meant Navarro would be even more desperate to track down Reece and end her before she had a chance to testify. There was no way in hell we were going to let that happen. Not on my watch. I was on my way out to relieve Riggs from his post when Gunner came barreling in from outside. As he started taking off his hat and gloves, I asked, "Did you complete the perimeter check?"

"I did." He removed his thick winter coat and tossed it onto the back of one of the kitchen chairs. "All clear."

"And what about Crow? You check in with him?"

"Yep. He's good, as always." Gunner reached for the coffee pot, then added, "The kid has a knack for this shit. Might be time for us to consider patching him in."

"Yeah. He's a good kid. I'll be sure to mention it to Gus."

As Gunner headed straight towards the fridge, he asked, "Is there any more of that lasagna left from last night?"

"I don't think so. I'm pretty sure T-Bone finished it off for breakfast."

"Damn. We're gonna have to put a muzzle on that man before he eats us out of house and home."

"At least we don't have to worry about having a garbage disposal."

"You ain't lying there, brother," he chuckled. "There's nothing that man won't eat."

"Maybe we should get Reece to cook him up a mess of brussels sprouts and see what he does with those."

"Hell, yes. And maybe some beets and liverwurst. I'd pay money to see that."

"Knowing him, he'd scarf them down like there's no tomorrow." I pulled on my hat, grabbed my thermos filled with hot coffee, and started towards the door. "I'm gonna go relieve Riggs. Let me know if anything comes up."

"You know I will."

Just as I was about to walk out of the kitchen, he tossed his scarf over to me. "You're gonna need that. The wind is blowing out of the east, and it'll chill ya down to the bone."

"Thanks, man."

I wrapped it around my neck, but it did little to protect me from the arctic wind as I stepped out onto the porch. The fresh fallen snow glittered and shined like diamonds under the light of the full moon, which made the forest look like a winter wonderland. The only sound I could hear was the icy layer crushing beneath my feet as I trampled through the knee-deep white stuff and made my way over to Riggs. When I walked up to him, he looked up at me and smiled. "Before you ask ... Yes, I did the perimeter check, and everything's clear."

I shrugged. "Wasn't even gonna ask."

"Yeah, right. We both know you can't help yourself," he teased.

"What can I say?" I glanced back over at the house as I said, "Gotta keep Reece and that boy of yours safe."

"You got that right."

Riggs was the club hacker, and with his particular

skillset, he was able to get the most updated information on just about anything. Knowing the trial was just two weeks away, I asked, "Any news about Navarro?"

"Not a damn thing." Concern crossed his face as he continued, "I gotta tell ya, brother ... the closer this trial gets, the more nervous I get. Navarro knows that with Reece's testimony he's toast. He has to be feeling pretty fucking desperate right about now, and desperate people do some fucked-up shit."

"I'm sure Reece feels the same way." I shook my head and added, "She has to be nervous about testifying."

"Yeah. She's been trying to put on a brave front, but I know it's worrying her. I don't think she's been sleeping all that well. That's one of the reasons why I have something special planned for her tonight."

"Something special, huh? Well, don't keep her waiting. Get your ass inside."

"You don't have to tell me twice." As he started towards the house, he handed me the two-way radio. He hadn't gotten very far when he shouted, "It's gonna be a cold one tonight."

"No different than last night. At least the snow has finally stopped falling."

"You're right about that. I'll check in with you in a bit. Try to stay warm!"

The bitter wind howled through the trees, biting at my flesh as I headed towards the back gate. I wanted nothing more than to go back to the cabin and sit by the fire, but it would be hours before that happened. As I tromped through the heavy snow with my teeth chattering and my bones aching, I found it hard to believe that I ever enjoyed a single moment of winter, but when I was a kid, I loved the snow. Hell, I couldn't get enough of it. There was nothing better than putting on a pair of my old man's coveralls and heading out into the blistering cold with the kids from my neighborhood. We'd spend the entire day building forts and having snowball fights with our buddies. We wouldn't head home until our clothes were soaked through and our fingers and toes were completely numb. But now, I was over it, and I was thankful that I'd finally made it to my post. We'd made two enclosures on either end of the property that were similar to deer stands. Each of them gave us a clear view of the grounds while protecting us from the elements. As soon as I'd climbed inside, I reached for the binoculars and started searching the woods for any sign of intruders. I'd been sitting there for over an hour with not so much as a critter climbing a tree when I heard Crow's voice on the radio saying, "Guys ... I think we've got company."

My stomach twisted into an anxious knot as I responded, "What the fuck are you talking about?"

"I'm out here on the west bank of the creek, and there's a UTV parked back here in the woods." Everything came to a screeching halt as I listened to the sounds of his feet crunching through the snow. Seconds later, he told us, "And the engine's still warm. Whoever is out here ..."

His voice had suddenly trailed off, and my blood ran cold when I heard a faint gurgling sound in the background. I had been coming down from my post when I heard Riggs shout, "Crow ... Crow! You there, brother?"

I already knew the answer. Whoever was out there

had already ended him, and if I didn't move fast, there would be more death to follow. I was racing towards the house when I heard T-Bone's voice on the radio. "Murphy's Law."

Since there was a chance that Crow's radio had been compromised, we all changed our frequencies, which made it more difficult for the invaders to monitor our conversations. It was a plan I'd implemented for this very reason. Once we were all on the same channel, Riggs ordered, "Everyone to your posts!"

My adrenaline was pumping at max speed as I rushed towards the house. Once I'd gotten inside, I met Gunner at the living room closet, and we started collecting the M249s and the extra ammo. We were both busy pulling everything out when Riggs had come up behind us. "Do you think it's them?"

"Got no idea," I answered.

His voice was filled with panic as he asked, "How in the hell did they find us?"

"No way of knowing." I tried to remain calm as I continued, "You gotta remember who we're dealing with here, brother. If Navarro hired someone to take us out, he'd hire the best. Someone who knows how to watch for our mistakes. One fuck up is all it would take."

"We were careful! We played everything by the book!"

Knowing we were wasting time, I ordered, "Keep one of these for yourself and give the other to T-bone. He may need something with a little more punch. He's out on the front porch."

Before he walked out, Riggs asked, "Where's Rider?"

"Out back."

"Reece and Tate are upstairs in the closet."

"Good." With a stern voice I told him, "I know you're worried and I get that, but brother, we've prepared for this. We've got to stick to the plan. It's the only way we're going to get out of this alive."

He nodded and headed out the front door. From there, things had gotten interesting. Riggs had only been gone for several seconds when there was a commotion outside and shots were fired. It was clear to see that whoever was out there was getting closer. I didn't realize *how close* until Riggs came busting through the front door and announced that T-Bone had been shot. As things started to escalate, we all knew time wasn't on our side, which made each of us a little rattled. Once we'd tended to T-Bone's wounds, I sent Riggs upstairs to guard Reece and Tate. After he was gone and in position, I grabbed two rifles and headed for the roof. One way or another, I was going to find the asshole who'd just put a bullet in my brother. He had to be dealt with before another one of us was taken out.

I crawled out of one of the upstairs' windows and carefully stepped out onto the snow- and ice-covered roof. After taking several treacherous steps, I spotted Crow's body sprawled out in the snow. He was planted face down with blood pooling around his neck and chest, leaving no doubt that he was dead. Anger surged through me as I scanned the woods, searching for the man who'd killed one of our most promising prospects, but my view was obstructed by the low-lying branches that were weighted down with snow. I eased forward and adjusted my footing in the snow and then lifted my rifle. As soon as I looked through the scope, I saw a slight movement coming from the west side of the creek. I zoned in on the area, and just as I noticed a branch start to quiver, the gunman stepped out into the open and started shooting several rounds towards the rear of the house. He was aiming for Gunner and hadn't noticed that I was on the roof. Taking the opportunity, I aimed for his head and quickly took the shot.

A sense of satisfaction washed over me as I watched the motherfucker's lifeless body drop to the ground. I was checking to see if there was anyone with him when Riggs's voice came over the radio. "What's happening out there?"

After one last look around, I answered, "I just got him."

"You sure?" he asked sounding hopeful.

"He's got a bullet between his eyes, so yeah, I'm sure." I was just about to tell him that we still needed to stay vigilant until the grounds were checked when the radio clicked over, letting me know that he was no longer listening. I cursed under my breath as I radioed over to Gunner, "We need to do another perimeter check before we head inside."

"You got it, brother. Jed's just showed up to give us a hand. I'll take him along with me."

"Good." Remembering our fallen prospect, I ordered, "Rider ... tend to Crow. Don't want him left out there alone."

"I'm on it."

I turned and started back towards the window, and just as I was stepping inside, I heard several rounds of gunfire followed by the sound of shattering glass coming from beneath me. My blood ran cold when I realized there was a second shooter, and he'd made his way into the house. Fuck. Horrified that either Riggs or Reece might've been hurt, I hurried through the window and raced down the stairs. I was almost to the second floor when I heard more shots being fired. Panicked, I continued towards Riggs' room, and just as I was about to come up on his door, I ran into Gunner. It was clear from his expression that he was just as worried as I was. "Any word from Riggs?"

"Nothing."

I eased over to his door and listened for any sounds coming from the other side. All I could hear was silence, so I took a step back and kicked the door down. Gunner and I charged into the room but stopped dead in our tracks when we found Riggs on the floor. A man dressed in all black was lying next to him with a bullet wound in his head. I wasn't sure how it had all played out, but Riggs had managed to kill the second shooter on his own. As soon as we realized the second shooter had been taken out, we quickly turned our attention to Riggs. He'd been shot numerous times, and it was clear from all the fucking blood that he was in pretty bad shape. I said a silent prayer as I knelt down beside him and placed my hand on his arm. "It's gonna be all right, brother. Just stay here with me."

Gunner walked up next to us and asked, "How the hell did he get up here without us seeing him?"

"He must've crawled up the side of the balcony. I

should've known something was up when I noticed the light was out."

"Not on you, brother," Riggs tried to comfort me. His voice was weak as he continued, "I should've been watching for him."

My chest tightened when Riggs closed his eyes and groaned. Unable to hold back any longer, Reece tapped on the closet door and asked, "Murphy? Is that you?"

"Yeah. It's me." I motioned over to Gunner, giving him the okay to open the door. I heard Reece gasp as soon as she saw Riggs, and when I turned to look at her, she was as white as a ghost. Fearing she'd pass out, I told her, "You're gonna have to keep it together, Reece. I know this looks bad, but Riggs needs you to be strong right now. You got me?"

She nodded and lowered herself down on the floor next to Riggs. As she wiped the tears from her eyes, she whispered, "I need you to stay with me, Jackson. Do you hear me? You can't leave me."

He tried to reach for her, but simply didn't have the strength. "I'm right here, beautiful ... I'm right here."

There was no denying that they both loved one another. Hell, you could almost feel it whenever you were in the room with them. I'd accepted the fact that a love like theirs wasn't in the cards for me, but that didn't stop me from feeling a little envious from time to time. At that moment, though, jealousy was the last thing on my mind. Instead, I felt nothing but remorse for them both. I sat there silently and listened to them whisper back and forth, telling each other those little things that needed to be said in this difficult situation, and as much as I knew they needed this time together, *time* wasn't on our side. We were out in the middle of fucking nowhere with very few medical supplies and no fucking doctor, and if we didn't tend to Riggs's wounds, we were going to lose him. Reece had been pleading with him to hang on when Jed came barreling through the door. "Just did another check. No one in sight. You boys got 'em all."

"Thanks, Jed." I looked behind him and asked, "Rider with you?"

"He's still taking care of your boy, Crow. Sure am sorry you lost him like that." Then he stepped towards Riggs and said, "Looks like we might lose him, too, if we don't get moving quick. We need to get him downstairs, *now*, before he loses any more blood."

We all gathered around him, and as we lifted him up, Riggs said to Reece, "Tell Tate about me ... tell him how much I loved him."

Reece didn't like that one bit, and she let him know it as we carried him downstairs. Jed motioned us towards the kitchen, and once he'd swiped everything onto the floor, we lay Riggs down on the kitchen table. As Jed started to survey his wounds, he said, "He's losing a lot of blood. I need one of you to run and get Sue Ellen. He's gonna need a blood transfusion, and since I don't know his blood type, we're gonna need Sue."

"Why do we need her?"

"She's O+ blood type, so she's compatible with anyone. Blood transfusions are usually done with packed red blood cells and not whole blood, but this is our best option."

"How the hell do you know all that?"

"I'll explain later. For now, we need Sue."

"I'm on it," Gunner told him as he rushed for the door.

Before he ran out, Jed shouted, "Tell her to grab my medical bag out of the closet."

Just as the door closed, T-Bone came shuffling into the kitchen. He was still holding the blood-soaked towel to his chest as he looked over to Riggs. "What the fuck?"

"Riggs was shot."

"Yeah. I can see that, Murphy." He stepped towards him as he said, "He looks like he's barely hanging on."

"That's because he is."

"Then, what the fuck are we gonna do about it? We can't just let him lie here and die."

Reece gave him a scolding look, then whispered, "Jed is going to help him."

"Jed? How the fuck is Jed gonna help him?"

"T-Bone," I warned.

"I was a medic in the Army," Jed informed him.

"And that was how long ago?" T-Bone snapped.

"I'll admit ... it's been awhile, but there are some things a man doesn't forget, T-Bone. And I'm not completely out of practice. The nearest hospital is two hours away, so people around these parts come to me when they need a doctor. Since I've retired, I've delivered more babies than I can count, set broken bones and stitched up wounds. That doesn't even count the cattle I've tended to."

I looked over at Riggs lying on the table. Reece was whispering to him, but I found it doubtful that he was actually hearing anything she said. I understood T-Bone's concerns. Our brother looked like he was hanging on by a thread, and I found myself saying, "This is bit more serious than setting a broken bone or delivering a baby, Jed."

"Maybe so, but trust me when I say, I've dealt with worse under harsher conditions." A confident smile spread across his face, "Besides, I've always liked a challenge."

It wasn't like we had any other option, so I asked, "What do you need me to do?"

"Put some water on to boil and grab me some towels."

"And me? How can I help?" T-Bone offered.

"Go back and lay down. I'll tend to your wound as soon as I finish with Riggs."

T-Bone hesitated, but eventually nodded and headed back into the living room. I gathered up some towels and put on some water to boil while Jed removed Riggs's clothes. He was completely out of it as Jed checked his pulse once more. I could hear the concern in his voice when Jed looked over to me and said, "We're losing him."

He'd barely gotten the words out of his mouth when Gunner returned with Jed's wife, Sue Ellen. She was calm and steady as she walked over with Jed's medical bag and said, "Where do you need me?"

"Pull up a chair and sit down." Jed started riffling through his bag, and as he pulled out an IV kit and other supplies, he told her, "We're running out of time, so we need to move fast."

To my relief, Jed was right when he said that there were some things a man never forgets. As soon as he inserted the IV line into Sue Ellen's arm, his entire

24

demeanor changed. His every move was precise, like it was something he'd done a thousand times before. In no time, he'd completed the first transfusion and was preparing to remove the bullets from his shoulder and abdomen. I was in complete awe as I watched him shift from one wound to the next, taking every precaution to ensure that he'd done everything he could to repair the damage the bullets had caused. There were several touch and go moments, especially when Jed had removed the bullets from Riggs's abdomen. Jed informed us that none of his major organs were hit, but his blood loss was significant and Jed worried that Sue Ellen's donation wouldn't be enough. Unfortunately, that wasn't the only thing he was concerned about.

The kitchen wasn't exactly sterile, so the strong possibility of infection setting in was a huge concern. We'd have to monitor him closely until Mack, the club's doctor, arrived with the antibiotics. Once Jed had done everything he could for Riggs, he gave us the okay to move him into one of the bedrooms while he tended to T-Bone's wound. By sunrise, we'd cleaned up the mess, and the pandemonium of the night had turned into an eerie calm. We were all gathered in the living room, trying to make sense of everything that had happened, when my burner started ringing. I looked down at the screen and saw that it was Gus. As soon as I answered, he said, "How's it going over there?"

"Things are starting to settle down ... at least for the moment."

"Riggs?"

"Jed did everything he could, but Prez ... he don't look

good. What if he doesn't have the strength to pull through this?"

"You gotta remember, Riggs has a lot to live for. No way he's gonna give up without a hell of a fight," he assured me. "Just give him some time."

"I hope you're right."

"I am. You'll see." He paused for a moment, then said, "I know you boys went through a lot last night, but we need to think about our next move. Your location has been compromised, and whether we like it or not, it's only a matter of time before he sends someone else to finish the job his hired men started."

He was right. Reece and Tate's lives were still in danger, and they would have to be moved to a safer location. I just had no idea where. "What are you thinking we should do?"

"I've already spoken with Cotton. He's expecting us to be in Washington with Reece and Tate by late tomorrow night."

"And what about Riggs? He's in no condition to travel, especially not a run like that. From the looks of him, it'll be a while before we can move him."

"I already thought of that. Shadow and Blaze will stay behind with Mack to keep an eye on things."

"You know ... Reece won't be happy about leaving him. When we tell her, she's liable to pitch one hell of a fit, and if Riggs was able, he'd probably do the same."

"I'm sure she won't be happy about it, but she doesn't have a choice. I told Riggs that we'd keep her and their son safe, and I plan on doing everything in my power to keep my word—no matter what the cost."

2

RILEY

*H*elping my father raise and breed horses was my greatest joy. From the time I could walk, I spent every waking moment out at the stables—not only because I was crazy about the horses, but because my father was there. I loved my father dearly, but seeing the way he handled the horses, how he cared for them and talked to them like they actually understood what he was saying, made me love him even more. I also loved the fact that he was sharing the splendor of these beautiful creatures with me. There were so many wonderful things about breeding horses, but nothing tickled me more than a pregnant mare. Nothing compared to the hope and excitement that came after seeing a fetus on an ultrasound. I would spend months anticipating the delivery, and when the moment finally came, my heart would nearly leap out of my chest when I saw the new foal stand and nurse for the first time. It was one of nature's greatest gifts, and almost as rewarding as the smile it brought to my father's face.

While our life on the farm had its advantages, it wasn't all rainbows and butterflies. It took a great deal of hard work—lots of blood, sweat, and tears—to keep a farm like ours going. The day was never truly done, and when things didn't go as planned, they could be both emotionally and financially crippling. Like all horse breeders, we'd encountered many misfortunes over the years, but some more tragic than others. We'd dealt with countless failed in vitros, many difficult, life-threatening pregnancies, and stillborns. Each time they were hard to accept, but we always found a way to move forward. Unfortunately, the same didn't hold true when we lost my mother. I was nineteen and in the middle of my first year of college when we got the news that Mom had stage-three breast cancer. I was devastated by the thought of losing her. Not only was she beautiful, she was kind-hearted and always put everyone else's needs before her own. Mom loved each of us without question or condition, making us all love her even more. Hunter, my older brother, and I adored her, and my father worshipped her. When she'd started to get worse, I decided to move back home. I wanted to spend every second possible with her and had even made plans to put school on hold so I'd be there if she needed me, but she was totally against it. She'd wanted me to graduate on time, so I continued taking my classes, commuting back and forth each day. It wasn't always easy, but it was worth it to have that extra time with her. As time went on and Mom's health had worsened, my father was determined to save her, and over the next three years, he'd take her to see every specialist he could find. They'd tried every treatment known to man, but in the end, it just wasn't enough. The cancer had won out, and we were all heartbroken, especially my father.

The first year after her death was the hardest, but by the second, we'd finally started to recover. We all turned our focus to the farm and eventually managed to find our way back to our old routines. Things were just starting to get back to normal when lightning struck our barn, causing it to catch fire. The blaze quickly grew out of control, and before we could put out the flames, we not only lost our barn, but we also lost Prancer, one of our very best stallions. I thought our days of raising and breeding horses were over, but I was wrong.

Just days after the fire, my father started rebuilding the barn, making it even bigger and better than before. He made plans to start the breeding process with one of our other stallions, Casper's Run, thinking that he would sire many beautiful, healthy foals. Unfortunately, that didn't happen. Casper was never the same after the fire. After several months with no foals being born, my father had to accept the fact that he was no longer able to reproduce. That's when he decided it was time to buy a new stallion, but not just any stallion. He wanted to buy Requiem—a three-year-old chestnut stallion who was known in Australia for being a phenomenal show horse. His sire potential was off the charts, but buying a horse like him would take an unbelievable amount of money. I didn't know all the ins and outs of the financial side of the farm. Dad kept that to himself, but it didn't take a

L. WILDER

numbers wizard to see that it was a huge risk to buy such an expensive stallion.

I can still remember the day I finally decided to voice my concern to my brother. It was a day I would never forget. My greatest joy would become my greatest disappointment—the day I realized my father wasn't the man I'd always thought him to be.

When I got out to the stables, I found Hunter humming to the melody coming through his headphones as he cleaned out one of the stalls. He was wearing his typical Wrangler jeans with a dark-colored t-shirt and a Cubs baseball hat, and he was completely oblivious that I'd walked up behind him. Hoping to get his attention, I picked up one of his old gloves and tossed it at him. When it hit him in the side of the head, he turned towards me with a startled jolt. With his pitchfork pointed right at me, he shouted, "What the hell, Riley?"

I waited for him to remove his headphones before I said, "Sorry. I didn't mean to spook ya, big brother."

"You didn't spook me, smart one."

"Really? So, you make a habit of jumping a mile high whenever someone tosses a glove in your direction?" I asked with sarcasm.

His dark-blue eyes narrowed as he grumbled, "How 'bout you get off my ass and just tell me what you want."

"Did you know that Dad was planning on buying a new stallion?"

"Yeah. He mentioned something about it."

"And?"

"And what?"

"What do you think about it?"

"I'm guessing from the look on your face that you aren't exactly keen on the idea."

"No. Actually, I'm not."

He turned his attention back to the messy stall, and as he scooped up a pitchfork full of straw, he asked, "And why's that? We haven't bred a foal in months. We need a new stallion around here."

"I agree, but Requiem isn't just any stallion, Hunter. That horse is going to cost us fortune, and we haven't sold a foal in over six months! God only knows what Dad spent on rebuilding this barn, and Mom's medical bills were astronomical!"

"Yeah, well, there's this thing called 'insurance,' Riley. Ever heard of it?"

"Yeah, I've heard of it, smart-ass, but if I had my guess, I'd say that the insurance didn't cover half of the cost of that barn. And Mom's last few treatments were considered experimental, so insurance wouldn't cover it. Add in the costs of the funeral and my college tuition and ..."

"Just give it a rest, Riley. You don't have a clue about what really goes on around here. You're too wrapped in your big, fancy college degree to even care. You focus on your studies and stop worrying about how we do things around here," he huffed.

I might've been younger than Hunter, but I wasn't just some naïve kid who had her head in the clouds. I'd been helping out at the farm since I could walk, and through the years I'd learned how things worked. I was also a few months away from getting my finance degree. I knew the kind of money a strong, healthy foal like one of ours could bring, but I also knew how much it cost to breed them. The in vitro, the veterinarian's fees, our farmhands' salaries—just basic feeding and maintenance costs could be substantial. There were times when we should've been just breaking even, but in the past couple of years, we were spending money like we were making it hand over fist. The barn expansion, the extra hired hands, and now the purchase of a million-dollar horse. Things just weren't adding up. I knew something wasn't right, and I could feel it in my gut. I placed my hands on my hips as I huffed, "Okay. Then enlighten me, big brother, because I know for a fact that things aren't adding up."

"Dad has always taken care of everything. Stop asking questions that you shouldn't even be asking, and just let him handle it."

"Why don't you just tell her?" a voice called out behind me. When I turned around, I spotted Travis, one of our horse trainers and my brother's best friend, walking in our direction. I glanced over at him and groaned when I saw the snarky expression on his face. He'd been working at the farm for years and acted like he knew more than anyone, especially me. I couldn't understand why my brother chose him to be his best friend. To me, they seemed like polar opposites. While my brother was all about making a good impression and being the best he could be, Travis was the black sheep of his family. If there was trouble to be found, he'd find it, especially if there was a girl involved. I always thought of him as a selfish asshole, but Hunter saw another side to him—a side I'd never had the pleasure of seeing and doubted that I ever would. Travis only cared about Travis, and I hoped that my brother would figure it out.

Hunter gave him a warning look as he asked, "And what do you know about it anyway?"

"I know plenty, Hunter. It's not like your dad has been trying to hide it," Travis argued. "I've seen what's been going on."

"I haven't seen anything," I added.

"That's because your always at school when ..."

"Travis!" Hunter clenched his fist at his side and shouted, "It's nothing, Riley. Just go back to the house and get ready for class."

"It's clearly something. I just don't get why you won't tell me what it is."

"Not now. Just go inside and get ready, Riley," Hunter demanded.

"It's not like y'all are going to be able to hide it forever, so you might as well tell her."

Hunter's expression softened, and for a split second, I actually thought he might spill the beans, but all hopes of that died when my father came walking into the barn. His tone was foreboding as he said, "Travis, I didn't realize you were working today."

"I wanted to get an early start," he answered with a nervous smile. "How you making it this morning?"

"I'd be better if I could get the tractor up and running." Then he turned to my brother. "I'm gonna need a hand if you're done cleaning out the stalls."

"Yeah, I'm done," he answered and leaned his pitch-fork against the wall. "Do you need me to grab your tool bag?"

"It's out in the shed. Travis ... why don't you give him a hand?"

"Sure thing."

When they all started outside, I quickly asked, "Is there anything you need me to do?"

"You can go get ready for class like your brother told you to."

My stomach twisted into a knot when I realized that he'd heard some, if not all, of our conversation. I gave him a quick nod, and before I started back towards the house, I replied, "Yes, sir."

"And Riley?"

"Um-hmm?"

His voice was full of warning as he growled, "If you have a question about this farm or how I run it, you come ask me about it ... *not your brother*. You got me?"

"Yes, sir. I understand."

I knew my father well enough to know that he was saying one thing but meant something else altogether. He didn't want me asking questions of any kind—not to my brother and especially not to him. If I wanted to know what was really going on, I would have to find out on my own, and that's exactly what I intended to do. I went back into the house, and after I got changed, I headed out to my car. Before I drove off, I waved to the guys, making them think that I was headed to campus, but it was all for show. I had no intention of going anywhere. I backed out of the driveway and started down the main road. After driving about a mile, I pulled behind an old, abandoned house that was just down the road and parked. I grabbed my phone and got out of the car. Hoping I'd go unnoticed, I trudged through the cornfield back towards our house. It took some careful maneuvering, but I was able to make it over to the old treehouse my father had built me when I was a kid. It was just a few yards away from the barn, but I managed to get inside without anyone seeing me. When I looked out the small, side window, I had a clear view of the house and the stables. I had no idea what I was expecting to see, but I certainly never thought I'd find out that my father had been deceiving me for years.

I'd been sitting up in that damn treehouse for over an hour, and I hadn't seen anything that looked suspicious. My father and Hunter were working on the tractor while the farmhands tended to the mares. I thought it was just going to be another typical day until I saw a black SUV with dark-tinted windows coming down our drive. Like they'd done it many times before, they pulled up to the back of the barn and waited as my father made his way over to them. As soon as he approached the vehicle, the driver lowered his window. "You got the goods?"

"I do, and I also have a few new options your boss might be interested in."

"Let's see what you've got."

"You got it."

With that, my father and Hunter disappeared into the tool shed, and moments later, they came out with a dolly carrying four large wooden crates. The SUV's door opened, and a tall African-American male with a thick goatee got out and stood next to my father. He looked out of place in his baggy jeans and thick, gold chains, especially since my father was wearing a pair of old coveralls with stained knees and a tattered hem. The stranger seemed eager to see what my father had to show him and leaned over him as he opened the crate. I could feel my pulse racing as I watched him reach into the wooden box and pull out a large rifle. As the man took the weapon from my father's hand, he asked, "How many do you have in this shipment?"

"We've got fifteen Colt AR-15 rifles and another fifteen of the Ruger 10/22 rifles with pistol grips," he answered as he reached inside the crate again. He pulled out a different weapon, this one smaller, like a pistol with an odd-shaped barrel. "And I just got these beauties in last week."

"Intratec DC-9s?"

"That's right ... with a barrel extension and a 32-round magazine. I've got twenty-five I'm looking to unload," he answered proudly.

"How many more can you get your hands on?"

"Can't say for sure, but I'll tell you this, Devon. These are hot ticket items. If your boss is interested, he better act fast before they're gone," my father warned.

"I'll let him know."

"All right, then." He returned the weapon back into the crate, then told him, "Today's shipment will be 10K as usual."

The man reached into his pocket and pulled out a large wad of cash. As he offered it to my dad, he said, "I'll be in touch about the others."

They loaded the crate into the back of the SUV, and then the man was on his way. I couldn't believe what I'd just seen as I sat there for several minutes in utter dismay. Once the SUV was no longer in sight, I glanced back over at my father, and it was all I could do to keep myself from crying. I'd always thought he was a good, decent man who always tried to do the right thing, and it broke my heart to discover that I was wrong. He wasn't a good man. He wasn't a man I could look up to and respect. My father was a gun-trafficker—a criminal who risked his life and others' just to make a damn dollar, and to make matters worse, he'd involved his own son in his wrongdoings. I thought back to the moment when I asked Hunter what was going on with Dad and the farm, and I couldn't believe that he'd lied straight to my face. They'd both lied to me, deceived me in unforgivable ways, and I couldn't help but wonder if they'd lied to Mom as well. The more I thought about it, the angrier I became. Before I even realized what I was doing, I was climbing down from the treehouse and headed in their direction. Rage consumed me as I charged up to my father and shouted, "Did she know what you are doing?"

"Riley? What the hell are you doing here?"

"Answer the question, Dad," I demanded. "Did Mom know what you and Hunter are doing?"

"What are you talking about?"

"I'm talking about the guns," I spat. "Did she know you were selling illegal weapons, or did you lie to her like you've been lying to me?"

"But how did you know?" He turned to Hunter and growled, "Did you tell her?"

"No one told me. I was here ... I saw it all for myself!"

"You were here? I thought you'd gone to class."

"Well, I didn't, and now, I know everything. I know about the guns ... about the money." I tried to fight back my tears as I cried, "My God. What were you thinking? How could you get involved with something like this?"

"I didn't have a choice, Lee." I could hear the sincerity in his voice when he said, "We were in real trouble. Money wasn't coming in like it used to and with all the different expenses, we were going broke. Then, your momma got sick. You know how much she meant to me ... how much she meant to all of us. I didn't want to lose her, so I did what I had to do to get the money for her treatments."

My anger started to subside when I heard the anguish in his voice. I'd always known that he would do anything for us, but I never dreamed he would go to such extremes. There were so many things going through my head at once, making it difficult to know what to say. After several minutes, Hunter looked over to me and said, "Don't you see? He did all of this for us, so we didn't lose the farm ... so we could keep a roof over our heads and you could go to college. It wasn't an easy decision to make, but he did what he had to do."

My words were strained as I asked, "But selling guns? Wasn't there another way?"

"The opportunity arose, and I took it." Dad stepped towards me as he said, "I know it was the wrong thing to do, and I promise you, Lee, we're gonna stop. You have my word on that."

"But when? How much longer are you planning to do this?"

"Not much longer. We just need to sell a few more shipments so we can buy Requiem. Once we have him and start breeding him, we'll be set. Then the farm will be able to sustain itself, and we'll be done with this gun thing forever."

While I knew he had good intentions and was trying to do the right thing by his family, he'd gone about it in all the wrong ways. He'd lied to me, deceived me, and on top of that, he'd gotten my brother involved. It would take some time for me to trust him again, but in the end, he was still my dad. I loved him, and because of that I would have to find a way to forgive him and to accept things for what they were. As I wiped the tears from my cheeks, I looked up at him and said, "I hope you know I'm going to hold you to that promise. This thing you're doing is dangerous. These people who are buying these guns are criminals. They aren't like us."

"I know that, sweetheart, but I'm always careful about who I do business with."

"Good, because I don't know what I would do if something happened to either one of you."

"Nothing's going to happen to us. You'll see."

3
___

MURPHY

*T*he days that followed the shooting were chaotic at best. After Gus and the others arrived at Jed's cabin, we headed out back to tend to our fallen brother, Crow. I'd hoped that we would be able to bury him in the club's cemetery, where the other brothers could be present, but we were almost six hours from Memphis and it was simply too risky to try to move him that far. Once the trial was over and everyone was back home, we would have a celebration-of-life gathering for him. I hated that we couldn't do more for him, but I knew Crow wouldn't want us to fuss over him. We were the only family that he had, and we'd make damn sure to pay our respects whenever we'd come to stay at the cabin. With heavy hearts, we had taken him over to Jed's family plot and buried him in the grave that Jed had gotten ready for him. After Gus had said a few words, we headed back inside and started making preparations to take Reece and Tate to Washington.

Just as I'd expected, Reece wasn't thrilled about leaving Riggs behind. Gus tried to assure her that Mack would help Jed take care of him, but it did little to comfort her. He still hadn't woken up and a high fever was setting in, so there was no way of knowing if he'd actually pull through. She wanted to stay there with him, to watch over him until his condition had improved, but Gus quickly let her know that wasn't an option. He reminded her that Navarro's trial was fast approaching, and her life was still in danger. He explained that moving was the only way he could ensure her safety and keep his promise to Riggs. Blaze and Shadow also chimed in, each had given her their word that they would keep an eye on things at the cabin, and if Navarro's men came snooping around, they'd deal with them accordingly. While she still had her reservations, Reece finally gave in and stopped resisting. After a long, heartfelt goodbye, she and Tate got in the SUV, and we were on our way.

We spent the next two weeks in Clallam County with our brothers from the Washington Chapter. Cotton set us up at their clubhouse where we would be safe with Big's high-tech security system and around-the-clock surveillance. Gus had made the right move. Under their watchful eyes, Navarro wouldn't be able to touch us, and Reece and Tate would remain out of harm's way. We'd been there for a couple of days when I'd noticed I hadn't seen much of Reece. Other than grabbing a quick bite to eat, she'd been keeping to herself, so I decided to go check in on her. When I got down to Reece's room, I knocked and waited for her to answer. Seconds later, the door eased open, and my chest tightened when I saw her standing on the other side with red, puffy eyes. It was clear that she'd been crying, so I asked, "You okay?"

"I've been better."

"I imagine you have." She walked back over to her bed and sat down next to Tate. "But give it time. Things will get better."

"I wish I could believe that, but I just got off the phone with Mack." I could hear the fear in her voice. "He told me that Riggs isn't doing much better. The infection is taking a toll on him. His blood pressure dropped, and he keeps slipping in and out of consciousness."

"Yeah, I heard." Like her, Gus had been calling Blaze every couple of hours to check on things. He'd mentioned Mack's concern about Riggs, and we knew it was a strong possibility that he might not make it. I hated the idea of losing another brother, especially Riggs. As a skilled computer hacker, he was a real asset to the club, but more than that, he was a good friend. Trying my best to hide the concern in my voice, I said, "Gus called earlier to check in, and Jed mentioned that he wasn't doing well."

"We could lose him, Murphy." Tears filled her eyes as she complained, "He should be in the hospital where they can give him the medical treatment he needs."

"We've already discussed this, Reece. You know that's not possible." I let out a deep breath as I ran my hand over my beard. "There would be questions ... and they'd want answers we can't give. Riggs knew what he was signing up for. He knew there were risks, but that didn't stop him. Nothing would. The man would give his life to protect you, your son, and his brothers."

"I know you're right. Riggs loves his club and wouldn't do anything to jeopardize it. I just wish there was something else we could do"

"I know it's hard, but Riggs wouldn't have it any other way. He's seen firsthand what Mack can do, and he would have no problem putting his life in his hands."

"And you? Do you trust that Mack and Jed can handle this?"

"I do." I walked over and leaned against her desk. "He'll pull through this. You'll see. You just have to have a little faith."

"I'm trying, but it's all I can think about. He's on my mind every second of every day." She wiped the tears from her eyes and took a deep breath. "Can I ask you something?"

Feeling a little leery, I answered, "Sure, but I'm not promising I can answer."

"Okay." She looked up at me with an intense expression as she said, "When we went up to the cabin, you and the others did everything possible to keep us safe. We were miles away from anyone, and we were careful. Really careful. I never would've dreamed that Navarro would find us. So, how'd he do it?"

"You asking me how he found us?" She nodded, and a feeling of dread washed over me. She was already having a hard time, and if I told her the truth, it was only going to make her feel worse. Hoping that she'd accept a vague answer, I told her, "Men like him have their ways of making things happen."

"Yes, and men like you block them at every turn." Her back stiffened as she continued, "So, how did he

43

find us? I know you must have some idea how he did it."

"I have an idea, but ... there's no way to be certain."

"Okay. What do you think happened?" she pushed.

"Ughhh, okay ... You know how Riggs did something to protect our phones and computers?" She nodded. "Well, he wasn't aware that Tate had an iPad, and they might've used it to ping our location."

"*Oh, no.* You're right. I'd forgotten I even had it." Her eyes widened as she cried, "That means ... this whole thing was my fault. I'm the reason Navarro found us. I'm the reason why Riggs was shot! And oh, my God ... Crow!"

"No, Reece. None of this was your fault." I tried to explain, but she wasn't listening. Instead, she lowered her head into her hands and started crying. After several moments, I walked over to her and placed my hand on her shoulder, "Reece ... you can blame yourself all you want, but it isn't going to do anybody any good. Things happen, and you have to find a way to move on."

"But Riggs and ..."

"Riggs wouldn't want you beating yourself up over this," I interrupted. "You need to find yourself a distraction ... something to keep your mind off things for a little while." I thought for a moment, then continued, "What about the article you were working on? Couldn't you focus on that while you're here?"

Doing what she could to pull herself together, she wiped the tears from her eyes and shrugged. "I don't know ... I have my laptop with me, so I guess I could try."

"I think you should. It would be good for you. Think

of it as your way of getting a little revenge on Navarro. The asshole certainly has it coming."

"Okay."

I stood up and started for the door. "You'll get through this, Reece. We all will."

"Thanks, Murphy."

As I walked out of her room, I told her, "No thanks necessary. Now, get to work on that article."

Once I was out in the hall, I closed her door and headed down to Big's room. Since Riggs was out of commission, I told Gus that I would check in with him to see if there'd been any news on Navarro or the trial. He was also a computer hacker and was known to be one of the best around—almost as good as Riggs. When I got down to his room, the door was open, and he was sitting at his desk working on his computer. I stuck my head inside his room.

"Hey, brother. You got a minute?"

He looked over towards the door, and when he saw it was me, he turned to face me and smiled. "Sure thing, Murphy. Whatcha need?"

"I'm looking for an update on Navarro. You think you could find out what he's been up to?"

"Already done." He reached for a file folder on his desk and offered it to me. "Apparently, there was some kind of disturbance down at the prison, and they had to put Navarro in solitary."

"Any idea what kind of disturbance?"

"He was attacked in his cell. Looks like someone was trying to take him out."

"Too bad they didn't finish him off."

"You got that right." He leaned back in his chair and added, "Other than that, it's been pretty quiet. His lawyer has been by to see him a couple of times, but that's about it. I'll keep an eye on him and let you know if anything comes up."

"Hopefully it won't, but I appreciate you staying on top of it."

"Not a problem." When I turned to leave, he asked, "Any word on Riggs?"

"He's struggling a bit today, but he'll pull through it."

"I have no doubt that he will." Big smiled. "He's too damn stubborn to give in without a hell of a fight."

"Yes, he is, and that's a good thing"—I started walking out of the room—"'cause he has a lot of people counting on him to make it through."

"He sure does."

"I'll catch up with you later, brother."

From there, I headed down the hall towards the bar. I needed a cold beer and a bite to eat before I called it a night. When I walked in, I found Cotton and Gus having a drink. They were in a deep discussion and hadn't noticed that I'd come into the room. I stood there for a moment, appreciating the fact that I was in the presence of two living legends as they sat there talking. They were both known for leading their clubs with an iron fist, neither of them backing down when faced with adversity. Instead, they faced it with strength and determination. They both had balls of steel, and never showed a moment's hesitation when it came to protecting the brotherhood. There wasn't a brother around who'd ever question their loyalty to the club, and I was grateful for the opportunity to work alongside them. When Gus noticed me standing in the doorway, he motioned me over and said, "Hey, brother. Come have a beer."

I walked over to the cooler, grabbed a cold one, and sat down next to him. I took a glance around and was surprised to see that we were the only ones in the bar. "Pretty quiet tonight."

"The guys decided to call it a night." Cotton took a drag off his beer before he continued, "It's been a long few days."

"Yes, it has."

Gus turned to me as he asked, "Did Big have any news about Navarro?"

"He's been moved to solitary confinement, but other than that, there wasn't much to tell."

"Good to hear. Maybe things will remain quiet for a few more days," Cotton replied. "So, what are your plans for getting Reece to that trial?"

"It's a two-day drive from here to Tennessee, so we'll leave here early on Tuesday, and time it where we get to Memphis just before the trial begins," Gus reached into his pocket for his cigarettes, and as he lit one, he continued, "This damn trial has been hanging over us for months. I'm ready for this shit to be over. Once Reece testifies and Navarro is behind bars for good, we can get back to some normalcy in our lives."

"Thankfully, it won't be much longer." Cotton took a drink of his beer before he continued, "On a good note, our last pipeline run was one hell of a success."

"Yeah, it's really coming together. Hopefully, they'll just keep getting better." Gus turned towards Cotton. "If

47

my source is correct, we might have the opportunity to add twenty or more Intratec DC-9 pistols with screw-on barrel extensions to the shipment."

"Intratec DC-9s? Those would definitely bring in the money, but they aren't easy to find unmarked. Where are you going to get your hands on those?"

"The supplier is in Somerville ... about an hour from our clubhouse. He runs a horse ranch or something. Not clear on his full story, but I'm planning to check him out when we get back." He paused for a minute, then shook his head. "Riggs could get me anything and everything on this guy, and it wouldn't take him long to do it. The kid amazes me with his tech knowledge. Don't know what we'd do without him."

"I could have Big look into him," Cotton offered.

"I appreciate the offer, brother, but we still have some time." The club often faced new opportunities, like a new supplier or new buyer, but each were laced with their own challenges—like not having Riggs when we needed him. Gus took a drag off his cigarette, then told Cotton, "Me and the boys will plan a visit to his place as soon as the trial is over. We'll get a feel for him, and if he's legit, we'll make something happen."

"I'll be interested to see how things play out."

"You and me both." Gus dropped his cigarette butt in his empty beer bottle then stood up and said, "It's been a long one, boys. I'm gonna call it a night."

"I'm right behind ya." Cotton quickly finished off his beer and tossed it in the trash. "I'll see you two first thing in the morning."

"Sounds good. Have a good one," I told them as they

walked out of the bar. I sat there for a few more minutes, sipping on my beer and listening to some sappy love song playing on the jukebox. It wasn't long before I'd had enough of the depressing lyrics and decided it was time to put an end to this horrendous day. As I'd headed towards my room, I'd hoped that the following days would be better, but they weren't.

As the trial date drew closer, we were all feeling more and more on edge, and the fact that Riggs wasn't improving didn't help matters. Thankfully, by the time the weekend arrived, Riggs started to come around. His fever had broken, and he was finally able to keep food down and had begun to gain back some of his strength. Reece was beaming when she heard his voice for the first time since the shooting. While she was relieved that he was finally doing better, she couldn't hide her disappointment when Mack informed them both that Riggs wouldn't be able to make it to the trial. He simply wouldn't be well enough to travel that far so soon. Riggs hated the thought of Reece walking into the courtroom and facing Navarro without him, but he found comfort in knowing that we would be there by her side. When it finally came time for us to leave Washington, Big and Two Bit helped us load everything into our SUVs. As he closed the back latch, Two Bit asked, "You sure you don't want us to follow you back?"

I shook my head. "I don't think that'll be necessary, but I appreciate the offer."

Cotton came over and patted me on the back. "It was good having you boys up for a visit."

"Thanks for letting us crash for a few days. You really came through for us."

I'd barely gotten the words out of my mouth when Reece walked up beside me. Tate was propped on her hip as she told Cotton, "Thank you for everything, Cotton. Your hospitality has meant so much to me, especially under the given circumstances."

"That's what family is for." He smiled and added, "Next time you come, bring Riggs and Gus along. Hell, bring the whole crew. We'd enjoy having you."

"We'll do that," Reece replied with a smile.

She gave him a quick hug, then walked over to the truck and put Tate into his car-seat. Once he was buckled in, she got in next to him and waved goodbye before closing the door behind her. I looked over to Cotton and the others and said, "I guess we better get on the road. We have a long-ass drive ahead."

"Be careful, brother, and let us know how it all goes."

Rounding towards the driver's side door, I nodded. "Will do."

I hopped in the truck, and as soon as I'd checked to see that everyone was set to go, I pulled out of the gate and onto the main road.

After two long days of driving we made it back home, and just as Gus had promised Riggs, we got Reece to the trial safe and sound. She was able to testify without any complications—except for Navarro's douchebag lawyer. He did everything he could to undermine her testimony and turn the jury against her, but the jury didn't buy into his manipulations and found Navarro guilty of two counts of first-degree murder.

Even though Navarro would remain behind bars, the brothers and I knew it was only a matter of time before another round of trouble would come knocking at our door again. There was always some gang, some up-and-coming MC, or some big shot with an overactive ego looking to take us down. It's just the way things were. I just didn't expect it to be so soon. None of us did.

4

RILEY

*I*t had been weeks since I'd discovered that my father was selling illegal weapons at the farm, and even though I pushed it to the back of my mind, I was still struggling with the notion. I knew my father well enough to know that his decision to do something so extreme hadn't come easy. My heart ached when I thought about how desperate he must've felt knowing that Mom was dying, and all of his attempts to save her were in vain. He had to have felt utterly hopeless, especially when he learned that we might lose the farm along with his wife. I understood he had his reasons for doing what he did. Sadly, that didn't change the fact that what he was doing was wrong—utterly, grossly wrong, and his actions had me second guessing everything. I wanted to believe that we were still the same family that we'd always been, and that the farm was still the same place I'd always known and loved, but I just couldn't do it, especially when everything felt so different. I no longer found joy in watching the sunrise across the pasture or riding Anna Belle, my favorite mare. I couldn't even go out to the barn without thinking about the guns that were stored in the shed next door. They haunted me, making me wish I never knew they existed. I tried to push it all to the back of my mind, to force myself to forget, but every time I saw my father on his cell or whispering something to my brother, I kept wondering if he was talking about those damn weapons. It was driving me crazy. I needed some time to clear my head, and I knew just the place to do it.

Whenever things were at their worst, I knew I could count on Grady to make me feel better. Not only was he my first cousin, he was my best friend. Our fathers were brothers and had lived in the same small town since they were born. Hunter and I grew up with Grady and his two brothers, Levi and Jasper, and from an early age, we were inseparable. Our friendship had always come easy. We'd always seemed to understand one another, and even after all these years, he was the person I trusted with my secrets. There wasn't anything we didn't share with one another—until now. I couldn't tell Grady about my father and the illegal guns he was selling. That was one secret I could never share, *not with anyone*, but I could have a few drinks and a couple of good laughs with my best friend.

It was just after ten when I walked through the front doors of The Smoking Gun. It was one of the hotspots on Beale Street, so I wasn't surprised to see that it was already packed. As usual, the music was blaring, and the dance floor was covered with hoochie mommas, each of them dancing around in their revealing low-cut tops and shimmery miniskirts. I felt a little out of place in my blue jeans and boots, but there was no way in hell I was going to wear something seductive when I was just going to be hanging out with Grady. Hoping to find a relatively quiet place to sit, I started inching my way through the sea of people and headed towards the bar. It took some time, but I eventually made my way over to the counter. Unfortunately, there were no empty seats and it was far from quiet. I could literally feel the music vibrating through my chest as I searched for a place to sit, or at the very least, get out of the way. I was about to give up hope when Grady slipped up beside me and smiled, "Hey, stranger."

"Grady!" I reached up and wrapped my arms around him as I shouted, "Man, am I glad to see you!"

"It's good to see you, too, squirt." I stepped back and gave him a good look. He was at least a foot taller than me with a broad, muscular build that would've made him look threatening if he wasn't such a pretty boy. On that particular night, he was wearing a pair of dark-gray slacks with a white button-up dress shirt and a black leather jacket, making him look casual but professional. His blue eyes sparkled as he spoke loudly, "I've got us a place over in the corner."

I nodded and followed him over to the small table. Once we were seated, I leaned towards him and said, "Looks like you've got yourself another busy night."

"Yeah. Things have been going really good lately." I still couldn't believe that my Grady, the goofy prankster who threw a round of firecrackers into the principal's bathroom, had become one of the youngest entrepreneurs in the area when he opened The Smoking Gun.

While there were plenty of people who had their doubts that he'd pull it off, including our family, I always knew he could do it. There wasn't anything Grady Nichols couldn't do if he put his mind to it, and he loved proving people wrong, especially when it came to his two older brothers, Levi and Jasper. A proud smile crossed his face as he told me, "So good—that I've been approached by some bigwigs up in Nashville to open a place down on the strip."

"Really? That's incredible, Grady! You must be so excited!"

"Yes and no. It would take a lot of work, and I'm not sure I'm up for it. At least, not now." He motioned his hand, beckoning one of the waitresses over. "You want something to drink?"

"Absolutely."

As soon as the waitress approached the table, she asked, "What can I get ya?"

"I'll have a Long Island Iced Tea," I answered.

"You got it." A seductive look crossed her face as she turned her attention to Grady. "And what can I get you, Mr. Nichols."

"I'll have a Scotch on the rocks."

"Sure thing."

"Thanks, doll," he told her with a flirty wink.

Once she was gone, I shook my head as I snickered, "You are too much."

"What?" Feigning innocence, he added, "I was being nice."

"Yeah, right," I scoffed. "You and I both know better than that."

"Maybe." He shrugged. "So, what about you? How are you doing?"

"I'm okay. Just trying to finish up my classes."

"You know I don't give two flying fucks about your classes, Lee. I was asking about you," he scolded.

"I said I was fine."

"I'm not buying that for one second. You sounded like you were about to lose it the other night when you called," he fussed. "I know something's up, so why don't you just save us both some time and tell me what's going on."

I'd never been able to hide anything from him. He'd always been able to read me better than anyone. He liked to think he had a sixth sense when it came to me, but that wasn't it: I was a terrible liar and I had a bad habit of revealing my true feelings with my facial expressions. Regardless, I had to come up with something to tell him, so I said, "I've just been feeling a little down in the dumps lately. It's probably just this stupid weather. It's been rainy and cold for weeks. I don't know if I can take another day without a little sunshine."

"Um-hmm. I see. It's just the weather." The waitress brought our drinks over and placed them on the table. He picked up his Scotch as he asked, "It has nothing to do with the fact that you haven't gotten laid in over a year?"

"No, but thanks for reminding me."

He studied me for a moment, and when he determined that I wasn't being completely forthright, he said, "So, you aren't going to tell me?"

"I'm just having a hard time understanding why good people have to do bad things."

"I guess that depends on what bad things you're talking about."

I shrugged. "Just bad things in general."

"You aren't giving me much to go on here, but I'll say this ... Just because someone does something bad doesn't make someone a bad person. Sometimes, it's just a simple fuckup, and other times, there's just no way around it. So, maybe it's just a matter of you accepting that things aren't always so black and white. Sometimes, there's a gray area that needs to be taken into account, but I can't really say for sure unless you tell me what the hell you're talking about."

"I can't. *Not this*. Besides, I get what you're saying, and you're right. Things aren't always black and white, and I'd be doing myself a favor if I just learned to let things go. Starting now." I smiled as I said, "How about we have ourselves a drink or two and forget about everything else ... at least until tomorrow? Can we do that?"

"Yeah. We can do that, but Lee ... you know I'm here for you. No matter what."

"Yes, Grady, I know, and I really appreciate it." As I picked up my drink and took a quick sip, I noticed a couple of women were gawking at Grady from across the bar. It was clear from their wanton expressions that they were interested in him, and from the "come hither" look he was sporting, he was equally interested in them. I didn't try and hide my annoyance as I huffed, "Can you turn that off ... just for a little while?"

"Turn what off?"

"I don't even know what it is," I grumbled. "It's whatever you do that makes women throw themselves at you."

Clearly amused, he chuckled. "I'm not so sure that I can just turn it off, but I'll do my best."

"Much appreciated." I reached for my Long Island and took a long sip. "These are really good. I think I might need another."

"You got it." He called the waitress back over and ordered us another round of drinks. "I hired a new bartender."

"Oh, really?" I glanced over at the bar and became immediately intrigued when I spotted a smoking hot guy standing behind the counter. To say he was tall, dark, and handsome wouldn't do him justice. He looked like a model with his jet-black hair and crystal-blue eyes. "Are you talking about him?"

"Yep. That's Earl. He's pretty cool. Works his ass off on busy nights."

"Wait—" I started laughing. "Did you say his name is Earl?"

"Yeah," he sighed, "but don't let the name fool ya. He's a really great guy. I'm sure he would show you a good time."

"I'm sure he's perfectly wonderful, but I don't need him to show me a good time. That's what I have you for."

"I'm not talking about *that kind* of good time, Lee," he fussed.

"I know, but *Earl*? I don't think I could say his name with a straight face."

I shook my head, and just as I was about to continue, I noticed several bikers sitting across from us. I was about to turn my attention back to Grady when, for reasons I may never understand, one of them caught my eye. He was beyond hot in his tightly fitted white t-shirt and black leather vest. His muscular arms were covered in tattoos, and I couldn't help but wonder if there were more scrolled across his broad chest. He had a thick, unruly beard, and his long, shaggy blond hair was brushed away from his face, revealing the most beautiful eyes. Every inch of him was wickedly sexy, and I longed to reach out and touch him. Unfortunately, that was never going to happen. There was no way in hell I'd ever have the courage to speak to a man like him, much less get close enough to touch him. He was too far out of my reach, but that didn't stop my heart from racing at the thought of spending a night wrapped in his arms. I was in the midst of imagining his mouth on mine when Grady's voice brought me back to reality. "Okay, I get it. You aren't interested."

Shaking off my overactive hormones, I let out a deep breath and said, "No, I'm not interested in Earl. Besides, it's been ages since we've had a chance to catch up. If it's okay with you, I'd rather just finish my drink and relax here with you."

With a look of pity, he mumbled, "You know it's fine with me. I was just trying to help out."

"I don't need any help getting a guy, Grady. I can find one on my own." My eyes drifted over to the biker across the room, and a warmth washed over me when I found him staring in my direction. The second our eyes met, I panicked and quickly turned my attention back to Grady. "I'm ... uh ... just taking some time to find the right guy."

"Taking some time?" he argued. "It's been over a year since you broke it off with Lance. You're twenty-four years old, and all you do is work out at the farm and study for your classes. One of these days you're going to have to get back out there and start seeing people again. You don't have to jump into anything serious. You just need to learn to cut loose and have a good time."

At the mention of having a good time, I found myself looking across the room, gazing once again at the hot biker. Maybe it was the slight buzz from the alcohol, but he looked even hotter than he had two seconds earlier. As I sat there gawking at him, I considered what Grady had said. "So, you're saying that I should be more like you?"

He cocked his eyebrow as he replied, "I would say yes, but your tone tells me I should say no."

"I just don't think you're the one who should be giving me advice on guys and relationships. I mean, let's be honest here ... When was the last time you were actually interested in spending more than one night with a girl?"

"I'm busy. I don't have time for a relationship right now, besides, how did this conversation get to be about me? It was you who came here looking for an escape from whatever the hell is going on with you." He ran his fingers through his hair and smiled. "I'm good. I've got nothing to complain about."

"And so am I ... at least for the most part." Hoping to change the subject, I asked, "What about Levi and Jasper? How are they doing these days?"

"You know Jasper. He's not one for keeping in touch, but the last I heard, my big brother was still locked away in his cabin in the woods, hiding from life as we know it." He took a tug off his drink and sighed. "As for Levi, he's been busting his ass to get his new garage up and running. He's always had a gift for fixing engines, so it won't take him long to make a name for himself."

I giggled as I said, "I have no doubt ... *he's a Nichols after all.*"

"Exactly."

My stomach started to growl, so I asked, "Do you think we could get a bite to eat? I'm starving."

"How about a burger or something?"

"A burger would be great ... and some fries too."

"You got it."

He ordered us a couple of cheeseburgers and fries, and we talked and laughed the entire time we were eating. Just as I'd hoped, Grady had helped me forget about my troubles on the farm—at least for the time being. When it got close to closing time, I leaned over to Grady and said, "I'm going to run to the bathroom before we go."

"I need to check in with our night manager and make sure he has everything covered, so just meet me up front when you're done."

"Okay."

As I started towards the bathroom, I remembered that I hadn't checked my messages, so I reached into my purse for my phone. I was scrolling through my texts when I saw that my class for the following day had been canceled. Relief washed over me when I realized I wouldn't have to get up early in the morning. I rushed into the bathroom, and once I was done, I headed up front to find Grady. On my way, I found myself glancing around the bar, looking for the hot biker I'd seen earlier, and was disappointed to see that he'd already left. I don't know why it mattered. It wasn't like I'd ever have the nerve to just go up and talk to a guy like him, especially with his burly buddies at his side. The sexy biker was quickly forgotten as I followed Grady out of the bar and over to his loft apartment across the street. With a stunning view of the river and the Memphis-Arkansas Bridge, his place was amazing. He'd spared no expense making it exactly the way he wanted it to be with lavish furniture and expensive artwork. It was a shame he didn't have someone special to share it with.

He didn't have to bother showing me to my room. I'd been there enough to know my way around. As soon as I'd gotten into my pajamas, I curled into bed, and with an improved state of mind, drifted off to sleep. Unfortunately, I didn't wake up in the best of moods and had no idea why I was feeling so grumpy. I headed into the bathroom for a shower, hoping that the hot water would help wake me up, but I had no such luck. I managed to get dressed but had no desire to put on makeup or fix my hair. Instead, I just threw on one of Grady's baseball caps and called it a morning. I grabbed my things and headed downstairs to my car. Since Grady was already at work and my class had been canceled, I decided to just go home and take Anna Belle out for a ride.

I had it all planned out. I'd completely bypass Dad and Hunter and head straight to the stables. Once I had Anna Belle all saddled up, I'd spend the afternoon riding and try to rekindle those feelings of hope and possibilities I'd had the night before when I was with Grady. I thought I had it all planned out until I turned into my driveway and noticed four motorcycles parked by the barn. As I got closer to the house, I could see several men talking to my father. Over the years, we'd had all kinds of people come out to our farm, even bikers, so I didn't think much about it. I just went along my merry way and pulled up next to the house. When I got out of my car, I glanced over at the men with my father and was surprised to see that they were all staring at me. I rarely made quick judgements about people, but I knew right away that these men weren't like the bikers who typically came out here. They were big and beefy with fierce expressions on their faces, and it was highly unlikely that they had any interest in going to the stables to see the horses.

I was standing there, frozen, with a mix of fear and intrigue when my father called out to me, "Lee! What are you doing here? I thought you had class."

"My class got canceled."

"Well, uh ... I have some business to discuss with these fellas. Why don't you head inside, and I'll be in when we get done?"

"Business, huh?" I asked sarcastically. If I hadn't seen it for myself, I would've never known that my father was selling illegal weapons. He'd purposely never done business when I was home, but it was clear from the looks of these men that they hadn't come to the farm to discuss buying one of our foals. Even though something told me it was a bad idea, I asked, "What kind of business?"

He didn't answer. He simply looked at me like I'd grown a third head.

Maybe it was my ill mood, or maybe it was the animosity I felt towards him for bringing men like these to our home, but I couldn't stop myself from pushing him further. "Are they here to see Dasher? Man, he's a two-year-old beauty ... Oh, wait. I bet they're here to see Merrick. Am I right?"

"Lee," he warned. "Go inside. I'll be there in a minute."

Being as snarky as possible, I smiled and said, "I'd be happy to show them around for you. I'm sure they'd love to see the stables and check out the horses, or are they here for some *other* reason?"

I knew I was walking on thin ice. These men were most likely dangerous, but I couldn't seem to stop myself. It was like I'd been possessed by a crazy person, and she was determined to ruin whatever business they had together. I probably would've kept at it if one of the bikers hadn't taken it upon himself to get involved. As soon as he stepped forward, I realized he was the man from the bar, and it was all I could do to keep my wits about me. With his leather jacket and ass-hugging jeans, he had a rugged look about him, but that didn't make him any less attractive. In fact, just like the night before, I found it sexy as hell. My interest in him took me by complete surprise. He and his buddies were more than likely criminals, doing God-knows-what to God-knows-who. I knew I had no business finding him or anyone like him appealing, but I couldn't seem to help myself. I was trying to pull myself together when he removed his sunglasses and his blue eyes locked on mine. Damn, I couldn't move. I couldn't think. I was a complete mess. Thankfully, the spell was broken as soon as he opened his mouth.

"Hey, Lee. Why don't you do us all a favor and just go inside like your father said?"

I was equally hurt and appalled by his unwarranted suggestion, and while I would've loved to tell him where to stick it, I wasn't stupid. I knew I was up against a grizzly bear of a man. Choosing to play it safe, I replied, "I was just trying to be helpful."

"I think we both know that isn't true." The look on his face left me as breathless as it did enraged. Damn. I had no idea why he got to me the way he did. His voice was low and menacing as he growled, "Now, if you don't mind … we have business to discuss."

Again, I had to fight the urge to snap back at him. Trying to play it cool, I took off my baseball cap and ran my fingers through my hair. With sarcasm dripping off of every word, I gave him a forced smile and replied, "Certainly. I wouldn't want to interrupt."

When I started for the barn, my father shouted, "Where are you going?"

I removed my sunglasses and turned towards him. "I'm taking Anna Belle for a ride. I'll be back in a few hours."

"Are you going alone?"

"Yep." I continued forward, and when I strolled by the biker, I gave him a disapproving scowl. "It was a real *pleasure.*"

He didn't respond. Instead, he just stood there silently as I walked away. I was close to the barn when my father called out to me. "Riley, be careful. You know the river's up. You'll need to go down to the east bank if you want to cross over," he warned.

I just held up my hand and waved as I entered the barn. I found it ironic that he seemed more worried about that damn river than he was of the ominous bikers he'd brought to our home. I glanced back over my shoulder and my heart stopped when I noticed the hot biker's gaze was still fixed on me. Good or bad, it seemed I'd made an impression on the handsome stranger, but it didn't matter. I knew a man like him was trouble, and I had no intention of seeing him again.

But like it's been said before—"the road to hell is paved with good intentions."

5
___

MURPHY

*A*s soon as the trial was over, Gus called the brothers into church. Since our concerns about Reece's safety were behind us, and Riggs was on his way home, he was eager for the club to move forward. It was time for us to start making plans for the next pipeline run, which meant meeting up with the new supplier—Daniel Nichols. He supposedly had a large shipment of Intratec DC-9s, and Gus wanted us to check them out before another buyer got their hands on them. I knew he was hoping this Nichols guy was going to be the real deal, but after looking over the small amount of intel Riggs had been able to find on him, I was feeling skeptical. Nichols was a horse breeder who'd done pretty damn well for himself. He had an unbelievable place with a ranch-style house sitting on three hundred and twenty acres of land. He'd just built new stables and had new training grounds in the works. It was clear that he was doing well, but that hadn't always been the case. After going over his bank statements, Riggs discovered that Nichols had started selling almost three years ago, right after his wife had gotten sick with cancer. Money had been tight, so he was looking for a way to bring in more funds. The fact that he'd started supplying out of desperation didn't sit well with me, and my feelings towards Nichols didn't improve when I rode out to his farm with Shadow, Gunner, and Blaze to meet him.

When we pulled up to the house, Shadow was the first one off his bike. He took a quick glance around before he asked, "Are you sure this is the right place?"

"Yeah." I got off my Harley and removed my helmet. "This is it."

"I know you said the guy bred horses and all that, but *damn*," Gunner was obliviously impressed as he added, "this place is incredible."

Blaze walked towards us and asked, "Where the hell is everybody?"

"Got no idea." I took a moment to scan the property, and I was surprised to find that there wasn't a single guard on watch, only a couple of farmhands out in the stables. "It's the perfect location. It's miles away from everything, but from the looks of it, he actually lives here. At the very least, you'd think he'd have more security than this."

Gunner shrugged. "Maybe the guy's a badass and people know not to fuck with him."

"Nobody is that big of a badass." Shadow looked over to me and asked, "Is Gus sure about this guy?"

"No. That's why we're here. He wants us to check him out."

I'd barely gotten the words out of my mouth when a man stepped out onto the front porch. He was wearing dark denim jeans with a cowboy hat and boots, and as he started towards us, he reminded me of John Wayne when he was younger. I assumed he was Nichols when he walked up to us and asked, "Which one of you fellas is Murphy?"

"That would be me, and these are my brothers, Shadow, Gunner, and Blaze. You must be Mr. Nichols."

"The one and only. Glad you boys could make it out."

"You've got yourself a nice place. From the looks of it, I'd say you've been doing pretty well for yourself."

"Yeah, I guess you could say that." He shoved his hands in his coat pockets. "But I haven't done all this on my own. This farm has been in my family for as long as I can remember."

"Your family always breed horses?"

"No. My father raised cattle and made a good living out of it, but when the market changed, I decided it was time for me to try my hand at breeding. It served me well for many years, but then my wife got sick ..." He shook his head and mumbled something under his breath, and then he said, "You know how it is. Circumstances change, and you have no choice but to deal with it the best you can."

"Are those changes in circumstances the reason why you decided to branch out into the weapons trade?" I asked, trying my best to put a positive connotation to it.

"The opportunity arose, and I took it."

"Until then, had you ever had any experience with it?"

"No, not exactly."

"Have you always done your business from here at the farm?"

"I figured it was the safest place for me to do it. We're miles away from town, so it's not like I have to worry about anyone being suspicious or anything like that."

He was doing business from his home and *that* was a huge issue for me, not to mention the fact that they had so little security. It was like he had no idea that he was putting his family and his farm in danger by bringing his buyers to his home. Hoping I was wrong, I asked, "What kind of security do you have in place?"

"Security?" he asked, then chuckled. "You looking to rob me or something."

"No, sir," I flatly answered. "Just need to know what kind of situation we're dealing with."

"I have a security system for the house, which has all the basics, and cameras out at the barns and the front gate. I keep all the weapons locked away in a safe. No one can get to them without the combination, and I'm the only one who has it."

"So, no guards?"

"Nah. Got no need for 'em." Fuck. My gut was right. This guy was in way over his head. Even though Nichols seemed like a decent guy, I saw more red flags than I could count. I was debating on walking away from the deal when Nichols said, "Gus mentioned that you were interested in checking out some of my merchandise."

I nodded. "We are."

"Good deal. I just got a new shipment in if you'd like to have a look at it."

"We would."

"Just give me a minute, and I'll go ..." He stopped mid-sentence when he noticed a car coming down the driveway, then shook his head and mumbled, "Damn."

Blaze glanced over at the car as he asked, "Is there a problem?"

"No ... Well, not exactly."

The car pulled to the house, and we all watched in silence as his daughter got out. It was difficult to get a good look at her with that damn baseball cap, but it was clear from the way that she spoke to her father that she wasn't happy we were there. If I had to guess, I'd say she didn't like the fact that he'd branched out into this new line of sales, especially when it brought men like us to her home. While I didn't blame her for being pissed, this wasn't the time for her to make her feelings known, so I decided to intervene, hoping I could put an end to her little display. As soon as I stepped forward, I knew I'd made a mistake. With the brim of her hat pulled down low, I couldn't see her face, but her body language told me everything I needed to know. "Miss Goodie Two-Shoes" was into me, but sadly, her interest vanished the second I opened my mouth. She didn't take my suggestion lightly that she should go inside, but she didn't lash out, either. Instead, she simply walked away but not until she'd removed her ballcap and sunglasses, giving me my first good look at her. It was at that moment when I realized she was the woman from the bar. From the minute I'd spotted her staring at me, I couldn't take my eyes off her, but I knew right then that she was out of my league.

I'd seen my fair share of gorgeous women but never anyone as beautiful as her. From her long, wavy brown hair to her round, full lips, she was all kinds of perfect. And those eyes—*damn*, I'd never seen eyes like hers. They were black as coal and shined like diamonds, and every time she looked at me, it felt like she could see right through to my soul. I was enamored by her—not just for her beauty, but for her fiery spirit. I couldn't remember the last time I'd been so drawn to a woman, and I didn't like it. I didn't like it one fucking bit. Knowing I had no business having such thoughts, I tried to shake it off, but then she winked at me and I was done. Fuck. It was all I could do to keep myself from reaching for her and throwing her over my shoulder like a fucking caveman.

"I'm sorry about that," Nichols mumbled, pulling me out of my head. "I didn't know she was going to be here."

"No offense, Mr. Nichols, but that's why you don't shit where you eat."

I knew I had no right to call him out. If I didn't like how he was running things, I could've just walked away and cut our losses, but not before I warned him. Obviously offended by my remark, Nichols crossed his arms and gave me a smug look. "What the hell is that supposed to mean?"

"You seriously have no idea how bad you've fucked up, do you?" I shook my head in aggravation. I had to make him see what he's been doing was wrong. "It's one thing to get involved in this line of business, Mr. Nichols, but it's another to do it right from your home without a major security detail. If something goes wrong ... if someone isn't happy with the product or demands more than you have to offer, what are you going to do about it? You've left yourself completely exposed."

"I'm not exactly new to the gun trade business, Murphy, and besides that, I've been in sales for longer than you've been alive." His voice was low and strained as he continued, "I understand your concerns about my security, but you've got to remember, my main focus has been and always will be this farm and selling my horses. We have people come out to these stables every day. They want to see the horses. Touch them. Dream about having one of their own. They have always felt comfortable coming out here because they know they can trust me. I start putting armed guards out here, then all that changes."

"If something goes wrong, you're putting them and yourself in danger."

"No, I only work with people who I've looked into first. That's right. I looked into you boys ... the same way you looked into me. I knew all about Satan's Fury. I knew who you were and what you represented long before I allowed my guy to contact Gus." He gave me a stern look as he told me, "I know what I'm doing, Murphy. I'm careful. Hunter, my son, has helped me out a few times, but I never do business when Riley is here."

"She was here today," Shadow barked.

"That was a mistake," he argued. "I never wanted her to know that I was even doing any of this. I've always done business when she was at class or in the city with her cousin."

Shadow was quick to reply. "Clearly, she knows."

"Yeah." He let out a deep breath. "She witnessed a deal going down a few weeks ago."

"If you're planning to keep this thing up, you're going

to have to make some changes, Mr. Nichols. If you don't, it's going to bite you in the ass," I warned.

It was clear that he was done listening when he snapped, "Look, I appreciate your concern, but I have things I need to tend to. Do you want to see the goods or not?"

I looked over to Shadow and Blaze, and they each gave their nod of approval. "Yeah. We want to see them."

"Then, let's get this thing done, so you boys can be on your way."

When he started towards his storage shed, Gunner nudged me and said, "Look, I know you're pissed about how this guy is running things and all, but did you check out his daughter? Damn, she was smoking hot."

"I didn't notice," I lied.

"Wonder if I could talk her into taking me for a ride," he joked, but his smile quickly vanished when he noticed my expression. "I meant on one of their horses."

Before I had a chance to respond, Nichols returned with a large wooden crate. As he opened it, he said, "Here are five of the Intratec DC-9s with a barrel extension and a 32-round magazine. I've got twenty more just like them in the safe."

"How much?"

"I'll be discussing that with your president."

"No," I growled. "You will *discuss it* with me."

He paused for a moment, considering his next move, but eventually responded, "Fine. Have it your way. I'll take twenty-five grand for the whole lot."

"Twenty-five? You've gotta be kidding me," I complained.

"That's a fair deal, Murphy. We both know you can sell them for twice that."

"I'm not looking for a fair deal, Mr. Nichols. I'm looking for *the deal*, so either get right with the price or we're walking."

He ran his hand over his chin and sighed. "The best I can do is twenty. Take it or leave it."

I looked over at the crate of guns and studied them just long enough to make Nichols squirm. When I saw that he was becoming flustered, I answered, "We'll accept the offer."

"Good. Glad to hear that."

"We'll be back in the morning to pick them up."

"Before you go, I've some Colt AR-15 rifles and some Ruger 10/22 rifles, too, if you're interested."

"I'll need to see them."

He turned and headed back into the shed. When he returned, he was towing a second large crate with a dolly. After he opened it, he turned to me and said, "These are some of the best on the market."

As I checked them over, I asked, "How many?"

"Thirty of each. I'll give you a good deal on 'em, too."

"I'll let Gus know." I shook his hand, then we started towards our bikes. "We'll see you in the morning."

He nodded and watched as we took off down his driveway. Heading back home, I found myself thinking about Nichols. He was a good, decent man who'd found himself in a bad spot. I just couldn't understand why a man like him would've chosen to get into gun trafficking —one of the most dangerous industries on the planet. There had to be someone out there who'd persuaded him to give this thing a go and provided him with goods he'd need to make a quick turnaround. Too bad they didn't take the time to tell him to use some common fucking sense when it came to being safe. If Nichols continued down the path he was on, he was destined for trouble—the kind of trouble that could cost him his life or worse, his kids.

Once we got back to the clubhouse, we headed to the bar to meet up with Gus. When we walked in, he was sitting at the counter talking to Riggs. It was good to have my brother back. He'd had us all worried, and it was a relief to see that he was doing better by the minute. As we sat down next to them, Gus looked over to me and asked, "Well?"

"We made the deal, but I have my concerns."

"Oh, really? What concerns?" I took a few minutes to share our experience at the farm, and once I was done, I gave him some time to reflect on everything I'd told him. After several moments, he ran his hand over his goatee and sighed. "So, how did you leave things?"

"I gotta admit. His Intratecs were top of the line, and his AR-15s and Rugers were pretty fucking good too. Since the price was right, I told him we'd be back in the morning. I figured we'd clean him out while we were there."

"You think we should do business with him again, or is this a one-time deal?"

"He's a good enough guy, and I think we can trust him. It's his other buyers I'm not sure about. Either way, I'm just relaying my concerns. The final say is up to you, Prez."

Gus turned his attention to Riggs as he asked, "You

think you can find out who Nichols is doing business with?"

"I already tried, but at the time, I wasn't at the top of my game. I'll do some more digging and see what I can find out."

"Good." Gus patted him on the shoulder. "Sure is good to have you back, brother. I don't know what we would've done without ya."

"Glad you don't have to find out." Riggs winced as he started to stand. "Guess I'll get to it. I'll let you know what I find out."

"Hold up, Riggs. It's late. This thing with Nichols can wait until tomorrow. Get home to Reece and that boy of yours," Gus urged. Like me, he knew how concerned she'd been. Those nights when he was hanging in the balance did a number on her, and it would take her some time to get over it.

"You sure? I don't want to hold you up."

"Positive. You're still on the mend, and I don't want you pushing it." He chuckled. "Besides, Reece would raise all kinds of hell if she thought we were working you too hard."

"I'm good, Prez. You don't have to worry about me. It'd take a lot more than a few bullets to put me down." As he started for the door, he told us, "I'll be back first thing in the morning. I should have something by the time you get back from the Nichols' place."

"Sounds good, brother."

When he was about to pass by me, he stopped and placed his hand on my shoulder. "I haven't had a chance to thank you for all you've done for Reece and Tate. I know it was a group effort and all the brothers had their part in looking after them, but Reece told me how you went out of your way to make sure she was keeping it together while I was laid up. I really appreciate you doing that."

"No need to thank me, brother."

"No. It needs to be said. You went above and beyond, Murphy. You always do."

"You would've done the same for me."

"No doubt." He patted me on the back as he continued forward. "I'll see you in the morning."

After he was gone, we each had a beer and discussed the plan for the morning's pickup. Once we had it all sorted, I decided to call it a night. Even though I had my own room just down the hall, I wasn't up for staying at the clubhouse. After the long day, I was ready for some peace and quiet, and the ride over to the house would give me a chance to clear my head. I said my goodbyes, then headed out to the parking lot to my bike. In a matter of seconds, I was pulling out of the gate and onto the main road. The weather in Memphis was usually fairly mild, but on this particular night, it was downright frigid. The cold wind nipped at my flesh as I rode down the streets of downtown. I wasn't surprised to see that there weren't many folks out barhopping. Nights like these were meant to be enjoyed by a fire with a drink in one hand and a smoke in the other. As I continued towards the house, I found myself thinking about Riley. I had no idea why my mind had wandered to her. I'd only seen her for a few brief moments, but there she was, dancing around in my thoughts. I couldn't stop myself from wondering how she was spending her night. Was she out in the stables with the horses she loved, or was she up in her room studying? Was she alone, or was she with someone? It seemed odd to me that I even cared.

I knew what became of relationships and love, and I wanted no part of either. I refused to put myself through the bullshit—not again. It just wasn't worth it—not even for a girl like Riley Nichols.

6

RILEY

I couldn't sleep. Every time I closed my eyes, I saw him—the enigmatic, hot biker with the intense blue eyes. I tried to force myself to think about something else, an old movie I'd seen or a crazy night I'd had with Grady, but I kept coming back to him. I would imagine him lying next to me, and as I lay there curled up in my bed, I would think about all the wicked things he would do to me. His lips on my neck. His possessive hands on my body. The glorious orgasms he'd give me over and over again. It wasn't like me to have such fantasies. Not like these. Not with a man like him, so rough and demanding, and certainly not in such fevered detail. I didn't understand my enchantment with him. Not only was he intimidating with his fierce exterior, he was also rude. It just didn't make sense. There was a good chance that he'd come to see my father to buy illegal weapons. I couldn't understand how I could be so upset with Dad for selling them when I wasn't troubled by the fact that he was there to buy them. He was a criminal, involved in who knows what, and yet, I couldn't stop thinking about him in the most sinful ways. I was always one who liked to play it safe, never getting involved in things where I wasn't in complete control, but for one reason or another, a part of me liked the idea of him having a bit of control over me.

I was lost in a world of lustful desire when it hit me. I was fantasizing about a guy who would never be interested in a woman like me. He would want a woman who was beautiful and confident. A woman with experience—real experience. A woman who would know exactly how to satisfy a man like him. A woman who wasn't me at all. The thought made my stomach twist into a painful knot, making it impossible to think about him any longer, so after a long night tossing and turning, I got out of bed. After I put on my bathrobe and slippers, I headed downstairs to make myself a cup of coffee.

When I walked into the kitchen, I found my father standing at the sink. He was staring out the window, watching silently as the sun just started to rise over the back pasture. He was lost in his world of thoughts when I walked over to the coffee pot and said, "Morning."

"You're up early."

"I couldn't sleep." After I poured my coffee, I went over and sat down at the table. "What about you?"

"The same."

"You have something on your mind?"

He shrugged. "No more than usual."

I knew he was lying, but I was scared to push, fearing that his sleepless night might have something to do with the hot biker and his friends. Instead, I sipped on my coffee and asked, "Has Hunter already gone out to the barn?"

"Yeah. He wanted to get an early start, so he left a few minutes ago." After several long moments, he finally asked, "What about you? Do you have class today?"

"No. My professor is sick with the flu or something, so it will be Monday before we meet again."

"So, what are your plans for the day?"

"I don't know. I guess I'll get some studying done. I also have a paper that I have to work on, and if get that finished, I was thinking I might take Anna Belle out for a ride."

"Do you mind waiting until later this afternoon to take that ride?"

"Yeah. I can do that, but why? Is something going on?"

He let out a deep breath before he explained, "I know you don't want to hear this, but I have some buyers coming in today and it would be better if you weren't around."

"Are they the same guys who were here yesterday afternoon?" When he nodded, I asked, "Why don't you want me around? Are they dangerous or something?"

"Yes and no. They seem like decent fellas, but I've heard some things."

"What kinds of things?"

"It doesn't matter. I just don't want to take any chances where you and Hunter are concerned. It's better if you just steer clear during the exchange." When he noticed the expression on my face, he continued, "I know you don't like any of this, but we're getting really close. I just need to unload a couple more shipments, and then we'll be done with this whole thing. We'll have the money we need to buy Requiem, and we can put this all behind us."

"Really?"

"Really." He sat down next to me, and I could hear the anguish in his voice as he spoke, "I know this hasn't been easy for you, and I want you to know, it hasn't been easy for me either. I've always wanted to be someone you and your brother could look up to, but I failed you. I've let you both down by getting involved in all this. But I promise to make it up to you."

Overcome with emotion, I leaned towards him and wrapped my arms around his neck, hugging him tightly. I whispered, "You haven't failed us, Daddy."

"I have," he muttered. "But I'm going to do whatever it takes to make things right again."

"I know you will." I loved my father, and while I hadn't approved of his methods, I admired him for doing whatever it took to take care of his family. I gave him a tight squeeze before letting him go. As I eased back into my seat, I looked over to him. "Can I ask you something?"

He nodded.

"How did you get started in all this? How did you know where to get those guns? Who to sell them to? How to go about it all without getting caught? It's not like you could just Google something like that."

"I had some help." He shifted in his seat as he continued, "When things started to go south, I called Uncle Roger. I told him about the situation with your mother's medical bills and the farm, and you know my brother, he's got an answer for everything."

"So, he's the one who got you started?"

"Yes and no. Actually, it was your cousin, Jasper, who played the biggest part in getting things started."

"Jasper?" I gasped.

"I was just as surprised as you are. Apparently, he's made some unlikely friends during his stint in the military. He reached out to them and was able to get us in contact with a supplier up north and several potential buyers here in our area."

"I can't believe that Jasper would be involved with people like that."

"You know Jasper. He's always been a little different, especially after the war." He shrugged. "Regardless, he came through for us, and after Roger fronted me the money for the first shipment, I had everything I needed to get the ball rolling."

"You weren't scared?"

"I was terrified," he scoffed. "But after the first few sales, I was able to pay your uncle back, and every sale after that was put towards our debt."

"And this supplier ... is he going to be okay with you walking away, or is he going to try and force you to keep going?"

"He knew I wasn't in it for the long haul, so he wasn't surprised when I told him the news." Then he reached for my hand. "Like I said, this isn't something that I'm proud of, but I was desperate. I didn't know what else I could do to make this kind of money in such a short time."

"I understand." I gave his hand a squeeze. "I appreciate you taking the time to explain everything to me."

He stood up and as he looked down at me, he asked, "So, you'll wait to take that ride until later this afternoon?"

"Yes, Dad. I'll wait."

"Thank you, sweetheart." He stood up and as he put on his coat, he said, "I'll let you know when they're gone."

"Okay."

With that, he headed out the door and towards the barn. As I sat there finishing off my coffee, I thought about my father's request. While I was a little disappointed that I was going to miss a chance to see my hot biker again, I knew it was for the best. My fascination with him was starting to reach an unhealthy level, and I had way too much going on to waste my time dreaming about something that would never happen. It was time for me to let it go and put him out of my head for good. With a newfound resolve, I grabbed a muffin and headed upstairs to take a hot shower. Once I was dressed, I emptied my backpack and got everything I would need to start on my paper. Thankfully, it was a topic I was familiar with, and it wouldn't take me long to get it done.

Once I pulled my laptop out of my backpack, I took it over to my desk and sat down. I had every intention of finishing the assignment in record time, but I couldn't seem to concentrate. I was too intrigued by what was going on outside my window. From where I was sitting, I could see the entire farm, and it only took the slightest movement or sound to distract me from my assignment. Knowing I couldn't afford to procrastinate, I started to move over to my bed, but stopped when I noticed Travis entering the training ring with Starlight, one of the younger mares. Even though we'd been working with her for months, there were times when she could still be cantankerous and difficult to handle—especially when it came to men. I was busy watching Travis lead her slowly around the fence when my attention was drawn over to a black SUV that was coming down the driveway. I wasn't sure if it was the same bikers who had been here the day before until they parked and got out of the vehicle. When I saw that it was them, I leaned towards my window, trying to get a better view as they approached my father. One of them offered my father a thick envelope, and once he'd put it in his back pocket, he and Hunter started for the shed. It wasn't long before they came back out with several large crates. Just as one of the men knelt down to examine the contents, there was a commotion over at the training ring, drawing my attention over to Travis and Starlight. I had no idea what had happened, but Travis was sprawled out on the ground with Starlight bolting and bucking around him. I looked to see if Hunter was around, thinking he might've seen what happened, but he was nowhere in sight.

Without thinking, I rushed out of my room, down the stairs, and put on my boots before racing out the back door. When I got out to the ring, Travis was still laid out on the ground. Worried that he was either seriously wounded or he'd been knocked out from the fall, I raced over to him and knelt down beside him. Just as I'd feared, he was out cold. Starlight was stomping her feet with annoyance as I gave him a gentle nudge. "Travis? Are you okay?"

When I got no response, I nudged him a little harder and shouted, "Travis!"

After blinking several times, he mumbled, "Fucking horse."

"Travis ... I need to get you out of the ring. Are you okay to move? Do you think anything's broken?"

"Nah, I'm good. I can get up," He eased himself into a sitting position and was about to try and stand when Starlight started galloping in our direction. "Watch it, Riley!"

"It's okay. I've got her."

I slowly moved towards her and could see she was rattled. Her head was raised high with her ears pinned back, and she was swishing her tail back and forth as she rounded her back. When she neighed with a high-pitched squeal, it was clear something wasn't right, but I had no clue what had gotten her so agitated. Knowing things could go from bad to worse very quickly, I eased closer to Starlight and kept my eyes on hers as I reached for one of the reins. When she squealed again, I whispered, "Easy, girl. I'm not gonna hurt ya."

She continued to buck and jolt as Travis warned, "If you aren't careful, she'll rear up on you."

Ignoring him, I gently eased the rein down, forcing her to lower her head. I knew there was a chance she could intentionally run into me or ignore my commands, but I tried my best to remain calm as I stepped even closer to her. When she didn't try to jerk away, I whispered, "That's my girl. Easy does it."

Knowing she could sense it if I showed any sign of fear, I continued to speak softly but firmly as I ran my

87

hand down the length of her nose. It wasn't long before she'd settled back down, but I was worried it would be short-lived the minute Travis came up beside us. When she gave him a defiant snort, he grumbled, "I know, I know. You don't like me right now."

"You might want to check the saddle or the bridle. Something seems to be bothering her," I suggested.

"I was thinking the same thing." As he ran his hand under the saddle straps, he chuckled and said, "There had to be a reason for her to send me flying."

"I would give you a hand, but I've got a paper to finish."

"You've already done enough. Thanks for helping me out."

"No problem."

I had hoped to get back inside before anyone noticed me, but it was too late. As I made my way back over to the entrance gate, I spotted my hot biker leaning forward against the fence with his arms crossed and his attention focused solely on me. Those gorgeous blue eyes never left mine as he said, "Man, that was really something."

"Thanks, but it really wasn't a big deal. She was just a little rattled and needed some help settling down."

"Regardless, you handled her like a pro."

"I've had a lot of practice."

His eyes skirted over me as he said, "I'm sure you have, but that doesn't make it any less impressive."

"Thank you, but really ... it was nothing." When I reached the gate, I smiled as I said, "But you being all nice *and giving me compliments*? Now, *that's* really something."

"Hey, I can be nice," he replied sounding slightly wounded.

"Um-hmm." I shrugged as I stepped through the gate. "Could've fooled me, especially with that whole badass biker thing you've got going on."

His lips curled into a smile as he asked, "Badass biker thing?"

I thought he was hot from the start, but when he smiled, I nearly lost my breath. It just wasn't fair for a man to be so damn good-looking. "Yeah. You know what I mean."

"No, I'm not sure that I do," he lied.

I let my eyes quickly skirt over him as I continued, "Let's just say you've got a look about you."

"Oh, really?" Clearly amused, he asked, "And what kind of look is that?"

"A kind of look that says, I'll kill you in your sleep, but I'll tuck you in all nice and cozy before I do. There's not many who can pull that off ... but *you certainly can*."

"Thanks for clarifying." He chuckled as he extended his hand and said, "My name's Murphy, by the way."

"It's nice to meet you, Murphy." As I shook his hand, I found myself questioning my sanity. He was a member of a biker club, and if I had to guess, I'd say it was a bad one. And on top of that, he'd come to my father to buy weapons, and not just any weapons, he and his buddies were buying big, powerful, *illegal* assault rifles that gang-bangers used. To make matters worse, I had a feeling he wasn't there buying weapons because he was worried about financial woes like my father. I should've been terrified, completely and utterly terrified of him, but I wasn't—not in the least. Standing next to him, I felt safe and secure, like there was nothing in this world that could harm me as long as I was close to him. "I'm Riley."

"You were at the Smoking Gun the other night, right?"

I found it interesting that he'd asked when he already knew the answer. I'd spent most of the night staring at him like a horny teenager, and there were many times when he was doing the same to me. Feeling a little embarrassed, I replied, "Yes, I was there."

"I thought that was you." He paused for a moment, then asked, "But you weren't alone. Was that your boyfriend or something?"

"Boyfriend? *Um ... no*." I chuckled as I told him, "I was with my cousin, Grady. He actually owns the bar, so I go there sometimes to hang out with him."

"Grady Nichols is your cousin?"

"Our dads are brothers," I explained. "Why? Do you know him?"

"Not personally, but I've heard of him. I'm sure you know he's made a name for himself."

"Yeah. He might've mentioned it a time or two. He's not exactly humble." The way he was looking at me made it difficult to function. Since I couldn't think of anything else cute or flirty to say, I figured it was best for me to go before things got awkward. I motioned over to my father and his friends as I said, "Well, I guess I better get going. I wouldn't want to keep you from your business."

He glanced over his shoulder and grimaced when he saw that they were almost finished loading the SUV. "Looks like business is just about done."

"So …" Trying not to sound desperate, I asked, "Does that mean you won't be coming back?"

"Not exactly sure. That decision isn't really up to me, but if I make my way back, maybe you could show me around."

"Sure. I'd love to."

"Why don't you give me your number, and I'll call sometime?"

Before I could respond, my father came up behind me and fussed, "Riley … I thought you had a paper that you needed to get done."

"I do. I just came out to give Travis a hand with Starlight."

"Travis can handle Starlight, Riley. It's his job after all," he scolded.

I could tell from his tone that he wasn't in the mood to argue, so I nodded and said, "You're right. I'll leave you boys to it. Sorry for interrupting."

"No reason to be sorry," Murphy told me. "Good luck with your paper."

"Thanks." As I started inside, I looked back over my shoulder and said, "Until next time."

He nodded, then turned his attention to my father. Even though I was curious about what they were saying, I headed back into the house and up to my room. As soon as I stepped through the door, I fell back on my bed and stared up at the ceiling. I started going over my brief conversation with Murphy, and a big, goofy grin spread across my face when I remembered the moment I'd called him badass. At first I cringed at the thought, but then I remembered the expression on his face when I'd said the word. He wasn't turned off by it. Instead, he was intrigued and egged me on, teasing and testing to see just how far I'd go. I was caught off guard by his playful side, especially after experiencing such a completely different side of him the day before, but I liked it. I liked it a lot. Something told me he didn't let many see that light-hearted side of himself, and I was glad he'd decided to share it with me, even if it was only for a few moments. Overall, I was pleasantly surprised by our little encounter. I just hoped he felt the same and there would be more of them in the near future.

7
___

MURPHY

I could see the train wreck coming from a hundred miles away, and yet, I was doing nothing to stop it. Hell, I was heading straight towards it with my eyes wide open, paying no mind to the laws I'd created for situations just like these. In my defense, I had good intentions. I'd gone out to the Nichols farm with the mindset that my brothers and I would get the goods and leave, but that plan was blown to hell the minute I spotted Riley racing out of her house like a mad woman. I watched as she ran towards the training ring, where one of their mares was having a damn fit, bucking and galloping around like she had a point to make. When I saw that the handler was out cold, I was worried that she was putting herself in harm's way, so I rushed over to give her a hand, leaving my brothers to tend to the exchange on their own. I'd barely made it over to the fence when I realized Riley didn't need my help. Hell, she didn't need anybody's help. She'd already taken ahold of the reins, and after a few soothing words, she had the mare completely under her control. It was an unbelievable sight to see, but her little show didn't stop there.

From the moment we started talking, I could feel myself being drawn in, like a moth to a fucking flame. I knew I'd get burned, but that didn't stop me from thinking about her relentlessly. I needed to get a fucking grip. I tried to block her from my mind, forcing myself to focus on the club and working overtime at the garage, but even after a week had gone by, she was still fucking with my head, haunting my thoughts and dreams. Out of frustration, I got on my bike and just started riding. I hoped that would help clear my head, but after a few hours of being on the road, I found myself out at the Nichols' farm. I told myself that I'd ended up there out of simple curiosity, that if I just had a chance to learn a little more about her, I'd be able to get her out of my head, but as I drove down their driveway, I was having my doubts. It had been a week or more since I'd last been there, and I had no idea if she was even home. Taking my chances, I pulled up to the stables and parked. By the time I'd gotten off my bike, one of their farm hands was walking in my direction. "Can I help you with something?"

"Is Mr. Nichols around?"

"No, sir. He's not. He and Hunter have gone to town to pick up some supplies. Is there something I can help you with?"

Realizing I'd made a mistake by showing up unannounced, I shook my head and said, "Nah, man. I'll just come back by another time."

"Want me to give Dan a message for ya?"

"You can tell him that Murphy stopped by,"

As he turned to leave, he replied, "Will do."

Silently cursing myself, I got back on my Harley and was just about to start up the engine when I heard, "Murphy?"

When I glanced over my shoulder, I found Riley looking at me with a puzzled expression on her face. I couldn't blame her for wondering why I was there. Like her, I had no idea why I'd shown up unannounced. As I sat there staring at her, I started to question everything, especially my sense of reason. It wasn't like me to act without thinking things through, but there I was—face to face with Riley Nichols and no clue as to what I should do. Trying to think fast, I got off my bike and started towards her. "Hey. I came by to have a word with your father."

"Why? Is something wrong?"

"No. Nothing's wrong. I just had something I wanted to run by him."

She slipped her hands into the back pocket of her form-fitting, Wrangler jeans as she replied, "I'm sorry, but he's not here."

"Yeah, I heard. I guess I should've let him know I was coming."

"I'm sorry you wasted the trip."

"Don't be. I enjoyed the ride over. It's really beautiful out here, and it's the perfect weather for being out on the bike."

"You're right. It is a beautiful day." Her cheeks blushed with a soft shade of pink as she said, "You know ... I could always give you that tour you were asking about. Unless you need to get back or something?"

"I've got some time."

"Great." She smiled brightly, nearly knocking me off my feet. "How about I show you around the stables first, and then we'll go from there?"

"Sounds good."

I followed her into the stables, and I was immediately impressed with how clean and organized the place was. She led me over to one of the stalls where they were housing one of the younger mares. Her eyes sparkled with pride as she scratched behind the horse's ear. "This beautiful girl is Anna Belle."

"If I had to guess, I'd say there's a story behind this horse."

"Yeah. You could say that." She glanced up at the mare with a solemn look as she said, "My dad gave her to me right about the time when my mother found out she had breast cancer. It was really hard to see her so sick, but it helped to have Anna Belle to distract me, not to mention that she's about the sweetest, most beautiful horse on the planet."

"I'm sorry to hear about your mother. Cancer can be tough, especially when it's effecting someone you really care about."

"It's the worst." She started walking towards the next stall as she continued, "Mom fought hard. I can't tell you how many different treatments the doctors had her try; they did nothing but make her feel worse. She died a couple of years later."

"Damn. I really hate to hear that. Must've been awfully hard on you."

"It was hard on all of us. To make things worse, the treatments were really expensive. Much more than we could afford, and we got in over our heads. That's one of the main reasons my father started selling those guns. I wasn't exactly pleased when I found out about it, but after the shock wore off, I realized he had good intentions." Riggs had already told me about her mother's death, and everything that had followed thereafter, but hearing it from her gave me a new perspective on things. Everyone knew that desperate times called for desperate measures, but some measures have greater consequences than others. When we made it down to the next horse, she let out a deep breath. "I'm sorry. I don't know why I'm telling you all this."

"I'm glad you felt like you could talk to me about it."

Quickly redirecting the conversation, Riley motioned her hand towards the horse in the second stall and said, "This is Starlight. She's the who showed out the last time you were here and bucked off her trainer."

"Yeah, she put on quite a show. Any idea what spooked her?"

"We're still trying to figure that one out. She's always been a bit of a handful. She does fine until you get her out in that ring. I don't know what it is, but something sets her off every time."

"Have you noticed her having difficulty transitioning between gaits?"

"I haven't noticed, but I'll watch the next time we take

her ... *Wait a minute*." She took a step back as she faced me. "What do you know about transitioning gaits?"

"My mother once dated a guy who raised horses, and we spent a lot of time out at his farm." Of all the men my mother dated, Joe was the only one I ever gave a shit about. He was a decent guy and tried to do right by my mother. Unfortunately, after years and years of being mistreated, my mother didn't know how to deal with a man who was actually good to her. Trying to be as vague as possible, I told her, "He saw that I had an interest in his horses and ended up hiring me as one of his hands. I only worked there a couple of summers, but I learned a lot from him."

"Obviously." She placed her hands on her hips and smiled. "I can't believe you worked with horses. You're just full of surprises, aren't ya?"

"You have no idea."

She tucked a loose strand of hair behind her ear as she started walking forward. "So, while you were out at his place, did you do any riding?"

"Some, but that was a long time ago."

"Would you be up for giving it another try sometime?"

"There's a chance I could be persuaded."

A light blush crossed her face as she turned to me and said, "Well, I guess I'll have to get working on my persuasion skills."

Damn. With every smile, every small twinkle in her eye, she was drawing me in closer. I wondered if she knew the effect she was having on me. "If I had to guess,

I'd bet you don't have any problem in that area. I bet you always find a way to get what you want."

"I wish." She chuckled under her breath, but her smile faded when we passed by several empty stalls. "I know it's hard to tell now, but there was a time when we would've had every one of these filled with foals."

"Oh, really? What changed?"

"We ran into some issues with our stallion."

"What kind of issues?"

"The breeding kind." She cocked her eyebrow and shrugged. "*You know how some men can be.* He wouldn't cooperate, so we're looking into bringing in a new one. Hopefully, that will get us back up and running again."

"You seem pretty invested in all this." As we left the stables and headed towards their enormous pond, I asked, "What are your plans for after you graduate?"

"I don't know. I've always pictured myself being here with my brother and dad, helping them manage the farm. I've always felt like I belonged here, that the farm and horses make me who I am, but lately I've been thinking I might want to try something different." She stopped and looked me in the eye as she continued, "I'll always love riding and spending time out here with the horses, but it's a big world out there with all these wonderful *possibilities*. Sometimes, I worry if I stay out here on the farm, I'll miss out on something really great."

"I get it."

"You do?" she asked, sounding surprised.

When we got closer to the water, she sat down on a patch of grass and waited as I sat down next to her. Once I was settled, I turned to her and said, "We all have doubts, Riley,"

"Even you?"

"Yes. Even me."

"Okay." Her eyes danced with mischief as she asked, "Here's a question for ya ... What's your biggest pet peeve?"

"Hmm. I might have to think a second on that one."

"Oh, you've got that many, huh?" She giggled.

"Yeah. I've got a few."

"Okay. Let's start with your biggest and go from there," she pushed.

"Well, for starters, I'd say dishonesty is a big one of mine." My eyes met hers as I added, "If somebody breaks my trust, there's no getting it back. From there, I'd say they're pretty typical: clicking the top of a pen over and over or hmmm ... someone who is constantly late, and .... uh, those people who scuff their feet on the floor when they walk. God, I can't stand that."

"Oh, I can't either. Man, those are good ones!" she announced excitedly. "For me, I really hate it any time someone chews with their mouth open or ... ugh, when skinny girls talk about the crazy diet they're on. Oh, the absolute worst is when people say 'no offense' and they know for a fact that they're being offensive but want to play it off as nothing."

"Yep. Those are good ones, too."

We spent the next hour talking about one random topic to the next. I was enjoying my time with her. It was easy, like we'd known each other for a lifetime, but the truth was, we didn't know each other at all. She had no idea who I really was, and her curiosity was growing by the minute. Her eyebrows furrowed as she looked over to me and said, "So, I've been trying to put the bits and pieces together, but I just don't get it."

"Not sure I'm following you. What don't you get?"

"*You*. It's not making any sense. How do you go from working out at a farm with your mom's ex-boyfriend to"— she pointed her finger towards me—"who you are now?"

"You mean, how did I become a biker?"

"Yes, but not just any biker." She motioned her hand towards me and her words were overly dramatized as she asked, "How did you become this *tough looking, muscled up ... badass* biker who belongs to a motorcycle club?"

I shook my head and chuckled as I answered, "It's complicated."

"I'm sure it is." As she toyed with a blade of grass, she said, "But I'd still like to hear about it."

"I don't know. It's not like I'd planned on joining Satan's Fury." I thought back to those days when it seemed like nothing was going my way, and it was hard to believe how much my life had changed. "After a tour in Afghanistan, I was faced with some hard truths and decided it would be best if I came home to find work. I managed to find some odd jobs here and there, but I had a hard time finding anything permanent. I was out of money and was about to find myself on the streets when I met Gus. He took a chance with me and offered me an opportunity to prospect. From day one, I knew I'd found what I was looking for ... a brotherhood like no other.

The brothers of Satan's Fury may not share the same bloodline, but they're family just the same."

"Not sure I would call that explanation complicated. I would guess that the brotherhood you found with the club is a lot like what you had in the service."

"In a lot of ways it is, but it's much more involved. We get to decide who's brought into the club ... who we think will be a good fit. That isn't the case in the military. There, it's just the luck of the draw, and that isn't always a good thing."

She shrugged and replied, "That makes sense."

"There are other differences, too, but I'll save that for another day." I stood up and added, "For now, I should probably get going. I've kept you long enough."

When she started to get up, I offered her my hand and helped her to her feet. "But what about my father? I thought you needed to speak to him."

"I'll catch up with him some other time." We headed back to my bike, I grabbed my helmet and said, "Thanks for showing me around."

"I really enjoyed it. I wasn't expecting you to be so easy to talk to."

"I could say the same about you, and I had a really good time, too. We'll have to do it again sometime," I suggested.

"I would like that. Maybe when you come back, I can persuade you to take that ride?"

"Only if you'll agree to take a ride on the Harley with me afterward."

"Your motorcycle?"

"Yeah, unless you're scared." I teased her.

"Oh, no. I'm not scared. In fact, I'd love to go for a ride."

"Consider it a plan." As I gave her one last look, I found myself wanting to reach for her, to kiss her long and hard, but I forced myself to resist. I got on my motorcycle and reached for the ignition. "Until next time."

"Be safe, Murphy."

"Always."

I started the engine, and while heading down her driveway, I realized I wasn't ready for my time with her to end. That's when I knew I needed to put Riley Nichols behind me even though it wasn't something I wanted to do. The plans I'd made to see her again would have to be broken. I didn't have a choice. I knew what would happen if I didn't. The one thing I'd learned from my mother and the fucked-up choices she'd made was when you care about someone, you protect them from the pain, you don't become the cause of it. Deep down I knew I was broken in every way that'd matter to a girl like Riley. I didn't believe in happy endings. To me, love was just a figment of the imagination, and if I pursued her, I'd only end up breaking her heart. I couldn't do that to her, and I sure wouldn't sacrifice her happiness for my own.

8
___

RILEY

*E*very time I thought back to that morning I spent with Murphy, a warm, fuzzy feeling would wash over me, and I'd start smiling like a loon. I couldn't believe it. The bad-boy biker had actually swept me off my feet. The very thought of it baffled me. I would've never dreamed a man like him could be such a gentleman, so charming and sweet, but he was. In fact, he was all of that and more—much more. I'd had a great time with him and the thought of seeing him again excited me, but sadly, that feeling didn't last. It had been three weeks since the day Murphy came out to the farm, and I was disheartened by the fact I hadn't seen nor heard from him since. I simply couldn't understand it. I'd seen the way he looked at me, and while I hadn't had a lot of experience with men, I knew enough; a man didn't look at you like that unless he was interested. It's possible I'd read him wrong. Maybe he was just suffering from allergies or the sun was in his eyes. Or maybe he was just being nice when he mentioned seeing me again and had no intentions of coming back. There was no way to know what was going through his head, so I was left with no other option. I had to face the facts and come to terms that I'd been blown off.

The notion didn't sit well with me. Instead, it made me feel even worse. I became angry and bitter, and my only solace was planning his demise—figuratively speaking, of course. I didn't want the man dead. I just wanted him out of my head, but it wouldn't be easy, not when it came to a man like Murphy. Thankfully, I had help. After I told Grady everything about Murphy—minus the fact that he was a biker and most likely a criminal—he insisted that I come down for a visit, promising a night that would erase all thoughts of Murphy. I was about to go upstairs to get ready when I heard my father talking in his office. The serious tone in his voice made me concerned that something might be wrong, so I eased over to the closed door and tried to listen to what he was saying.

He sounded hopeful as he asked, "Did the last shipment meet your expectations?"

There was a brief pause before I heard him say, "Good. I'm glad to hear it. I know your boys were concerned, especially that Murphy fella, but I was hoping you'd be pleased with the product."

At the sound of Murphy's name, I became even more curious and stepped closer to the door. "Yes. I understood why he'd be worried about that, and if I planned to stay in this much longer, I might consider making some changes, but the truth is ... I'm thinking it's about time to shut this thing down. Not until I get you the goods you requested, of course, but soon after."

There was another brief pause before he continued, "Well, I'm hoping that won't be a problem, but if it does become an issue, I'll handle it."

There were a few "um-hmms" and "hmphs" before my father said, "Sounds good. I'll have them to you by the end of next week. Thanks, Gus."

He hung up the phone, and moments later, he came barreling out of his office. Fortunately, I'd already made it back to the kitchen, and he had no idea I'd been eaves-dropping. He grabbed his coat off the hook and started for the backdoor. Before he had a chance to open the door, I called out to him, "Hey, Dad?"

"Yeah?"

"I'm not gonna be home tonight. I'm heading into Memphis to hang out with Grady."

Too preoccupied to care, he just mumbled, "Okay."

"I'll be back in the morning."

"You two have fun, but be careful."

With that, he walked out and shut the door behind him. I eased over to the window and watched as he headed out to the stables. As soon as he was out of sight, I rushed into his office and grabbed his cellphone off his desk, quickly searching for the number of his last call. Once I found the number, I wrote it down on a slip of paper and put in my back pocket. I had no idea what I planned to do with Gus's phone number, but somehow, having it made me feel more in control. I put my father's phone back on his desk and was about to run upstairs when Hunter asked, "What are you doing?"

I came to a screeching halt as I answered, "Umm ... nothing."

"Looks like something to me."

"Well, I hate to break it to you, but you're mistaken."

As I started passed him, he asked, "Did I hear you say you were going to see Grady tonight?"

"Yes. I'm leaving as soon as I get out of the shower. Why?"

"I had something I wanted to talk to you about, but it can wait."

"You sure?"

He nodded. "Yeah, it's no big deal. Tell Grady I said hi."

"Okay, I will."

I started up the stairs, and when I got up to my room, I took the paper out of my back pocket and studied it for a moment. I was such an idiot. There was no way I could call that number without looking completely and totally desperate. I crumpled it up in my hand and was about to toss it into the trash, when I stopped myself and put it in my purse instead.

Pretending that I hadn't just done something stupid, I headed into the bathroom and took a hot shower. When I got out, I was feeling a little anxious, so it took me longer than usual to find something to wear. Once I'd decided on the perfect outfit, I started to work on my hair and makeup. By the time I was done, it was after nine. Knowing how Grady hated it when I was late, I grabbed my things and rushed downstairs. After I said goodbye to Dad, I hurried out to my car, and in no time, I was on the interstate. Half an hour later, I arrived at the

Smoking Gun, and just as I had hoped, it was packed tight—exactly what I needed to take my mind off Murphy.

With a confident smile, I zig-zagged through the crowd towards the back of the bar. As soon as I spotted Grady, I went over to him and said, "What's shakin' bacon?"

He cocked his eyebrow at me. "You're in an awfully good mood."

"No, I'm not, but I plan to be real soon." I motioned towards the bar as I told him, "I need a drink."

"Okay ... You want a long island or something stronger?"

"A long island will do for now."

"You got it." After he placed our drink order, he led me over to a table in the back. Once we were seated, he leaned back to check out my outfit. "I can't remember the last time I've seen you so dolled up. You trying to impress someone?"

I glanced down at my little black dress and heels. "I didn't think it would hurt to put in a little extra effort."

"Well, the extra effort paid off!" The waitress brought over our drinks, and as soon as she placed them on the table, I looked up at her and said, "I'm going to need another one."

"So, you're planning to just drink him outta your mind?"

"Maybe," I answered as I leaned forward and took a quick glance around the bar.

"You looking for him?"

When I realized what I was doing, I sat back with a

huff and grumbled, "Good grief. What the hell is wrong with me?"

"Nothing is wrong with you, Lee. You got your hopes up over this guy, and that's completely understandable," he assured me. "You can't help that he was an asshole and ghosted you."

Grady was right. Murphy had ghosted me. It was the perfect word for what he'd done. He was there one minute, all sweet and charming, then gone the next—disappearing like he'd never existed. I took a long sip of my drink before I replied, "It's my fault. We only talked for a couple of hours. I don't even know the guy ... *not really*. I shouldn't have let myself get carried away, but I'm over it now."

"No, you're not, but you will be."

I let out a deep breath and said, "You know, finding the right guy shouldn't be this hard."

"No, it shouldn't." He shrugged innocently and added, "And you wonder why I don't do relationships."

"I'm beginning to think you're right. Relationships are for the birds."

"Exactly."

As we discussed all the reasons why relationships sucked, I finished off my first drink, then a second, and was well on my way with the third. I was just starting to feel the effects of the alcohol when another round appeared on our table. Even though I'd have a few from time to time, I'd never been a big drinker, so it didn't take much for me to get completely wasted. I knew that I should slow down, especially since I was drinking on an empty stomach, but it was nice to cut loose and forget about things for a while. Besides, with Grady at my side, I didn't have to worry about doing anything I would come to regret—or so I thought. I'd just started on my fourth drink when I started to feel really lightheaded. Thinking it might help to walk around a bit, I grabbed my purse and said, "I'm going to the ladies' room."

When he saw that I was a little wobbly, Grady asked, "Do you need a hand?"

"No, I'm fine."

"Are you sure?"

"I'm fine, Grady. I've only had ... like two drinks," I fussed.

"You've had more than two, and they were really strong."

"They weren't that strong." As I started towards the bathroom, I told him, "Stop your worrying. I'll be right back."

Trying my best not to run into anyone, I continued towards the back of the bar where the restrooms were located. Between the crowd of people and the loud music, I was starting to feel a little claustrophobic, which didn't help my spinning head. I was hoping to escape in the bathroom stall, but the line was wrapped around the corner. I tried to wait it out, but as I stood there, I couldn't help but notice all the different couples that were huddled up together. They all seemed so happy, so in love, and just looking at them filled me with a sense of hopelessness. I'd only had two relationships in my life, and they'd both ended in heartbreak. Then Mom died, and I gave up trying to find my Mr. Right. Until Murphy, it had been over a year since I'd met anyone who'd interested me, and even then, it was short lived. As soon as the guy opened his mouth, I saw that he was just another arrogant asshole, and I lost all interest in seeing him again. As I glanced back over at one of the couples kissing in the corner, I was hit with the revelation that it was my own fault that I was alone. I'd been too guarded, too resistant to finding anyone to love, and when I finally did let someone in, I'd chosen the wrong man.

I was teetering on the edge of tipsy and more towards drunk, which wasn't the best time for such a revelation. I wasn't thinking clearly, and all the self-loathing was making me feel like the walls were closing in on me. I needed to get some air before I completely lost it. Relief washed over me when I noticed a backdoor. Without a moment's hesitation, I rushed past the long line and darted outside. Even though it was dark and not exactly safe, the cold air did wonders to clear my head. I leaned back against the brick wall, and after several deep breaths, I was starting to feel better. Worried that Grady might wonder where I'd gone, I reached into my purse for my cell phone. As I pulled it out, I spotted the crumpled slip of paper that I'd written Gus's number on. I started to think about how rejected and hurt I'd been feeling over the last couple of weeks. It infuriated me that I'd let Murphy get to me the way he had. The more I thought about it, the angrier I became. Before I realized what I was doing, I'd taken the paper out of my purse and was dialing his number. Seconds later, I heard a man's voice answer, "Yeah?"

"Um ... This Gus?" I stammered.

"Who's asking?"

"I'm askin'."

"And who might you be."

"I'm might be Riley," I slurred, paying absolutely no mind to the anger I heard in his voice.

"Riley who? And how the hell did you get this number?"

There was no way I could tell him that I stole the number from my father, so I just pushed forward. "I need to talk to Murphyyy."

"Did you say Murphy?"

"Yessir ... Murrr-phyy. He's this biker guy. Is he around?"

"Um-hmm." He paused for a moment, then said, "Let me see if I can track him down."

I could hear men talking in the background, but I couldn't make out what they were saying—partly because it was muffled and partly because I was three sheets to the wind. I was fighting to keep my concentration when I heard Murphy's voice say, "Riley?"

"Hellooo, Murphyyy," I sassed. "Is s'good to know you're alive and well."

"Did you know you were calling Gus's number?" he snapped.

"*Mayy-be* I did. *Mayy-be* I didn'."

"What the hell were you thinking? You don't just call the president of Satan's Fury without having a good fucking reason, Riley!"

"I did have a g'reason, Murr-pphy! I've got sumthin I need to say to you. Then, I'm done." I had no idea if he could even understand me with all my slurred words, but I didn't care. I needed to clear my chest, so I told him,

"You might be a big, rrrough an tough biker guy with gorrrgeous, baby blues and great ass ... but that doesn't give you the right to be a complete jerk. And to think I actually thought you were a nice guy. Can you believe that? ... I mean, I actually *liked* you! I was 'slooking forward to seeing you again, but yooo had to go and blow me off."

"Have you been drinking?"

"Yep, and I'm about to drink me s'more."

His voice was low and threatening as he asked, "Where are you?"

Ignoring his question, I asked, "You know wha's really crazy? I actually thought you liked me, too. How sad is that?"

"Riley," he warned.

"You ghosted me, Murphyyy. Do you know wha' that means?" Before he could answer, I snapped, "It means, yooo made me like you, and then you disappeared ... I had no idea if you were alive or dead, *but whatever*. I get it. You aren't interested, and I'm *tow-tahh-ly* fine with that. Seriously. Do what you gotta do. As for me, I'm gonna have myself a grand old time and forget—"

Before I could finish my sentence, he barked, "*Riley*, where the fuck are you?"

I was just about to answer when the backdoor flew open, filling the alley with the sounds of people talking and loud music. As Grady stepped outside, he shouted, "Riley! I've been looking all over the bar for you. What the hell are you doing out here?"

I held up my cellphone as I sassed, "Uh ... I'm on the phone, *Gradyyy*."

"Well, get off the damn phone. It's thirty degrees out here and you're not wearing a fucking coat!"

"I'm jus' fine!"

"You're lips are blue, Lee. Stop acting like a child and get your ass inside."

"Fine! Jus' give me a second." I brought the phone back up to my ear and said, "Hey, Murphyy, I gotta go."

I waited for some kind of response, but I got nothing —just dead air. When I saw the disapproving look on Grady's face, I could tell he was upset with me. As I started towards him, I shrugged. "I'm not on the phone any moooorrree."

"Come on. Let's get back inside." I followed him back over to our table, and as soon as I sat down, he gave me one of his looks. "I'm not going to tell you that you made a huge mistake by calling him, because you'll figure that out tomorrow."

"He s'gonna think I'm a raging lunatic."

"Maybe, but who cares what he thinks." He placed his hand on mine as he said, "You are an amazing woman, Riley Nichols. Any guy who can't see that isn't worth having."

"I know."

"Then act like it and forget about the douchebag."

I let out a deep breath. "Okayyy. You're right. I'm over it."

"Good." When I reached for my drink, he placed his hand on my arm and said, "Easy killer. You need to slow down with the booze."

"Yeah, I probably should, but my buzz is starting to wear off and that's the last thing I need right now." I took a big gulp of my drink and hiccuped before I smiled and said, "But I'll try to behave."

"I'm going to hold you to that."

As I looked over towards the bar, I asked, "Is Earl working tonight?"

"I thought you were going to behave."

"I was just asking a question. Jeez," I complained.

Just as he was about to respond, one of his bouncers came rushing over to Grady. "Hey, boss. We've got a problem."

"What kind of problem?" Grady growled.

He was talking a mile a minute as he explained, "Some guy fell down the front steps. He busted his ass pretty good, and now, he's threatening to sue!"

"On what grounds? He wasn't drunk enough?" Grady scoffed.

"No, sir. I think this guy is a lawyer or something." The bouncer's eyes were wide with panic as he said, "He started spouting off some city penal codes about it being mandatory to clear off any and all ice from the front entrance of the building. I don't know if that's true or if he's just pissed."

"Well, fuck." Grady looked over to me as he said, "I'm sorry, Riley, but I've gotta go see about this guy."

"It's fine. Go ahead."

"I'll be back as quick as I can." As he stood up, he demanded, "Do not move from the spot. Is that understood?"

"Understood."

I watched as he followed the bouncer towards the front door. When they were both out of my line of sight, I turned my attention back to my drink. As I took another sip of my long island, my mind drifted back to my phone call with Murphy. I might regret it more tomorrow, but I was glad I'd gotten everything off my chest. As I tried to focus on the song that was playing, I took another long drink and then another and another. It wasn't long before that woozy feeling returned, and I was swaying to the rhythm of the music. All was well in the world until I caught the attention of a sleaze-ball with slicked-back hair and a thick gold chain. When I noticed him eyeing me from across the room, I quickly turned and looked in the other direction, hoping that he'd get the hint that I wasn't interested. Sadly, he didn't let my disinterest stop him from approaching my table. At the time, I didn't know it, but my night was about to take a drastic turn.

9
_____

MURPHY

*W*hen it came to Riley Nichols, it wasn't about wanting something I couldn't have. It was wanting something I shouldn't want. Knowing what was at stake, I'd done everything in my power to shake the pull I felt towards her, but no matter how hard I tried, she'd always find a way to slip back into my thoughts. The whole thing was driving me over the edge, and when she called, it was like throwing fuel onto the fire. As soon as I heard the sound of her voice, all I could think about was getting to her. I needed to lay my eyes on her, see for myself that she was okay, but from the way she was going off on me, it was doubtful that she'd be happy about seeing me. I wasn't surprised that she was angry. Hell, I would've felt the same if I was in her shoes, but I didn't expect her to call me out, and I certainly didn't expect her to use Gus's phone to do it. Oddly enough, Gus wasn't nearly as surprised as I was. I had no idea how, but he'd known from the start that Riley struck a chord with me. While he had his concerns about me becoming involved with our new supplier's daughter, he trusted me, knowing I'd never do anything to jeopardize my brothers or the club.

When I hung up the phone, Gus looked over to me and asked, "What was that all about?"

"She's drunk and wanted to give me hell."

"Well, I'll be damned. Another fiery one. It'd be nice if one of you boys could fall for a meek, timid chick," he grumbled.

"What's the fun in that?" Blaze argued. "Besides, we all know that the fiery ones are the only ones who can put up with our shit."

"You've got a point there." Gus reached into his pocket and pulled out the keys to his SUV. As he tossed them over to me, he said, "You might want to explain a couple of things to her ... like why she shouldn't steal phone numbers from her dad's cell."

"I'll make sure she understands."

"I know you will."

I couldn't stop thinking about the pain I heard in her voice—the pain I'd caused. I'd hurt her—the very thing I was trying not to do—and it gutted me. One way or another, I had to set things right, but before I could do that, I had to find her. When I started for the door, Gus called, "Murphy?"

I stopped and looked over to him. "Yeah?"

"You'll never know unless you take a chance."

I nodded, then headed out to the parking lot. When I got to his truck, I didn't take the time to consider what Gus had said. Instead, I cranked the engine and drove like a bat out of hell towards downtown. While Riley hadn't actually told me her location, I'd heard her say Grady's name right before the line was disconnected. It was my only clue, and I hoped it would be enough to find her. When I pulled up to the Smoking Gun, I wasn't happy to see that it was packed to the gills. I just wanted to find her and set things straight before she did something we'd both regret, but it wasn't going to be easy to find her in such a large crowd. I started towards the back of the bar, carefully maneuvering my way through the partygoers as I searched for any sign of Riley. I was starting to lose hope when I finally spotted her sitting at one of the tables in the back corner. She was wearing a little black dress that clung perfectly to her curves, and her hair was down around her shoulders. She looked stunning. Unfortunately, I wasn't the only one who'd noticed how beautiful she looked.

An overeager douchebag was standing next to her with his arm around her shoulder, and from the way he was drooling over her, he thought he'd found his companion for the night. Unfortunately for him, that was never going to happen. With my fists clenched at my sides, I started towards them, and as I got closer, I could see that Riley had her hand on the douchebag's chest, trying to push him off her. The guy clearly wasn't taking the hint and just kept whispering God only knows in her ear. She shook her head, clearly telling him no, but he wasn't accepting her answer. By the time I reached the table, I was ready to rip the guy a new one. I placed my hand on his shoulder and snarled, "It's time to move on, asshole."

The guy was at least a foot shorter than me with a slim, but athletic build. When he turned and looked at me, I could tell from his expression that he was feeling unsure of himself, but that didn't stop him from saying, "This doesn't involve you, so fuck off!"

I didn't miss the surprise in her drunken voice when Riley asked, "Murphy? What are you doing here?"

"You've got two seconds to get your fucking hands off her." When he didn't move, I brought my hand up to his throat, lifting him up in the air as I slammed him against the wall. With a look of utter panic, he started clawing at my hand, trying to pry himself free from my hold. The poor bastard looked terrified, but he had it coming. I gave his throat a firm squeeze, and when his face started to turn red, I leaned towards him and with my face just inches from his, I growled, "I'm going to let you go, and when I do, you're going to walk away. Is that understood?"

He nodded frantically.

"Good." I lowered his feet to the ground and released my hold on his throat. "Now, get the fuck out of here."

As he turned to leave, I heard him grumble, "No piece of ass is worth this bullshit!"

The second he was gone, Riley turned to me and asked, "What the hell was that?"

"That was *me* saving your ass from that asshole, which wouldn't have been necessary if you hadn't gone and gotten yourself drunk."

"Oh, no. You don't get to come in here acting all high and mighty trying to *save me*," she slurred. "You don't get to do that. Not after ..."

"*I just did.*"

"Well, you had no right to intervene. Besides, I was *handling it!*"

"Um-hmm. Sure, you were." I crossed my arms as I asked, "Where's your cousin, Grady?"

"Not that it's any of your business ... he had something he needed to take care of."

"So, he left you here alone?"

"Yes, but *he had something important he needed to take care of*," she repeated with an over-exaggerated eye-roll.

"Nothing is as important as you are, Riley. *Nothing.*"

A faint blush crept over her face as she said, "Tha's almost funny coming from you."

When she picked up her drink and took a long sip, I reached for her and said, "You've had enough. It's time to get you home."

"Whoa. Hold up there, Hercules," she argued. "Who are you to tell me when I've had enough? I'mmmm not going anywhere."

"This isn't up for discussion, Riley. You've had your little tantrum. Now, I'm taking you home."

"Tantrum?" Her words continued to be slurred and drawn out as she stood up and asked, "Are you kidding me?"

"Riley," I warned.

"You can 'Riley' me all you want, but I'm not leaving." As she pointed towards the front door, she said, "You, on the other hand, are more than welcome to do whatever you want."

"Is that right?"

With that, I stepped towards her, and with one quick swoop, I lifted her up and planted her across my shoulder. Once I had her situated, I noticed that her dress had shifted, and her tiny, black lace panties and perfect ass were completely exposed. My cock stirred to life, and I silently cursed myself when I felt the urge to touch her and feel her smooth, round flesh beneath my hand. It wasn't the time nor the place, so I gave the hem of her dress a quick tug, making sure she was completely covered. It was at that moment that Riley started hitting me in the back with her fists. "What the hell are you doing? Put me down!"

"You said I was welcome to do whatever I want, and I want to leave."

"I already told you I wasn't going anywhere!"

Unable to help myself, I gave her ass a quick, but memorable smack as I told her, "Considering your present situation, I would say you're wrong about that."

"Oh, my God! I can't believe you just did that! Put me down, Murphy!"

Ignoring her half-hearted protests, I grabbed her purse off the table and worked my way towards the front of the bar. She kept trying to wiggle her way out of my grasp, but that wasn't going to happen. Now that I had her, there was no way in hell I was going to let her go. I gave her ass another firm pop, and as I'd hoped, she finally accepted her fate and settled down. I'd almost made it to the front door when a tall, preppy mother-fucker stepped in front of me, blocking the exit. "What the hell do you think you're doing? Put her the fuck down."

"Not gonna happen."

"Oh, it's gonna happen, and it's gonna happen right now."

"You need to step back, asshole, or you're not gonna like what happens," I warned, tightening my grip around her waist. I could've let her down. Considering her current condition, it would've been the respectful thing to do, but I had a point to make, and I was damn well going to make it. Besides, there was no way in hell I was going to accommodate the asshole who'd left Riley alone while she was drinking. That shit was out of line, and I had every intention of letting him know it.

He took a charging step forward, and just as he was about to do something stupid, Riley stopped him by saying, "Grady, don't. I'm okay."

"Who the fuck is this guy?"

She turned her hips so she could face him, and with a hiccup she answered, "Um ... this is Murphy."

A surprised look crossed his face as his eyes skirted over me. "This is Murphy? *The* Murphy?."

"The one and only."

Grady looked up at me and said, "I don't know what you think you're gonna do here, but there's no way in hell I'm letting you leave with her. Not like that."

"She was under your watch tonight, and you dropped the ball. That fuck up is on you." I knew he was Riley's cousin, but that didn't mean I was gonna let him stand in my way. "If you're smart, you'll see that you're about to fuck up again."

"Grady, just leave it. Seriously, s'okay."

"Nothing about this is okay, Riley," he argued. "Just say the word and I'll handle it."

I eased my hand up and it rested on her ass. Taking the hint, she answered, "Don't. I'll be fine ... if the room will just stop spinning."

Grady reached in his pocket and pulled out his card. "Here's my number. Call me if she needs anything."

I nodded, and as I walked past him, he shouted, "Riley, call me as soon as you get home."

Seconds later, we were out of the bar and headed towards the SUV. When I got to the passenger side door, I carefully lowered Riley's feet to the ground and handed her the purse I'd taken off the table. She stood there silently scowling at me as I opened the door for her. In her act of defiance, she crossed her arms with an angry huff and asked, "Are you going to tell me what your plans are here, or am I just supposed to assume that I am being kidnapped?"

I stepped towards her and with my arms fully extended, I placed my hands flat against the truck, pinning her in place. As I looked down at her, I felt that pull to her grow even stronger, and from the way she was looking back at me, I knew she could feel it, too. "We both know you just got what you wanted, so why don't you just get in the truck and stop pretending that this is something it's not?"

"Oh, my God! You are such an asshole!" Once again, her words were slurred and her facial expressions over-dramatized. "You just carried me out of the bar on your shoulder, and you actually think I *wanted that*?"

"You wanted to see me again, and now, I'm here." I knew I sounded like a dick, but I couldn't stop the words from coming out of my mouth. "So, yeah. You got what you wanted."

"You're right. I *did* want to see you again, but that was before ..." she lowered her head and her voice grew soft, "when you were being nice ... when you actually talked to me instead of the way you're acting now ... barking orders and acting like a bossy asshole. It's hard to believe you're even the same person."

"We're one and the same, Riley." I took a step back as I motioned my hand towards the truck. "You can either come with me and give me a chance to set things right, or I can call you a cab. It's your call."

10

RILEY

*A*nd just like that, he'd put the ball in my court—which couldn't have come at a worse time. In my inebriated state, I had to decide if I was going to ask him to get me a cab and put an end to whatever was going on between us forever or get in his truck and take a chance on starting something real with him. I would've thought it would be a simple decision; after all, I'd pined over him for weeks, but I was completely at odds with myself. As I stood there looking at him, all brooding and sexy as hell, I had no doubt that he had the ability to turn my entire world upside down. My brain was screaming for me to just walk away and salvage what was left of my dignity and self-respect. While I was certain I had a pretty good idea of who he was and the kind of life he led and after dealing with the decisions my father had made, I wasn't sure I could handle it. My heart, on the other hand, didn't agree. I'd seen a glimpse of the man beneath that rough exterior. Murphy was no knight in shining armor, but there was a light hidden away in all that darkness—a good inside of him that I was drawn to in ways I couldn't begin to understand. There were plenty of reasons why I should be scared of wanting him, but the fact was I did, and I couldn't imagine walking away without taking a chance.

I mulled it over for a few more seconds, then let out a deep breath and started to get inside the truck. Once I was settled, he shut the door, then walked over to the driver's side and got in. Neither of us spoke as he started the engine and pulled out of the parking lot. When he started out onto the main road, I asked, "So, what's the plan here?"

"I already told you, I'm taking you home."

I tried my best to hide the disappointment in my voice when I replied, "Oh, okay."

Feeling dejected once again, I turned and leaned my head against window, completely ignoring him as we continued forward. Just as we were leaving the crowded streets of downtown, something caught Murphy's attention, and he mumbled something under his breath as he slammed on his breaks. Seconds later, we were parked next to the sidewalk and he was getting out of the truck. He grabbed something out of the backseat, and just before he closed the door, he looked at me and said, "Lock it and stay put."

"Um... okay?"

"No matter what happens, do not move from this spot, Riley. Is that understood?"

"Yes. It's understood."

With that, he closed the door and waited for me to

lock it behind him. Once he was sure that I was secured inside, he started walking towards a group of teenagers who were huddled together near the side of an old brick building. I had no idea what was going on until one of the boys happened to notice that Murphy was headed in their direction. When the boy took a step back, I could see that his friends were harassing an old homeless man, kicking and hitting him as they towered over him like a pack of wolves. The whole scene sickened me, and I hoped that Murphy would be able to put an end to it but feared that there were too many for him to handle. I wanted to call out to him and tell him not to risk it, but it was already too late. The others had seen him approaching, and their focus was now directed at him. Words were exchanged, and I thought they were about to jump Murphy, when instead, the teenagers started to scurry away. It was the craziest thing I'd ever seen. Together, they could've easily taken him down, but they all looked completely freaked out as they rushed out of sight. I watched in wonder as Murphy walked over to the homeless man and helped him to his feet. He spoke with him for several minutes, and once he saw that he was okay, he offered him the coat he'd gotten out of the backseat. After he'd put it on, Murphy reached into his front pocket and pulled out some cash. He gave the money to him, then turned around and walked towards the truck.

I unlocked the door, and as soon as he was back inside, he started up the truck and drove away. I wanted to ask him about what had just happened, but I couldn't form the words. I was too stunned. I couldn't believe that the same man who'd thrown me over his shoulder, smacked my behind not once, but twice, and carried me out of the bar like a caveman had shown such compassion and kindness to an elderly homeless man. It just didn't make sense to me.

Maybe it was the fact that I was intoxicated or maybe because I was so lost in my own world of thoughts, whatever the reason, I never even noticed that he didn't take the exit to the interstate. Instead, Murphy had pulled up to a beautiful cobblestone house and parked. He opened his truck door and said, "We're here."

As I sat up in my seat, I looked out the window and asked, "Wait. I thought you were taking me home."

"You're right. I did." I was beyond confused. I thought I was starting to sober up, but apparently, I still had a long way to go. Murphy got out of the truck and continued, "I just didn't say whose home I was taking you to."

"Hold on ... This is where you live?"

"Yes. This is where I live." He walked over and opened my door, then reached for my hand and led me up to the front steps. Even though it was dark, I could tell we were in a nice neighborhood, most likely in midtown. Like several of the other homes around him, it had a small front porch and a large fenced-in backyard, but unlike the others, his was landscaped with elegant shrubbery and flowers along the walkway. As he unlocked the front door, he shrugged. "It's not much, but it's home. Go see for yourself."

I stepped inside, and my mouth dropped open when he turned on the lights, revealing a quaint little entry way with checkered tile and an elaborate, crystal chandelier hanging above the hallway that led to the second floor. As I started towards the living room, I quickly realized that Murphy had spared no expense when it came to making his home just the way he wanted it. His furniture, the color of the walls, the newly refinished hardwood floors, and even the artwork hanging throughout the room looked as if they were all made specifically for him. When I walked into the kitchen, it was much of the same—elegant but comfortable. I could barely contain myself. "It's really incredible, Murphy."

"Glad you think so."

"Was it like this when you bought it?"

"I did most of it myself, but I had some of the brothers give me a hand." He took off his leather jacket and hung it on the back of a kitchen chair before walking over to the refrigerator. He opened the door and looked inside then asked, "Have you had dinner?"

I wasn't really in the mood to eat, so I answered, "No, but I'm not really hungry."

"You need to eat something, Riley." Before I had a chance to respond, he asked, "What are you in the mood for? I could make us a couple of burgers or a full on breakfast. The choice is yours."

"Actually ... breakfast sounds really good."

"Yes, it does."

He grabbed a package of bacon along with a pound of sausage and after he placed them on the counter, he pulled out the eggs and a couple of cans of biscuits. Once he had everything laid out, I walked over to the stove and asked, "What can I do?"

"Nothing. I've got this." Then, he offered me a large

glass of water and two Tylenol. "Just make yourself comfortable."

After the way he'd put me in my place at the bar, it was hard to believe that he could be so sweet. It was like the old Murphy had returned, and while I couldn't have been more pleased that he was back, I found myself wondering why he'd come to the bar to find me, especially after the way I'd talked to him on the phone. It didn't make sense. He should've been completely turned off by what he called my "little tantrum," but there he stood, preparing to cook breakfast for me. Either he really was interested in me or he simply felt sorry for me. I was curious to know the answer. "Can I ask you something?"

"Let's get some food in you, and then you can ask me whatever you want."

"And you'll give me an honest answer?"

"I'll do my best."

"Okay." After I took the Tylenol he'd given me, I went over to the kitchen table and sat down. As I sat there watching him with his broad shoulders, defined, muscular chest, and unruly dirty-blond hair, I thought how odd it was that such a gruff biker was actually cooking bacon and eggs *for me*. I couldn't have imagined anything sexier, and it was difficult to resist the temptation of going over to be close to him. Thankfully, my growling stomach distracted me, and as soon as he was done, I helped him carry everything over to the table. Once we'd made our plates, I dug in, and it was absolute heaven. With my mouth still full, I mumbled, "Oh, my. This is incredible."

"Yeah. I gotta admit, it's not half bad," he replied proudly. I took another bite, and it wasn't long before I'd cleared my plate. When Murphy noticed, a big smile crossed his face. "So, I take it you were hungrier than you thought?"

"Apparently so, or maybe it's just due to the fact that it was so good. You really outdid yourself."

"I'm glad you enjoyed it." When he got up to put our dishes in the sink, he asked, "How are you feeling?"

Then I remembered how I'd behaved earlier. "Mentally or physically?"

He chuckled. "Let's start with physically."

"Well, there, I'm doing okay."

"You think you're sobering up?"

I shrugged. "I guess so. The room has stopped spinning."

"Good." He brought me another bottle of water and placed it on the table in front of me. "You need to keep hydrated."

"Okay." After I took a sip of water, I told him, "By the way, it was really sweet of you to help that homeless guy like you did."

"He would've done the same for me."

"So, you know him?"

"He's a vet ... One of our brothers, Sam, was in a similar situation a few years back, so we try to keep an eye out for him when we can."

"He's lucky to have you do that for him. Who knows what would've happened if you hadn't come by there when you did."

"Good thing we don't have to find out."

With my buzz quickly wearing off, I was starting to feel cold and suddenly wished I was wearing something more than my little black dress. I ran my hands over my bare arms, then crossed my arms, hugging myself for warmth. Murphy noticed that I was cold and said, "Come into the living room and I'll start a fire."

"Okay." I grabbed my bottle of water and followed him, then I sat down on the sofa and watched as he lit the gas logs. Once the fire was rolling, he pulled a blanket off the back of the sofa and offered it to me. Wrapping it around me, I smiled and said, "Thank you, Murphy."

He sat down next to me and quietly watched the fire as it danced between the logs. I could tell by his expression that there was something on his mind, something that brought tension into the room. I could feel it radiating from him, and the longer we sat there without talking, the worse it became. I was beginning to wonder if he was ready for me to leave when he finally said, "You had a question you wanted to ask."

"Yeah. I guess I did." He turned to face me and waited silently for me to speak. It was much easier to ask intimate questions when you've been drinking with the courage of alcohol coursing through your veins. Now that I was sober, I wasn't sure I was brave enough to say the words. After several awkward moments, I finally wimped out and said, "It's really nothing. Just forget I mentioned it."

"Surely, you aren't about to chicken out on me."

"*Maybe.*"

"Ask the question, Riley."

"Well, one question might lead into another, so be

warned." He nodded, so I let out a deep breath and continued, "On that morning when you came out to the farm, why did you make me think you were going to see me again?"

"Because at the time, I intended to see you," he answered flatly.

"But then you changed your mind?"

His blue eyes grew intense as he answered, "Yes, but I had my reasons ... reasons you might not understand."

"Okay, so why don't you explain it to me," I pushed.

"It's complicated, but all in all, I did it for *you*."

"You did it for me?"

"I was trying to protect you."

"Protect me from what?"

"From *me*."

Of all things, I wasn't expecting that to be his answer. He hadn't tried to hide who he was. I'd seen his club's name embroidered on the back of his leather jacket. I was there when he came to buy illegal weapons from my father. I knew what I was getting into when he showed up at the farm that morning, and I never once thought I was in any kind of danger. Instead, I felt safe and free to be myself. I loved the time I'd spent with him and longed for more. Hearing that he felt the need to protect me from the man I'd grown so fond of didn't make sense to me, and I wasn't so sure that he truly believed what he was saying either. "If you honestly believed you were protecting me by staying away, then why did you come to the bar looking for me tonight?"

His eyes narrowed as he barked, "You called Gus's phone, Riley."

"And?"

"And that was a bigger deal than you realize, and a topic we will discuss again later."

"Okay, but you still haven't answered my question."

"I needed to make sure you were okay."

He was talking in circles, and I was more confused than ever. "I'm sorry, but I just don't understand."

"We have our obvious differences. That, in itself, is enough, but there is so much more than that." The confidence in his voice was replaced with unease as he said, "I'm not one of those guys who believes in happy endings. I don't believe in soul mates or love everlasting. In fact, I don't believe in love in any regard."

"Love? Who said anything about love?" I scoffed.

"After that phone call, you're gonna try and tell me that the thought of *us* hasn't crossed your mind ... You haven't wondered if there could be something more between us? You never once wondered if we could fall in love and have a happily ever after?"

"Touché." Trying my best not to lose my momentum, I narrowed my eyes as I looked at him and said, "So, let me make sure I got this straight ... You think love is just some word—nothing more, nothing less—and because of this particular belief of yours, you decided to blow me off."

"I didn't blow you off, Riley," he argued. "But yes. You deserve someone who can give you more ... someone who can love you."

"How do you know what I deserve? You barely know me." I shifted in my seat so I was facing him. "I could be the devil incarnate for all you know."

"I know, Riley."

"*How* do you know, Murphy?" I pushed.

"I can feel it," he answered nonchalantly.

"So, you can feel that I'm a person who deserves someone who can give me more, but you're incapable of feeling love?"

"Never said I was incapable of feeling love. I said I don't believe in it."

"But how can you feel something you don't believe in?" When his back stiffened, I knew I'd struck a nerve, but I didn't let that stop me from saying, "You know that doesn't make any sense, right?"

"Maybe not, but it is what it is."

"*Wow*. Somebody did a real number on you." He didn't verbally confirm my suspicions, but I could tell by the expression on his face that I was right. Someone had betrayed him, and the pain they caused was still there, tugging at him and refusing to be forgotten. I wanted to show him that he was wrong about love, but first, he'd have to trust me enough to let me in. I placed my hand on his thigh and said, "In case you don't know, not all relationships end bad."

"I've never known one that didn't."

"I find that hard to believe. There has to be someone you know who has a good relationship ... maybe a friend or one of your brothers." His eyes skirted upward, and I instantly knew that I was right. Even though he'd never admit it, it was clear he knew someone with a good relationship. I gave him a second to think about it before I continued, "My parents fell in love when they were just teenagers, and they were still madly in love thirty-five years later."

"And yet, he's alone now with a broken heart, selling illegal guns to keep from losing everything else he cared about."

He was clearly set on his beliefs and I was probably wasting my breath, but I told him, "True, but he had something really great for a long time. And I bet if you asked him, he'd do it all over again."

"A glutton for punishment," he mumbled in almost a whisper.

"Maybe so, but he wasn't scared to try. Can you say the same about yourself?"

"I'm not scared, Riley."

"Okay, then. *Prove it.*" I inched a little closer to him, and then I did something I never dreamed I would do. I looked into those beautiful, baby blues and with more confidence than I actually felt, I said, "Take a chance right now ... and *kiss me*."

I could see the wheels turning in his head as he considered my challenge, and for several moments, he didn't move. He just sat there with his eyes locked on mine, fighting an inner battle that might never have a victor. Tension coiled around us, making me want to take matters into my own hands. I wanted to know if his touch was anything like I'd imagined in my dreams, but I stayed planted in my spot. Like he'd done earlier, I'd placed the ball in his court, and it was his turn to make the move.

I was beginning to think he was going to pass on the chance to prove me wrong, when he brought his hands up to my face and slowly brushed his thumb across my bottom lip. He slowly leaned closer, and a warmth rushed over me when I felt a slight tickle from his beard against my jaw. He was so close, just inches away, but he didn't kiss me. Not yet. Instead, he hovered over me, lingering in that moment of anticipation and lust. When neither of us could stand it a moment longer, he lowered his lips to mine. My entire body tingled as he delved deeper into my mouth. I quickly realized that this was no simple kiss, no simple peck on the lips. There was no working up to something more. From the moment his mouth touched mine, it was a kiss full of passion and need that sent me spiraling into a storm of absolute ecstasy. Murphy's arm slipped around my waist, pulling me over to him as he continued to claim me with his mouth. I'd never felt anything so intense, so full of desire, as we clung to each other like we were taking in our last breath. I suddenly realized that I wanted more, much more, and the thought terrified me. Doubts rushed over me, and I found myself pulling back. And not just a little. I pulled back all the way, and without even realizing what I was doing, I'd slipped out of his grasp and down onto the floor. Mortified by my actions, I dropped my head into my hands and groaned.

With a surprised look on his face, he looked down at me and asked, "You wanna tell me why you're down there instead of up here with me?"

"I just need a moment."

"Okay? You wanna tell me why you need a moment?"

"No, not really."

"You having regrets already?" He teased.

"Um ... no. Not yet, but I'm afraid I might if you keep kissing me like that."

Clearly amused by my quandary, he asked, "Is there something wrong with the way I kiss?"

"No. I love the way you kiss." I looked up at him as I continued, "That's the problem."

"And why is that a problem?"

"I know it's a little late for me to be telling you this now, but there's a good chance I could suck at this. Unlike you, I haven't had a lot of experience with sex."

Using my own words against me, he teased me. "Sex? Who said anything about sex?"

"I'm just saying if we get to that point, and *I really hope that we do*, I don't want you to be disappointed."

"There's no way in hell I would ever be disappointed, not when you kiss like that." With his brows furrowed, he glanced down at the bulge between his legs and growled, "Hell, woman. Can't you see what you do to me?"

It wasn't until exactly that moment I noticed he was aroused, and my confidence returned with a warm rush after I realized I'd done that to him with just a kiss. I eased back up on the sofa, and as I settled in next to him, I wished I could go back in time and take back my momentary lapse of judgement. Wanting to pick right up where we'd left off, but knowing where it could lead, I needed him to take control of the situation, proving that he wanted this just as much as I did.

11

MURPHY

*S*he challenged me at every turn and made me rethink everything I believed in. I shouldn't have been surprised. I knew from the start that she was trouble. I could feel it in my fucking bones. Everything about Riley Nichols, from her sharp wit to her innocent smile screamed red flags, cautioning me to steer clear, and yet, I found myself wanting to ignore all the warning signs. I couldn't understand it. When I was with her, the walls I'd put up would disappear, like they never even existed, and instead of focusing on all the things that could go wrong, I wound up thinking of all the possibilities. That was Riley. She'd caught me in her spell and turned me inside out. I'd let myself get drawn in, and now that she'd pushed me into a corner, I had to decide what I was going to do about it. I could take a chance and see if she was right, or stick to my guns and walk away before things got even more complicated. The decision might've been easier if she didn't look so damn beautiful sitting there and staring at me with those gorgeous dark eyes, waiting to see if I was going to kiss her again.

For weeks, I'd imagined what it would feel like to have her mouth on mine, and now that I'd actually had a taste of her, there was no way in hell I could resist having another. As I leaned towards her, I said, "I'm going to take a chance here, and I'm going to kiss you, Riley. I'm going to kiss you long and hard. I'm going to make you forget every doubt you ever had and show you exactly what you do to me, but before I do, I need to tell you ... I'm going to want more than just a kiss. I'm going to want all of you ... every fucking inch, and once I have you, there'll be no walking away ... no letting you go."

"Okay."

"You need to be sure about this."

Without a moment's hesitation, she leaned in towards me and replied, "I am sure, Murphy."

"There's one more thing. Murphy is my road name. It's something my brothers call me. My real name ... the name I want you to call me whenever we're alone together is Lincoln."

"*Lincoln*," she whispered.

Hearing her say my name did something to me. I needed to hear it again, so I demanded, "Say it again."

Her eyes met mine as she repeated, "Lincoln."

Unable to wait any longer, I slipped my arm around her waist and drew her closer as I lowered my mouth to hers. I couldn't believe how good she felt in my arms, like her body was meant to be next to mine, and I cursed myself for the time I'd wasted trying to keep my distance from her. When she inched her way closer, I knew I was done. Even if it meant the end of me, I wouldn't waste another second. I pulled her over my lap with her knees straddling me as I delved deeper, tasting her, teasing her, driving us both crazy with need. Her hands slowly drifted over my chest as she grazed her center against my throbbing erection. Knowing there was just a tiny piece of fabric between us was driving me to the edge, and hearing all of her little moans and whimpers wasn't helping matters.

"Riley," I rasped. "I don't know how much more I can take."

"Me either. I want you so much."

"Maybe it's best that we just stop ... at least for now."

Her eyebrows furrowed as she protested, "I don't want to stop, Lincoln. I want this."

At the sound of my name, I lowered my hands to her hips, carefully lifting her as I stood up from the sofa. I took a step forward, and her legs instinctively made their way around my waist. My breath caught when I felt her body pressed against mine. Damn. Need surged through me like a fucking wildfire. I feared if I didn't extinguish the burn, it would completely consume me. As I started up the stairs, I had to fight the urge to stop and just take her right there on the fucking steps. When we finally made it up to my room, I carried her to the foot of the bed and slowly lowered her feet to the floor. With her standing before me, I brought my hand up to her face, and ran the pad of my thumb across her bottom lip as I said, "I can't tell you how many times I've thought about this moment."

"I've thought about it, too ... many times, but I never

dreamed it would feel like this." She took a step back and said, "I didn't know it was possible to want someone like I want you right now."

With her eyes trained on mine, she pulled her little black dress over her head, revealing her black lace bra and panties. I'd never seen a more incredible sight. From head to toe, she was absolute perfection. I watched in awe as she reached her arms behind her, removing her lace bra. She stood there in nothing but her lace panties looking at me with needful eyes, waiting for me to make my move. I could hardly restrain myself with her looking so unbelievably beautiful. I was barely able to keep it together, and seeing that spark of eagerness only made it more difficult as I kicked off my boots and removed my shirt.

I dropped my hands to her waist and slowly lowered her sexy little body onto my bed. Impatient for more, her hands quickly dropped to her hips as she slowly lowered her panties, inch by inch, down her long legs. Her eyes never left mine as she kicked them off the bed. She lay there, her naked body sprawled across my bed as she waited for me to come to her. "You're so damn beautiful."

"Lincoln, *please*."

I was done. I had to have her. I let my eyes drift down her body, and her delicious curves called me as I lowered myself down onto the bed next to her. I watched the goosebumps rise along her skin as I began to trace the slope of her breast with my fingertips. She was perfect, every damn inch of her. I'd waited so long to find her— someone who could make me feel again. My mouth moved to her neck, kissing and nipping gently at her soft skin before traveling to her collarbone and then her breast. I rolled my tongue around her nipple and watched with satisfaction as her back arched off the bed, silently pleading for more. I glided my tongue along her stomach ever so slowly, trailing kisses here and there as I settled myself between her thighs. "You've got no idea what you do to me, but baby ... *you're about to find out.*"

Without waiting for a response, I lowered myself between her legs. I needed to taste her, to see for myself just how turned on she really was. I slid my hands under her ass as I lowered my head between her legs and ran my tongue ever so slightly across her center, teasing her, tormenting her as she squirmed beneath me. Damn. Everything about her had me burning for more. I never dreamed I could want anyone like I wanted her. She gasped and her back arched off the bed as I pressed the flat of my tongue against her clit. I loved seeing her come apart, knowing that I was in complete control as I watched her body respond to my touch. I wanted to make her come undone. I wanted to hear all of her little gasps and whimpers again and again as I pushed her to the edge of her release.

"L-Lincoln," she stammered as her fingers dove into my hair, guiding me as her knees opened wider. With the sounds of her moans echoing through the room, I placed my hands on her thighs, holding her in place as I continued to lick and suck while easing my fingers deep inside her, searching for the spot that would drive her wild. When I found it, I covered her with my mouth, tormenting her until her body started to tremble beneath me. Her hands dropped to her sides as she clutched the sheets, tugging them tightly as her orgasm surged through her body like a bolt of lightning. As she gasped for air, I could hear her mumbling, "Oh, my God."

She was still lost in the haze of her release when I stood up and removed my jeans and boxers. I quickly pulled on a condom, then lowered my body on top of her. Eager for more, her thighs spread as she wrapped her legs around my waist, pulling me close and grinding her hips against mine. I raked my throbbing erection against her, and as soon as I felt the warmth of her center, I whispered, "Do you feel that? That's what you do to me, Riley."

"Lincoln," was the only word she could muster.

I knew right then that I would never get tired of hearing her say my name in that breathy, wanton tone like she wanted me just as much as I wanted her. She pressed her lips to mine in a possessive, demanding kiss as she used her legs to pull me forward, and I felt her tremble beneath me as I slid deep inside her, giving her every aching inch of my cock. Fuck. She was so tight, so warm and wet, engulfing me in splendor. After pausing for several breaths, I started to move, slowly rocking against her. I watched as she started to writhe beneath me, her neck and chest flushed red with desire, and her eyes clenched shut. For the moment, she was lost in all the sensations, and I couldn't take my eyes off of her. The mere sight of her called to me, making me want to claim her, and as much as the thought rattled me, it didn't stop me from wanting to make her mine. I lowered my mouth to hers, kissing her deep and rough before I started to increase my pace. I thrust against her, hard and demanding, and her head fell back with a pleasured moan when I hit that spot that drove her wild. Her hips rolled into mine with the same fevered rhythm as my own. She wasn't holding back. Instead, she met my every move, letting me know without words exactly what she wanted. Her nails dug into my lower back as she lifted her hips, trying to force me deeper, and when she started to tighten around me, there was no question that she was getting close. I could feel the pressure building, forcing a growl from my chest. Unable to resist, I began to drive deeper, harder, and her head reared back as she cried, "Yes! Lincoln! Don't stop!"

"That's it, beautiful." I couldn't wait to see her orgasm take hold once again, to hear those little sounds she made over and over. "Come for me."

Her body grew rigid, and she started gasping for air as her thighs clamped down around my hips. I knew she was close to the edge, unable to stop the inevitable torment of her building orgasm. The muscles in her body grew taut and still as she held her breath for several long moments. Finally, her muscles began to quiver and a rush of air escaped from her lungs. With my impending release quickly approaching, I continued to drive into her with the sounds of my body pounding against hers echoing throughout the room. With one last deep-seated thrust, I buried my cock inside her as my orgasm finally took hold. After several deep breaths, I lowered myself down on her chest. I rested there for just a brief moment, then I rolled onto my back, slid off the condom and tossed it in the basket by my night table. When I pulled her over to me, she rested her head on my shoulder with the palm of her hand on my chest and a satisfied smile on her face. After a few moments of recovery, I was pleased to see that Riley was more than willing to have another go, and then another. In fact, we spent the entire night tangled up together, and would've continued on even longer if my burner cell hadn't started ringing.

I reached down and grabbed my jeans from the floor then pulled my phone out of my back pocket. When I saw that it was Gus calling, I answered, "Hello?"

"Is Riley there with you?"

"She is. Why? Is something wrong?"

"Yeah. *You could say that*," he huffed. "Her father just called looking for her."

"He did? What made him think to call you?"

"Apparently, some guy has been calling her all night and all morning, and when she didn't answer, he called her father to see if she'd made it home."

"That'd be, Grady," I grumbled, catching Riley's attention.

"Yeah. That's him," Gus grumbled. "Seems he told her father that you came in the bar and carried Riley out on your shoulder against her will?"

"Wasn't exactly *against her will*."

"Um-hmm," he scoffed. "Well, now he thinks you've kidnapped his daughter."

"Damn."

"You might wanna have her call him and let the guy know she's all right before he does something stupid," Gus suggested.

"I'll have her call him right now and get it sorted."

As soon as I hung up the phone, Riley turned to me and asked, "What was that about?"

"Your father .... You need to call him and let him know you're okay."

"Why? What makes him think I'm not okay?"

"Grady called him looking for you, and after he told him about last night, your dad called Gus looking for you."

"Damn. Grady and his big mouth," she complained. "You're right. I better call him. Do you mind if I use your phone? Mine is downstairs."

As soon as I handed it to her, she took it and started dialing her father's number. She bit at her bottom lip as she waited for him to answer. When she heard his voice on the other end of the line, her back stiffened as she said, "Hey, Dad. It's me."

"Riley! What the hell is going on?"

"I'm fine, Dad. I'm with ... "

Before she could finish her sentence, I heard him bark, "I know who you are with Riley! Grady told me all about you and that Murphy fella."

"I am, and like I said earlier, I'm fine."

"No, Riley. You're not fine!" he roared. "That man is dangerous, and you damn well know it."

"I don't know that, and honestly, I don't want to talk about it right now. I was just calling to let you know I was okay," she snapped back in return.

"Listen to me, Riley. You need to get the hell out of there!"

"Goodbye, Dad. I'll see you in a couple of hours."

She hung up the phone and tried to act unfazed by

the conversation with her father as she handed it back to me. Once I'd laid it down on the side table, she returned to her spot in the crook of my arm and rested her head on my chest. As I ran my fingers through her long dark hair, I whispered, "You okay?"

"I'm more than okay."

"You sure about that?" I looked down at her as I said, "It didn't sound like your father was very pleased about you being here with me."

"No, he wasn't, but I'll talk to him when I get home." There was no hiding the concern in her voice as she asked, "What about you? Are you okay?"

I kissed her on the shoulder and answered, "Honestly, I'm better than I've been in a long time."

A beautiful, bright smile slowly crept over her face as she said, "I'm glad to hear you say that." She turned to her side so she could face me when she asked, "I've been thinking about something."

"Okay? What have you been thinking?"

"I was just wondering ... if your name is Lincoln, why do your brothers call you Murphy?"

"I was wondering when you'd get around to asking that." I chuckled. "Have you ever heard of Murphy's Law?"

Her brows furrowed as she asked, "Isn't that the saying ... if anything can go wrong, it will go wrong?"

"Yeah. That's the one. My brothers picked up on the fact that I like to be prepared. I try to think of the things that can go wrong in any given situation, and I do my best to ensure that those bad things don't happen. It's one of the reasons why they made me their sergeant-at-arms."

"What's that?"

"It's a position in the club." I didn't want to go into great detail, so I told her, "It's my job to make sure things go the way they're supposed to."

She smiled. "I bet that's not always easy when you're dealing with grown men."

"No, it's not, but it's nothing I can't handle." I leaned down and kissed her on the temple before easing out of bed. I walked over to my dresser and grabbed her a pair of sweats and a t-shirt. I knew they would be too big for her, but at least they were clean. As I offered them to her, I asked, "You hungry?"

"I could go for a cup of coffee, but afterwards, I should probably get going." She sat up on the bed and started to put on the clothes I'd given her. "I have a big test tomorrow, and I need to help clean out the stables or Hunter will never let me hear the end of it."

"Okay"—I grabbed some clothes for myself and started to get dressed—"but, I'm gonna have to see you again soon."

She walked over to me and wrapped her arms around my neck as she replied, "And I'm going to have to see you, too."

I leaned down and kissed her, long and hard, giving her something to remember before she left. As soon as she'd gathered her things, she followed me downstairs and I made us both some coffee. Before we left the house, I gave her my cell phone number, warning her not to contact Gus unless it was an emergency, then I took her back to her car. My chest tightened as I watched her get out of the truck and walk over to where she was parked. I waited as she unlocked the door and tossed her things in the backseat. Just as she was about to get inside, she stopped and turned back towards me. She looked at me for a moment, then rushed back over to the SUV. When I opened the door, she reached for me, kissing me tenderly before she asked, "Soon, right?"

"Very soon."

She smiled as she replied, "Good."

After one last kiss she headed back to her car, and seconds later she was gone. As I pulled out of the parking lot and made my way to the clubhouse, I thought back over the past few weeks and tried to pinpoint the second that everything took a turn. I'd always done everything in my power to guard against Murphy's Law, thinking if I was prepared for all those things that could go wrong, they wouldn't happen. I'd even made up a specific set of rules to follow to ensure that I would always be prepared for those things that would go wrong, but when it came to Riley Nichols, I'd failed to remember one of my most important rules—*never let your emotions rule you.* I just couldn't help myself. She made me feel things I never thought I could, so I took a chance and put everything on the line. It was a decision that would change everything, triggering more and more of my rules to be broken, and if I wasn't careful, it would cost me everything—including her.

12

RILEY

On my drive back home, I couldn't stop thinking about the night I'd shared with Murphy. It was hot, romantic, and everything in between. Murphy was absolutely incredible, more than I could've ever dreamed, and when I thought about the way he touched me, my entire body would tingle. I wasn't exactly surprised. I knew from the moment I laid eyes on him that he wasn't like any man I'd ever known. He was sin wrapped up in one wickedly, sexy package, and I found him positively, mouthwateringly hot. It wasn't just his good looks that I found so appealing. It was the way he exuded confidence that had me so intrigued. Murphy was one of those take-charge types with complete control of himself and those around him, and I simply couldn't take my eyes off him. At the time, I had no idea that there was another side to him, one full of kindness and compassion that took his hotness to a whole new level. After spending an incredible night with him, I was floating on cloud nine, but as I got closer to home, those blissful thoughts slowly started to fade.

I wasn't looking forward to facing my father, especially after the way he found out that I was with Murphy. It wasn't that I'd intended to keep it a secret from him. I'd just hoped that I'd have the opportunity to talk to him, to explain everything to him in a calm, rational way, but Grady had taken that chance away from me. I couldn't really blame him. When I finally returned his call, it was clear that I'd worried him, especially after the way Murphy carried me out of the bar. He had a million questions, but I put him off, telling him it was a conversation we needed to have in person. I promised to go see him soon so we could talk about everything, and thankfully, he agreed to wait. For the time being, I needed to focus my thoughts on what I was going to say to my father. When I started down my driveway, a feeling of dread washed over me which only got worse when I saw that he was waiting for me on the front steps. I took a deep breath and did my best to collect my thoughts as I parked the car. As soon as I got out, he started walking towards me with an angry scowl. "Do you have any idea how worried I've been?"

"I told you I was fine. Besides, there was no reason for you to be worried."

"No reason to worry? Are you kidding me?" he shouted. "Do you have any idea who this man is? What he's capable of?"

"I know him better than you might think."

"I sincerely doubt that, otherwise you wouldn't have been with him last night." He shook his head and sighed.

"That club he belongs to ... Satan's Fury ... they're not just a group of guys who ride motorcycles together. They're criminals, Riley. Those men aren't just buying weapons, they use them to kill anyone who tries to stand in their way, and your new boyfriend, Murphy, he's not only a member, he's one of their officers."

"You're the man who sold them the guns!" I glared at him as I said, "Oh, that's right. You had a good reason for doing what you did. That excuses everything."

"Is this what this is all about? Is this your way of punishing me for—"

"I'm not punishing you, Dad. Me seeing Murphy has nothing to do with you." I reached into the backseat and grabbed my bag. As I slammed the door shut, I looked at him and said, "You taught me that it's not right to judge anyone, especially when you don't know anything about them, and yet here you are doing exactly that. I expected more from you."

"I just don't want you throwing your life away because that's exactly what you'll be doing if you continue seeing him!" He was about to continue when his attention was drawn over to a black BMW that was barreling down our gravel driveway. A distressed look crossed his face as he ordered, "Get inside and lock the door."

"Who is that?"

I could hear the panic in his voice as he shouted, "Do what I said, Riley! Now!"

I'd never seen him quite so rattled, so I did what he said and rushed inside, quickly locking the door behind me. Knowing something was terribly wrong, I stood by the window and watched as the car came to a screeching halt. I held my breath as a man got out and started to approach my father. It didn't take me long to recognize him. As soon as I saw his face, I remembered seeing him that day I was hiding in the treehouse. He'd come to purchase weapons from Dad, but unlike today, his visit hadn't taken Dad by surprise. On that day, he didn't seem nervous or threatened by Devon, but that clearly wasn't the case today. While he was doing his best to hide it, I could tell Dad was feeling uneasy about the situation. His tone was short as Dad looked up at the man and said, "Hello, Devon. I didn't know you were coming by."

"You haven't been answering my calls."

"I've already told you. I sold the shipment you were interested in, so there's nothing left for us to discuss. Our business is done."

"That's where you're wrong. We aren't even close to being done." The man took a menacing step towards my father as he growled, "Those weapons were ours, and you sold them right out from under our feet."

"That's not how it played out, and you know it. You and your boss had your chance to buy, but you didn't move fast enough." Even though I was completely terrified by the menacing expression on Devon's face, my father seemed unfazed and his voice never faltered as he continued, "That's on you. Not me."

Devon's nose flared as he stuck out his chest and snarled, "You best remember who you're talking to, Mr. Nichols."

"Look, Devon. I don't want any trouble with you or your boss, but the deal is done." Dad shrugged. "Those guns are gone."

"Then, you need to get them back!"

"By now, they're halfway across the country."

"Fuck! Lynch is going to lose his shit." Devon ran his hand roughly over his face. "When can you get your hands on some more?"

"Not sure that I can. Like I told you last week, I'm getting out of the business."

With that, Devon sprang forward and grabbed my father's shirt, fisting it tightly as he jerked him forward. "You're not getting out of the business until the *Hurricanes* say you're getting out! You are going to do whatever it takes to get us that fucking shipment, or there'll be hell to pay. Is that understood?"

From the day I first learned about my father's new enterprise, I'd worried that something would go wrong, and now my worst fears were becoming a reality. I was completely terrified, and I wasn't the only one. Dad's courageous stance started to waver when he mumbled, "Yeah, I understand ... but it's going to take some time."

"I'm glad we're finally on the same page," Devon replied as he turned towards his car. "You've got forty-eight hours."

Before my father could respond he got into his car, and seconds later he was gone. Dad didn't move. He simply stood there staring off into space with a blank expression on his face. It was a look of defeat, much like the one he had on the day the doctors told him that Mom's treatments hadn't worked. I didn't know what to do. He wouldn't like that I'd eavesdropped, but I couldn't pretend that I hadn't heard Devon's threat. I unlocked the door and slipped out onto the porch without my father even noticing. I stepped up behind him and asked, "Are you okay?"

His eyes skirted over to me as he answered, "You were listening?"

"Yes. I heard everything." My voice trembled as I asked, "What are you going to do?"

"I'll figure it out."

"If you get them that shipment, won't they just keep coming back for more?"

"I said, I'll figure it out, Riley," he snapped.

"I'm sorry. It's just ... that guy was pretty scary." I looked him in the eyes and told him, "I don't want anything to happen to you."

"Now, you understand how I feel. I know you don't want to believe me, but that Murphy fellow is just as scary as Devon. You keep talking to him, and you'll eventually see that side of him. I guarantee it."

"Maybe, but it's a chance I'm willing to take." As I started back up the porch steps, I told him, "You know, there's more to you than just this farm and the horses you breed, and the same goes for Murphy. There's more to him than just that club. There's a lot of good in him, and it's a shame you can't see that."

"I've seen all I need to see to know that my beautiful daughter has no business messing around with the likes of him."

I shook my head with disgust as I opened the front door. Before I stepped inside, I told him, "I have some studying to do."

"Well, at least you haven't given up on your education. Maybe there's still a chance for you after all."

I didn't bother responding. Instead, I slammed the door and went up to my room. My mind was still reeling as I went into the bathroom and took a hot shower. Once I was done, I put on some clean clothes and lay across my bed. I stared up at the ceiling and was thinking about everything that had happened over the past few months when I was struck with a thought. I'd often wondered why I hadn't judged Murphy more harshly, especially after the way I'd reacted over my father selling illegal weapons. Both of them were involved in things I didn't condone, but there was one defining difference between them. My father had always portrayed himself to be an upstanding man who always followed the rules, never wavering for anyone. I'd always looked up to him for that, and even though I loved him and understood his reasons for what he'd done, I felt betrayed by his actions. Murphy, on the other hand, never once tried to hide who he was. He was upfront from the start, never apologizing for the life he led or the choices he made. My father would never understand why I liked Murphy the way I did. Sometimes, I didn't understand it myself, but in the end, the heart wants what the heart wants.

With all intentions of studying, I took out my binder and started flipping through the pages of notes, trying to make sense of what I was reading. Sadly, I wasn't having much luck. My mind just wasn't in the right place, and I was having a hard time focusing. I'd started to become frustrated when I heard my phone chime with a text message. I smiled when I noticed I had a message from Murphy.

MURPHY:

You make it home okay?

ME:

I did. I just got out of the shower.

MURPHY:

Really? I hate I missed that.

ME:

You're not the only one.

MURPHY:

How did things go with your dad?

ME:

As well as could be expected.

MURPHY:

That well, huh?

ME:

He'll come around.

MURPHY:

Not so sure about that.

ME:

He will. You'll see. Besides, I didn't get much time to talk to him. We got interrupted by one of his buyers.

MURPHY:

Interrupted how?

ME:

I don't know all the details. I just know he wasn't happy about a shipment.

MURPHY:

Did you father get him sorted?

ME:

Not yet, but he will.

MURPHY:

You sound pretty confident about that.

ME:

That's because I am.

MURPHY:

Good. You got plans after class tomorrow?

ME:

Not that I'm aware of. Why?

MURPHY:

I want to see you.

ME:

Good, because I want to see you, too.

MURPHY:

I'll text you later to sort out the when and where.

ME:

Sounds like a plan.

MURPHY:

Now stop messing around and get to studying for that test.

ME:

I'm trying, but this hot guy keeps messaging me.

MURPHY:

Tell him to fuck off. You're taken.

ME:

I'm not sure he will believe me, but I'll find a way to convince him.

MURPHY:

And how are you planning to do that?

ME:

You'll see tomorrow.

MURPHY:

I'll be looking forward to that. I'll text you later.

WITH A GOOFY GRIN on my face, I tossed my phone on the bed and started studying. It took some time, but I was eventually able to make sense of all my notes. I went downstairs when I felt certain that I had everything down, and after I put on my coat and boots, I headed outside. I wasn't in the mood for another confrontation, so I was pleased to see that Dad was nowhere in sight as I headed out to the barn. After greeting each of the horses, I grabbed a pitchfork and started cleaning out one of the stalls. I was just about to finish when Hunter came up behind me and said, "Is it true?"

Confused, I turned to face him as I asked, "Is what true?"

"Are you screwing around with one of those biker guys?"

Damn. Round three was about to ensue. "I'm not screwing around, Hunter."

"You know what I mean, Riley. Are you seeing that dude or what?"

"His name is Murphy, and yeah, I saw him last night." My eyes narrowed as I grumbled, "If you're about to give me one of your big brother lectures, I really don't want to hear it right now. I've already heard it all from Dad."

"I wasn't gonna give you a lecture, sis." He leaned against the gate as he said, "I don't care who you date as long as you are happy."

It wasn't like Hunter to be so understanding, so I asked, "Seriously? That's all you're going to say."

"I'm not going to waste my breath on telling you things you already know. I'm sure you have your reasons for liking this guy." I couldn't believe my ears as he said, "Just be careful and don't do anything stupid."

"Are you up to something?"

"No. What makes you think I'm up to something?"

As soon as the words came out of his mouth, I knew he was trying to hide something. "I know you better than anyone, Hunter Nichols, so tell me. What did you do?"

"It's not as bad as you fucking around with that biker."

"*Hunter*."

He grimaced as he answered, "I got arrested last night."

"Arrested! For what?"

"Public intoxication and indecent exposure."

"Seriously? Where were you, and what were you doing?"

"Travis and I were down on the strip, and we met up with some friends of ours from school." His eyes skirted to the floor as he continued, "We got to drinking, and then we drank a little more. A bachelorette party came in, and everything after that was kind of a blur."

"So, what did you do to get arrested?"

"Apparently, the girls convinced me that I should get up on the table and strip for them. You know how I aim to please, so ..."

"Hunter," I fussed. "I can't believe you did that!"

"Yeah ... It wasn't my proudest moment, but at least I gave that bride-to-be something to remember," he boasted.

"Maybe so," I stepped towards him as I said, "but Dad is going to have a conniption fit when he finds out you were arrested."

"I'm fucked."

"You might as well go on and tell him. You know how Dad is. He'll find out one way or another."

"You're right. I'll talk to him."

"No time like the present." I motioned my hand

towards the training ring as I said, "He's out back with Starlight."

"Damn."

When he started walking towards the door, I called out to him, "Hey, Hunter?"

"Yeah?"

"There is one good thing about all this!"

"Really? What's that?"

I smiled as I told him, "Once Dad hears about you getting arrested for giving a striptease, he's going to forget all about me and Murphy."

"Not a chance, sunshine," he scoffed. "Not a chance."

13

MURPHY

I'm not sure that I've ever known what it felt like to be content, to be able to lay my head down on the pillow without feeling like a dark void was devouring me from the inside out, but as I sat there reading Riley's last text message, content was the only way I could describe how I was feeling. There was always the chance that the feeling wouldn't last, that our worlds were just too different and it would tear us apart, but I wasn't going to let that stop me. Something in my gut told me that the connection we had was worth taking the risk, so I messaged her back and made arrangements for us to meet later that afternoon. As soon as she confirmed, I put my phone in my back pocket and turned my attention back to my brothers. We'd gathered at the bar to go over the plan for our upcoming pipeline run, but Blaze was running late. He'd told us earlier that he was taking his son, Wyatt, for another six-month checkup. Wyatt had been in remission for quite some time, and knowing what they'd been through, we were all concerned that they might've gotten bad news. Thankfully, that wasn't the case.

We were all talking amongst ourselves, when the backdoor flew open, and Blaze walked in with a big smile plastered on his face. As he sat down beside us, he announced, "We got good news. Wyatt's remission is still holding, and his stats are better than ever."

"That's awesome, brother," Riggs told him as he patted him on the back.

"Yes, it is." Blaze chuckled as he added, "Wyatt was pretty pleased with himself."

I smiled as I replied, "I bet he was. He's just like his old man ... taking credit where credit is due."

"You got that right." Blaze looked over to Gus and said, "Sorry for holding y'all up."

"No need to apologize, brother. We're just glad to hear that everything turned out okay."

Blaze nodded, then asked, "So, what's the plan for the run tomorrow?"

"Same as last, only this time, Rider will be filling in for Riggs." Gus looked over to Riggs as he told him, "I know you think you're up for it, but I'm not sending you on a run like this until I know you're at a hundred percent."

I could tell from Riggs's expression that he wasn't happy about Gus's decision, but he knew better than to argue. "Whatever you think is best."

"I think you all will agree that Rider has proven himself to be an asset to the club. If he's able to step up to the plate tomorrow, I think we should consider patching him in."

"Agreed," I replied without reservation.

"Plan to start loading tomorrow morning at five. That should put you on the road well before six and in Mobile by noon." He then turned to Shadow and said, "As always, I'll expect you and Blaze to have all artillery checked before nightfall."

"You got it," Blaze answered.

"Good deal." As Gus stood up, he announced, "I'll see you boys first thing in the morning."

Once he was gone, I pulled out my phone to see if I had any messages from Riley. When I saw that she hadn't texted, I quickly returned my phone to my pocket. As soon as I looked up, I found Blaze and Riggs smiling at me like two schmucks who were up to no good. "What?"

"You expecting a call from someone?" Riggs taunted.

"No."

"You sure about that?" T-Bone taunted.

Blaze had a mischievous grin on his face as he snickered, "You looked pretty disappointed when you checked your phone. Did your girl, Riley, forget to touch base?"

"You guys got nothing better to do than give me a hard fucking time?" I complained.

"Nope."

"That's what I was afraid of," I groaned.

"So, what's the deal? You got a thing for the farmer's daughter or what?" Blaze asked.

"And if I do?"

"Then, I'd say it's about damn time," Riggs scoffed.

As I stood up, I looked over to my brothers and said, "I'll see you boys in the morning."

"That's all we're gonna get?" Blaze fussed.

"Yep, so stop acting like a bunch of girls and let me get out of here. I've got somewhere I need to be."

As I started for the door, Riggs said, "You should take her some flowers."

"No way. It's too soon for fucking flowers," T-Bone argued. "You start that shit now and you'll never hear the end of it."

Blaze shook his head, leaving no doubt that he disagreed with their suggestions. "Just take her somewhere cool ... like Graceland or the Brooks."

"I've got it covered," I shouted as I walked out the back door.

As I started towards my bike, I wondered if I should've taken the time to listen to my brothers' advice. Over the years, I'd had my share of hookups, but I couldn't remember the last time I'd seen a woman for a second time, much less actually taken them out. There was always the possibility that Riley wouldn't like what I had planned for our afternoon together, but I decided to go with my gut and take a chance. When I arrived at the address she'd given me, I found her waiting in the parking lot. I was pleased to see that she was wearing a jacket with her jeans and boots. I pulled up next to her, and when I offered her a helmet, she asked, "We're taking your bike?"

"If you're up for it, I thought we'd take advantage of this nice weather."

A smile crossed her face as she lifted the helmet to

her head and started to fasten the strap. "Yes! I'm definitely up for it."

"I was hoping you would say that." I extended my hand and helped her get on behind me. Once she was settled, I asked, "You ready?"

"Wait ... give me some pointers first."

"You ride horses, Riley. Just do what comes natural." I gave her a wink as I said, "You've got this."

She placed her hands on my hips, and seconds later we were out of the parking lot and traveling towards Mississippi. The wind was brisk, but it wasn't too bad with the sun shining. Riley's grip tightened as I sped through busy streets, letting me know that she was nervous, but it didn't take her long to relax and loosen her hold. As we started towards the interstate, Riley leaned against me, resting her chin on my shoulder. "This might be better than horseback riding."

"You think so?"

"I don't know. It's pretty close." When we started down Riverside Drive, she turned and looked out at the Mississippi River and sighed. "The views are just incredible."

"I'm glad you're enjoying yourself."

When I eased off the main road and took the Mississippi exit, she asked, "Where are you going?"

"It's a surprise."

As we continued towards our destination, she became more and more curious. "I don't think I've ever been on this road."

Considering it was the only road into Tunica from

Memphis, I was hoping she hadn't ever been. "I've only been on it a couple of times."

"How long will it be before we get there?"

I smiled to myself as I asked, "Do you need a break? We can stop at the—"

"No," she stopped me. "I was just curious."

"It won't be much longer. Maybe fifteen minutes or so."

She remained silent for the next twenty minutes, and then, suddenly, she tapped me on the arm. "Wait! Is that one of the casinos?"

"It is."

"You're kidding me! I've always wanted to go, but I've never gotten the chance!"

Hearing the excitement in her voice was like music to my ears. "So, this will be your first trip to a casino?"

"Yep. My very first!"

I could feel the excitement rolling off of her as we pulled up to the Horseshoe Casino and parked. Once we'd removed our helmets, I reached for her hand and led her inside. I was thankful to see that it wasn't very crowded, so we wouldn't have to worry about waiting in any lines. I glanced over at Riley and smiled when I saw the wide-eyed expression on her face. She looked spellbound as she studied the various slot machines. I gave her hand a gentle squeeze as I asked, "Where do you want to start?"

"I have no idea. There's too many to choose from."

I reached in my pocket and pulled out a twenty-dollar bill. As I offered it to her, I said, "Why don't you start with one of the slots?"

"Are you sure?"

"That's why I brought you here."

She hesitated, but she eventually took the twenty from my hand and carried it over to one of the machines. Once she inserted the money, she looked over to me and asked, "Okay. What do I do now?"

"This is a penny slot, so just choose the amount you want to bet and push the button. If the lines match up, then you win."

"That seems easy enough." She chose her wager, then pressed the button. The music started playing and different colored fish started jumping around on the screen. When the fish all lined up and the machine fell silent, Riley looked up at me and asked, "What happened?"

I chuckled as I told her, "You lost."

"I did?"

"You did, but it happens." I motioned my hand towards the machine. "Give her another go."

"Okay." She tried again and again, hoping for a different result. Unfortunately, she wasn't having any luck. After losing fifteen out of the twenty dollars, she looked up at me and said, "I'm losing all your money."

"It's not mine anymore. As soon as it touched your hand it became yours." I reached in my pocket for another twenty. "I'm about to give it a go myself, so don't stop on my account."

She watched as I sat down at the machine next to her and inserted my money. Once I started playing, she turned her attention back to her game and started playing once again. She nearly leapt out of her seat when all the fish finally lined up. "Look! I won six dollars!"

Before I could respond, she was back at it, and after a few more hits, she was up forty bucks. Just as I'd hoped, she was having a great time, but something told me, she wasn't hard to please. Riley was one of those women who appreciated the small pleasures in life, and it was a characteristic that I was growing fond of very quickly. After several more rounds, I looked over to her and asked, "Do you want to try a different game?"

"Sure!"

Once we'd cashed out, Riley followed me over to the high-stakes slots and watched as I entered my credit voucher into one of the ten-dollar machines. I was up a couple hundred bucks, so I decided to go for it. I placed my bet and immediately lost. I tried again, only to lose once more. I was about to hit it again, when she asked, "Wait ... are these ten dollars a bet?"

"Yeah."

"But you're betting five lines at a time. Doesn't that mean you just lost fifty dollars?"

"No. I lost a hundred."

"Murphy! That's crazy," she fussed.

"You gotta play big to win big." I hit it again, and this time I won. "See. I'm up three hundred."

"Holy cow!" She went over to one of the five-dollar machines beside me and inserted her voucher. After her first try, she squealed, "Look at that! I won a hundred dollars!"

As we continued to play several more rounds, we won some, then lost some more. I played a few more bets, then walked over to see how Riley was doing. "How's it going?"

"I was up a hundred and twenty, and now I'm back to eighty." As she hit the cash-out button, she said, "I think I'm gonna stop while I'm ahead."

"You sure? We could go over and hit the blackjack table or roulette?"

"You can play whatever you want and I'll watch with bated breath, but I'm good." She held up her paper voucher as she announced, "I'm tickled with my eighty-dollar win."

"All right, then. How about something to eat? There are several restaurants to choose from if you're hungry."

"Yeah, I could go for a bite to eat."

"We'll need to redeem our winnings first."

She followed me over to the cash kiosk and got in line behind me. I had gotten my cash, and when I turned around, I quickly noticed that Riley was no longer behind me. Apparently, she'd decided she needed to give it one more go and hit one of the machines close by. Just as I was heading over to her, the machine she was using lit up and music started blaring, announcing that she'd gotten a big win. I had no idea how much she'd won, but from the look on her face, I thought she'd won a million or more. With an animated gasp, she asked, "Are you seeing this?"

"I am. How much did you just win?"

"I have no idea!" she shrieked.

With all the noise and flashing lights, it was hard to tell. I took a step closer and noticed that she was playing one of the penny machines. For a moment, I was worried that she might be disappointed by her winnings, but she wasn't. Not even close. When everything finally stilled and her final total flashed on the screen, she jumped out of her seat and cheered, "I won three hundred dollars!"

"How about that." I couldn't get over it. By the expression on her face, you would've thought she'd hit the jackpot. I couldn't believe that a girl who'd grown up the way she had would be so tickled over so little. There was a lot more to Riley than I ever imagined, and I looked forward to finding out everything about her. I smiled as I told her, "You've got beginner's luck working in your favor."

"I can't believe it! I've never won anything like this before."

Seeing that smile got me right to the core, and I knew right then, I would do everything in my power to see it again and again. "Do you want to give it one more go?"

"Not a chance!" She pressed the cash-out button, and as soon as she had her voucher, she headed straight for the cash kiosk. Once she was done, she looked down at the money and studied it for a moment before offering the whole wad to me. "It wouldn't be right for me to take this."

"You won that money fair and square, Riley. There's no way in hell I'm gonna take it from you." I placed my hands on her hips and pulled her closer. "I would've paid that and a hundred times over to see that smile on your face."

"Thank you for all this. I can't remember when I've had so much fun."

"Right back at ya." I leaned down and pressed my lips to hers. I'd intended on the kiss being brief, but the moment our mouths met, I ached for more. Feeling that same deep longing, she wound her arms around my neck, inching closer as we both got lost in the moment. Just as I was about lose all self-control, I heard someone behind me clear their throat. I quickly pulled back, breaking free from our embrace. When I looked over my shoulder, I found an elderly lady who was five feet tall at best. She was wearing a pale-pink sweater with a strand of pearls, and she was scowling at me like I'd just kicked her poodle. Apparently, we were blocking her path to one of the games she wanted to play, so I eased Riley out of the way. I took out a five-dollar bill from my winnings, and as I offered it to the lady, I said, "Sorry about that. Have a round on us."

"Don't mind if I do." She took the money from my hand, and Riley's mouth dropped open in surprise when the lady shuffled past us, grumbling, "You kids need to get a room."

I figured we'd caused enough of a scene, so I reached for Riley's hand and, hoping they'd have something quick and easy we could eat, led her into one of the smaller restaurants. It wasn't much, just your typical café, but Riley didn't seem to mind as we made our way over to one of the tables in the back. We hadn't been sitting long when a waitress came over to us. Once she'd taken our order and left, I looked over to Riley and asked, "How did your test go this morning?"

"I think I did okay. I won't know for sure until my professor posts the grades."

"I don't think you ever mentioned what you were getting your degree in."

She grimaced as she replied, "Finance. I was thinking that I could use it to help my dad out at the farm, but with this degree, I'll have options. I could be a financial planner, a financial analyst, or an investor relations associate."

"Not sure I know what any of those are, but they sound pretty impressive."

"I don't know about that," she scoffed. "It can be a little boring, but I thought if I could find a new company … one that really speaks to me, then it would be kind of cool to help them get off the ground."

"I think that would be very cool."

Before I had a chance to respond, the waitress brought our food and drinks over and placed them on the table. As we ate, Riley explained how torn she felt. Even though a lot of things had changed over the past few months, she still felt obligated to help her father at the farm. "I'm not sure what I'll do. I won't graduate until this summer, so I still have some time to figure it out."

"You've gotta do what makes you happy, Riley. I'm sure that your father would agree."

"I know. I just need some time to figure things out." After she took a bite of her sandwich, she asked, "What about you?"

"What about me?"

"What do you do for work? You do have an actual job, right?"

I chuckled. "Yeah, I got a job. Several, in fact. The club has a garage where we do small renovations and engine repair. I work there mainly."

"Is working on engines something you learned from your brothers, or did you pick it up somewhere else?"

"A little of both, I guess. I've always had a thing for engines." I shrugged. "It's just one of those things that came easy to me."

"I'm impressed. I wouldn't know the first thing about fixing an engine."

"And I wouldn't know the first thing about finance, so we're even."

When we finished eating, we got back on the bike and rode back to Memphis. The sun was just starting to set as we pulled into the parking lot at her college campus. When I parked, Riley got off and quickly removed her helmet. She wore a somber look as she said, "I had a great time."

I pulled off my helmet, then tugged her close. "I did too."

"Well," she shrugged, "I guess I better get going."

There was something about the hesitation in her voice that made me think she wasn't ready for our time to end any more than I was. Hoping she might be up for staying out a little longer, I told her, "It's still early."

"Yes, it is."

"Stay."

Her brows furrowed as she asked, "I guess I could ... if you're okay with that."

"I'm very good with that."

"Okay ... then what do you want to do?"

"Follow me over to my place. That way, you'll have your car and can leave whenever you're ready."

As soon as I saw the spark in her eyes, I knew her

answer long before she said the words. "Okay, but I can't stay too long. I've got another big test tomorrow."

"Understood."

Riley gave me a quick peck on the lips, then rushed over to her car. She followed me back to my place, and as soon as we stepped through the front door, I pulled her in for a kiss. I'd tried my damnedest to be on my best behavior during our little excursion, but having her on the back of my bike and feeling her body so close to mine without being able to do a damn thing about it had taken its toll. I reached for the nape of her neck and took a hold of her hair, gently tugging it as I deepened the kiss. A needful moan vibrated through her chest as she inched closer, pressing her hips against mine, and I was happy to see that I wasn't the only one who was feeling eager for more.

I knew we didn't have much time, so I lifted her up. As I tossed her over my shoulder, she shrieked, "Whoa! What is it with you and the caveman act?"

"It's all you, baby." I gave her ass a light smack as I told her, "You bring it out in me."

"Oh, really? Well, I'm not so sure that's a good thing."

"Oh, it's definitely a good thing. You'll see."

I carried her up to my bedroom and tossed her onto the bed. A flash of desire crossed her face as I eased down on top of her, hovering above her for a brief moment before I lowered my mouth to hers. Riley's mouth was warm and soft, and each swirl of her tongue made the blood rush straight to my cock. The feel of her body against mine sent me over the edge, and my hands suddenly became rough and impatient. I had to have her —all of her.

I lowered my mouth to her neck and whispered, "I never could've imagined"—I ran my lips leisurely from the curve of her jaw down to her shoulder—"that I'd find someone who can get to me like you do."

"I feel the same way about you," she rasped as she pulled her sweater over her head and tossed it to the floor. As she unfastened her bra, she whispered, "You're all I can think about."

I continued trailing kisses past her collarbone, and her fingers tangled in my hair, pulling me towards her when my mouth reached her breast. Heavy breaths and low moans filled the room as I flicked my tongue against her nipple. Her head fell back, and goosebumps prickled across her skin as my fingers worked their way across her abdomen, through the waistband of her jeans, and further down between her legs. A small whimper escaped her throat as my fingers grazed across her center, circling her, teasing her. Unable to contain herself, she rocked her hips forward, begging for my touch. Fuck. I could barely contain *myself*. Seeing her so wound up made my cock grow thick with need. I eased my fingers deep inside her, and I'd just begun to stroke her when she moaned, "Oh God, Lincoln ... Please, don't stop."

The moment I brushed my thumb against her clit, I felt her begin to tremble. Knowing she was close, I increased the pressure as I grazed my fingers over her g-spot. Her breath quickened, and her head dropped forward as her entire body tensed with her release. When I saw her body jolt and writhe beneath me, I was done. I couldn't wait a moment longer to have her; I withdrew my fingers and moved my hands to the waistband of her jeans. Once I had them unfastened, I gave them a tug, removing them in a blink and tossing them to the floor. Equally as eager, Riley reached for the hem of my shirt and pulled it over my head then started to work on my jeans. In a matter of seconds, we were both completely undressed, and we spent the next two hours tangled in each other's arms. I didn't want her to leave. I wanted her to stay there with me, safe and warm in my arms, but I didn't listen to that voice in my head and let her walk out that door. It was a mistake I would soon come to regret. Once again, I'd forgotten my rules. I let myself push them to the back of my mind, thinking they didn't apply to her, but I was wrong—very, very wrong.

14

RILEY

There was no denying that I was attracted to Murphy. From the moment I laid eyes on him, I'd had to fight to keep my hormones in check. Obviously, there was good reason for my lustful reaction—the man was gorgeous from head to toe with a confident, no-excuses attitude that was impossible to ignore. I was intrigued by him, both mentally and physically, but over the past few days, I'd gotten the chance to see that there was more to him than just his sexy exterior. Murphy was fierce, demanding, and strong. He liked to be in control in all aspects of his life, and he had a short fuse. It didn't take much to get him riled, but he also had a kind, compassionate side to him. Murphy put others first, even if that meant compromising himself and what he wanted. He was sweet and funny, and I felt good whenever I was around him. He made me happy, really happy, and because of that my feelings for him were quickly growing into something more.

After an amazing day in Tunica and a night wrapped in his arms, I went back home and found my father sitting at the kitchen table with a troubled look on his face. I wasn't sure if he was thinking about me, Devon, or my brother, so I asked, "Are you okay?"

Without looking up, he answered, "I'm fine."

"Have you eaten dinner? I could fix you ..."

"I'm not hungry." He sounded utterly defeated as he stood up and said, "I've got some things I need to tend to. I'll be in my office if you need me."

I wasn't used to seeing him like this, so I asked, "Are you sure you're okay, because you don't seem like you are?"

"I told you I was fine. I've just got a lot on my mind."

"Is it that Devon guy? Are you worried—"

"I'm handling it, Riley," he bit out. "I don't need you making things harder by asking questions."

"I'm sorry. I was just trying to help."

"If you want to do something to help, then stop seeing Murphy. That'll give me one less thing to worry about. Can you do that for me?" When he saw the expression on my face, he grumbled, "That's what I was afraid of. You've fallen for this guy. Dammit! A no-good-rotten-piece-of-trash has won the heart of my precious daughter, and I've got no one to blame but myself. I've made a mess of everything!"

"It's sad how you can't see that you're wrong about Murphy, Dad." I sighed as I started for the stairs. "I really hope you figure that out before it's too late."

"What's that supposed to mean?" When I didn't

answer, he stormed into his office and slammed the door. "Dammit!"

With a heavy heart, I went up to my room and crawled into bed. After I sent Murphy a text, letting him know that I made it home okay, I pulled out my books and tried my best to prepare for my test. I had no idea how long I'd been studying when I fell sound asleep. When I woke up the next morning, the house was completely empty with no sign of my dad or Hunter. Feeling relieved that I wouldn't have to face another confrontation, I made myself some coffee and headed to class. As soon as I finished my test, I went out into the hall and took out my phone. I was about to call Murphy when I remembered that he'd told me that he was going on a run with his brothers. I had no idea what a run was or how long something like that would take, but I could tell by the way he spoke that it was important to him. When I'd asked him about it, he told me that club business was never discussed outside of the club. At first, I took offense to it, thinking our newfound relationship gave me privy to such information, but then he explained their reasons behind their secrecy. It was then that I realized there was still a lot about the club and about him that I didn't know or understand, but Murphy assured me that when the time was right he would explain everything to me. I just had to be patient, which wasn't exactly one of my strong suits, but Murphy had left me with no other choice.

Since Murphy wasn't available, I decided to run by and see Grady. It had been a couple of days since that night at the bar, and I was hoping that he'd had a chance to cool off. Unfortunately, that wasn't the case. It was just after two p.m. when I got to the bar, so I figured he was working in his office. I walked in and found him sitting at his desk going over some paperwork. I put on one of my best smiles as I said, "Hey, you busy?"

"Hey." He glanced up at me and said, "I thought you were coming by yesterday after you got out of class."

"I was planning to, but something came up."

He didn't hide his disapproval as he asked, "Did this *something* have anything to do with that guy from the other night?"

"Maybe."

"And what did you two do?"

I couldn't help but smile as I told him, "He took me to one of the casinos in Tunica. It was so much fun, and I actually won three hundred dollars!"

"Sounds like you had a great time."

"I did."

"And the other night when he carried you out of my bar like some kind of animal, did you have a good time then, too?"

"Grady."

He paused a moment, then crossed his arms and leaned back in his chair. "Look, I hate to be the one who puts a damper on this ..."

"Then, don't." I went over and sat down in the chair beside his desk. "I've already heard it all from my father, besides ... you're supposed to be on my side."

"I am on your side, Riley. I always have been, but I can't help that I'm worried about you." Sincerity crossed his face as he said, "You mean a lot to me, and I don't want to see you get hurt."

"I know and you mean a lot to me, too." I placed my hand on his arm and added, "I appreciate your concern, but I really like Murphy, and I want to see where this thing goes."

"I just don't get it. What is it about this guy?"

"I don't really get it either. I just know I feel more like myself when I'm with him than anywhere else." I wasn't sure if I was making any sense. "Do you have any idea what I'm talking about?"

"Yeah. I know exactly what you're talking about." His mood turned somber as he continued, "A connection like that is rare at best."

"So, you get why I want to pursue this thing with Murphy."

"I do, but if he hurts you, I'll kill him. Be sure he knows that."

"I'll be sure to tell him," I scoffed.

"So, what do you have going on today?"

"I should probably get back to the farm." I stood up as I told him, "I've been a little busy, and I haven't taken Anna Belle out in days."

"You wanna grab a bite to eat or something before you go?"

I thought back to the night before and the worried look on my father's face. I knew he was concerned about Devon, and I didn't want him to face that alone, so I said, "I should really get home. Can I get a raincheck?"

"Sure."

"Thanks, Grady. You're the best." I leaned towards him and gave him a quick hug. "I'll see you soon."

"You better."

Once I'd left his office, I got in my car and drove back towards the farm. I wasn't too sure if I wanted to be there when Devon came for the weapons he was after, but I didn't like the idea of my father being there alone with him even more. When I got home, I was surprised to see that Travis was the only one around. Worried something might be wrong, I went over to him and asked, "Have you seen Dad?"

"Not since this morning."

"Did he mention where he was going?"

"Yeah." He continued to check Starlight's hooves as he said, "He said something about meeting up with some guy. He had a package to pick up or something,"

Assuming the package he was getting had something to do with Devon's threat, I asked, "Any idea when he'll be back?"

"No idea." He looked up at me and asked, "Why? You need something?"

"No. He never mentioned that he'd be gone, and I wanted to see where he was." As I started towards him, I asked, "Have you had a chance to check on Anna Belle's hooves?"

"Yep. I did a few minutes ago."

"Great. I'm going to work with her a little, then take her for a ride." As I started towards the house, I told him, "I'm just going to run in and change first."

"I'll saddle her up and take her out to the training ring for you."

"Thanks, Travis. I'd appreciate that."

I went inside and changed into my jeans. A cold front was coming in and it really was starting to get a little chilly, so I decided to put on an undershirt with one of my bigger hoodies. I grabbed an extra pair of socks and went downstairs to get my riding boots. Once I was ready, I put on my coat and headed towards the training ring. I was pleased to see that Travis was already there with Anna Belle. He was adjusting her saddle when I came up to them. "Thanks for getting her ready for me, Travis."

"No problem. I'm sure she'll enjoy some time out with you."

I reached my hand up and scratched behind her ear. "Hey there, sweet girl. Are you ready to stretch your legs a bit?"

"Don't be out too long. It'll be dark soon," Travis warned.

"I won't." I put my foot in the stirrups and pulled myself up. "I'll be back in an hour or so."

I tugged the reins and let her out of the training ring, and I was just about to head out to the back pasture when I noticed my father's truck coming down the driveway. Curious to see if he was okay, I stopped and waited for him to pull up to the house. I watched as he got out of the truck, and the minute I saw his face, I knew something was wrong. Panic washed over me as I heard him tell Hunter, "We need to be prepared for the worst here, son. I've got no idea how this is going to play out."

I got off Anna Belle and led her back over to the fence beside the driveway. After I'd secured her to one of the rails, I walked over to my father and asked, "You seem upset. What's going on?"

"Riley!" His eyes widened with fright as he asked, "What are you doing here?"

"It's after five, Dad. Why wouldn't I be here?"

"Damn. You've got to get the hell out of here before Devon—" his voice was filled with urgency, "You need to get your things and go to Grady's."

Knowing it wasn't a time to argue, I answered, "Okay. I just need to get Anna Belle back in the stable."

"Make it fast. There's no telling when he'll show up." As I turned towards Anna Belle, I heard Dad say, "Hunter … go get your rifle. Get one for me and Travis too."

He was trying to prepare for Devon's arrival, but he was too late. I'd only taken a couple of steps towards Anna Belle when his black BMW came barreling down our driveway, much like it had two days earlier, but this time was different. This time Devon wasn't alone. I glanced back over at my father, and he looked positively petrified. Seeing that he was terrified didn't help the dreadful fear I was feeling as I watched the BMW park and four men get out. Devon walked over to my father and asked, "You got my shipment?"

"I-I've been trying to call you," he stammered. "I've got everything lined up … but I need more time."

"You had time, Nichols." Devon turned to one of the men beside him and gave them a quick nod. He looked back to my father, and with a look of utter nonchalance, he told him, "Now, your time is up."

The tall, bulked-up brute-of-a-man took a charging step in my direction, and I knew I was in trouble. I turned and began to run, but the sound of gunfire stopped me in my tracks. I stood there frozen, and the world around me stilled as I watched my precious Anna Belle's lifeless body collapse to the ground. I thought back to the day my father had given her to me and how much she'd meant to me. My heart shattered into a million pieces when I saw the bullet wound between her eyes as I screamed, "No! Oh God, no!"

I'd only taken a few steps when I was quickly jerked back. "Where you do you think you're going?"

The man lifted my feet off the ground as he hurled me back over to my father. Devon took the gun that he'd used to kill Anna Belle and pressed it firmly against my temple as he growled, "I told you to have my shit here within forty-eight hours, and you disappointed me. I don't like being disappointed, Nichols."

"It's on its way. I just need some more time," my father pleaded. "It'll be here by morning. You have my word."

"You better hope it is, cause if it ain't …" He motioned his head towards Anna Belle as he continued, "The same thing that happened to your horse over there is gonna happen to your girl. You got that?"

The blood drained from my father's face as he said, "Yeah, I got it."

"Let's roll, boys."

Devon kept his gun pointed at my head, and my heart was racing as he led me over to his car. When my father realized what was happening, he shouted, "Wait! What the hell are you doing?"

"What the fuck does it look like I'm doing?" He chuckled as he shoved me into the backseat. Horror washed over me when I heard him say, "I'm taking this sweet ass with me to make sure you follow through. You've got till morning, Nichols, or she gets a bullet in this pretty little head of hers."

"Devon, please don't do this. I'll keep my word."

Unfortunately, he didn't listen. Once I was in the car, two men got in next to me, securing me on either side, then Devon and another man got in the front seat. Once they closed their doors, Devon started the car and whipped out of the driveway. When we drove by Anna Belle, my chest tightened, and I had to fight the urge to cry. My stomach was in knots, like I was stuck in a horrible nightmare, and no matter how hard I tried, I couldn't wake up. Only this was no dream. I was wide awake, and my life was hanging in the balance. I was lost in my own thoughts when one of the men next to me said, "Yo, Marcus. Did you see that dude's face when Devon killed that fucking horse?"

"Yeah, man. He about lost his shit."

"Well, he got the message."

Devon chuckled. "Yeah, I made sure of that."

Marcus glanced back at me as he asked, "You got a name?"

"Riley," I mumbled with fear.

"Well, sit back and enjoy the ride, Riley." A sinister smile crossed his face as he said, "'Cause you're going to be in for quite a night."

15

MURPHY

*A*s planned, the brothers and I made it down to Mobile by noon. When we pulled up to the dock, Ronin and his crew were already there waiting to help us unload. While there were times when he was a royal pain-in-the-ass, Ronin had proven himself to be an invaluable asset. Over the past couple of years, the club had been partnering with several of our affiliate chapters to create a pipeline that would enable us to move a large number of weapons in one haul, allowing us to gain a high profit. It had been going well, and we owed a great deal of that success to Ronin. After the weapons left our hands, it was up to him to see to it that they made it to our buyers, and he always went the extra mile to ensure that the deliveries went without a hitch. In the past, he'd used barges to move the goods from one secure location to the next, but recently, Ronin had changed his method of transportation. Just like the time before, he had a seventy-foot, high-performance yacht sitting at the dock waiting to move our shipment to the next location.

Like the last few times before, the brothers and I had to travel in two different SUVs. Our shipments had gotten bigger, so it was now taking us two horse trailers to carry the load. I'd driven one SUV with Blaze, Rider, and Gunner riding along with me, while Shadow had driven the second with T-Bone and Gauge. We'd had a long drive, so I was looking forward to stretching my legs as I got out of the truck. I'd barely had time to stretch out the kinks, when Ronin came over to me and said, "We need to move fast. There's a storm rolling in, and I want to get out of the bay before it hits."

There wasn't a cloud in the sky, so I asked, "What makes you think it's gonna rain?"

"Look at the radar. There's a hell of a storm brewing along the coast."

"Is that going to be a problem?"

He didn't sound exactly confident as he answered, "Not if we get this shit unloaded in the next fifteen minutes."

"Then, let's get this thing done." I pounded on the hood of the truck as I shouted, "Let's roll, boys."

When I spotted him standing by the truck, I called out to Rider, "Hey, brother. Come give me a hand."

He followed as I went over to the horse trailer and watched as I opened the back doors. Then, he helped as I got the two mares out and secured them on a nearby post. Once we were done, Rider asked, "What do you need me to do now?"

"We need to help the guys unload. Just follow my lead."

"You got it."

We both watched as Shadow and T-Bone unbolted the secret compartments beneath both of the trailers' floor. As soon as they got them open, we started removing the crates. One by one, we carried them over to the yacht and hid them away in the storage containers in the lower deck. I watched as Rider followed suit, never asking questions as he tried his best to do what was expected. It took several trips for us to get everything unloaded, but we got it done with time to spare. Knowing he had to get moving, Ronin didn't stick around for idle conversation. Instead, he said his goodbyes, and seconds later, he and the yacht were gone. When we returned to the truck, I sent Gus a message and let him know that all went well and we were on our way back home. As I started the truck, Gunner turned to me and asked, "You think he'll beat the storm."

"I got no idea."

"Well, it could be all kinds of bad if he doesn't." His face grew pale as he asked, "Have you seen that movie, *The Perfect Storm*? Those waves tore that boat to shreds. There's no telling what a storm like that would do to that fancy-assed boat of Ronin's."

"We're talking about a thunderstorm, Gunner. Not a fucking hurricane. Ronin and his boat should be just fine," I assured him.

"It was a great movie, though," Blaze added.

"Yeah, it was." Gunner looked over to Blaze with a

proud smile as he asked, "What about Kintzler and Quintana?"

"No surprises there, Gunner. We all knew they'd be back."

"Yeah. There's still no word on Hamels or Strop, but I don't see them going anywhere."

"Probably so, but not really concerned about them." Blaze shook his head as he said, "If the Cubs want to make it this year, then they're gonna have to find a reliable backup catcher. Contreras is good, but he can't carry the team alone."

They continued to talk baseball for the next half hour. I'd never been a fan of the Cubs, so I was relieved when the conversation died out. We were just about to come into Meridian when Shadow's voice came over the two-way radio. "We're going to need to fill up soon."

"Us, too. Let's get off at the next exit."

"You got it."

Once we'd taken the exit, I pulled over to the nearest gas station. None of us wanted to waste time stopping for lunch, so while Shadow and I filled up the SUVs with gas, the others went inside to grab us something to eat. Ten minutes later, they came out of the store looking like they'd just gotten a week's worth of groceries. When they started getting in the truck, I asked, "What the hell is all that?"

"It's lunch," Gunner answered innocently. He reached into the bag and pulled out a burger wrapped in foil. "Whatcha want? I've got a couple of burgers and hot dogs ... but I gotta tell ya, the hot dogs were looking a little sketchy. If I had to guess, I'd say they'd been there for a while."

"But that didn't stop him from buying them," Blaze complained. "And it also didn't stop him from buying a couple of pretzels that were as hard as rocks."

"I was hungry."

I chuckled as I took the burger from his hand and told him, "You've got a gut made of steel, brother."

"That I do, but if you had to eat the shit I did growing up, you'd have one, too." He shrugged. "Don't get me wrong. My momma tried, but damn. There's only so many times a man can eat undercooked chicken."

Blaze chuckled as he told him, "We've all heard the horror stories of your momma's cooking, but I've eaten over at your place. It's not that bad."

"Brother, she didn't cook that shit. That was takeout that she'd warmed up in her dishes to make it look like she made it, and she still screwed it up and burnt the damn mashed potatoes."

"Yeah, I remember." Blaze's face twisted into a grimace at the memory. "But at least she tried. Maybe one day you can find yourself a good woman who can cook."

"I'd be happy with just a good woman ... Don't give a shit about her being able to cook." He took a bite out of one of the old, rubbery hot dogs and said, "For the right woman, I'd live on beanie weanies and Vienna sausages."

I glanced up at the rearview mirror so I could get a look at Rider. He hadn't said two words on the entire trip, so I asked, "You're awfully quiet back there. You making it okay, brother?"

"Yeah, I'm good," he answered. "I'm just soaking all this in, so I'll be better prepared next time."

"You did good today," I told him. "I'm sure Gus will be happy to hear that."

"I hope you're right." He took a bite of his sandwich and said, "By the way, the chicken salad ain't so bad."

"Wait! You're eating the chicken salad?" Gunner asked with alarm. When Rider nodded, Gunner reached into the backseat and grabbed the sandwich out of his hand, quickly tossing it out of the window. "Never ... and I mean *never*, eat the chicken salad from a gas station, brother. Trust me. Not even *my* stomach can take the hell it will do to your intestines."

"Thanks for the heads up."

"No problem." Gunner reached into his sack and brought out another burger. As he offered it to Rider, he said, "Do us both a favor and eat this instead."

We all settled in and finished our lunch as we continued down US 45. We'd almost made it to Tupelo when my burner started to ring. I reached down and took it out of the cupholder, and when I checked the screen, I was surprised to see that Gus was calling. As soon as I answered, he asked, "How far out are you?"

"We've still got about an hour and a half to two hours."

"I was afraid of that."

There was something about his voice that set me on edge. "Why? Is something wrong?"

"It's Riley."

I could feel the weight of the world pressing down on me when I asked, "What about her?"

"I don't have all the details yet, but from what I can tell, she's been taken."

"What the hell are you talking about?"

While mine was frantic and full of anger, his voice remained calm while he continued, "There was a situation out at the Nichols' place ... an exchange that didn't go down as expected, and they took Riley at gunpoint."

My breathing became more rapid, more shallow, as I barked, "Who was it?"

"I don't know yet. Nichols called looking for you, and I couldn't understand much of what he was saying." The thoughts were racing too fast in my head. I wanted them to slow down so I could think as he told me, "I was trying to explain that you were out of town when the line went dead. I've tried calling him back, but I haven't gotten an answer."

"Fuck."

"Murphy," Gus warned. "I know this isn't easy, but you're gonna have to keep it together until we find out what the hell is going on."

"I've got to get to her, Gus."

"I know and we'll see that you do, but for now, you need to get back here in one piece. You got me?"

My ribs felt like they were bound in a vice as I tried to take in a deep breath. I was in full-blown panic mode which never happened—not to me. It was me who always kept a level head, but I'd let my rules fall by the way side and it cost me. "Yeah, I got you."

"I'll keep trying to get Nichols and see if I can get any more information on Riley. You focus on getting back home."

"I'll do my best."

I hung up the phone and threw it into the cupholder. "Dammit!"

"What's going on with Riley?" Blaze asked with concern.

As I told him what Gus had just told me, he didn't ask questions. He just took in the information and did his best not to get me any more worked up than I already was. Once I'd gone through everything, I said, "Gus is supposed to call me back when or if he gets back in touch with Nichols."

"I don't know, brother." He seemed certain when he said, "I think we need to head straight to the farm and see for ourselves what's going on. If Nichols is as upset as I think he is, he's gonna end up forgetting something important. Besides, it's on the way."

"Agreed."

"Good. I'll call Shadow and let him know what's going on."

When he picked up the phone, I eased down on the accelerator and hauled ass down the interstate. An hour later we were in Somerville, and I was hanging on by a thread as we turned into the Nichols' driveway. I was doing my best to keep it together as we made our way down the gravel road, but then I saw Riley's favorite mare sprawled out on the driveway with a pool of blood around her head. Once we'd pulled up at the house, I threw the truck in park and got out. With Blaze and Shadow at my side, we started walking towards the house. I hadn't gotten far when Riley's father and her brother came rushing out the front door. With his pale complexion and worried expression, Mr. Nichols looked like he'd aged twenty years as he raced towards me. He shook his head and said, "You were right ... you were right about everything."

"None of that matters now," I told him. "Right now, we need to focus on getting Riley back."

"I won't be able to live with myself if they hurt her."

"Who exactly are 'they'?" I pushed.

"I don't really know ... the Hurricanes or something. They're some inner-city gang." He went on to tell me about Devon, and the argument over the shipment that we'd purchased from him several weeks before. He explained how he'd reached out to his contact and a new shipment was in route, but there had been some bad weather up north and it had caused a delay. Tears filled his eyes as he told me about Devon shooting Anna Belle, and the devastated look he'd seen on his daughter's face when she realized he'd killed her. He continued talking, but I couldn't hear anything after he told me about Devon putting his gun against Riley's head. After that, it was all static. I clenched my fists at my side as I inhaled a deep breath, hoping it would help center me, but I was too far gone. I was going to end this guy Devon and every one of those asshole gangsters who were in that car with him. Nichols' voice trembled as he went on, "There was no way I could know that they'd just take her like they did. If I'd known that, I would've killed them myself."

"How long have they been gone?"

"Not quite two hours." He took a step towards me as he pleaded, "You've gotta help me get her back, Murphy."

"I'll do everything I can. You have my word on that."

After I gave him the number to my burner, I told him, "We're going to need to leave our horses and trailers here, or they're going to slow us down. You good with that?"

"Absolutely. Do whatever you need. Just unload the trailers, and I'll tend to the horses."

Once we unhitched the trailers, I turned to Nichols and promised, "We'll be in touch as soon as we know something."

I got in the truck and closed the door behind me. Once my brothers had done the same, I pulled out of the driveway, and as I started back towards Memphis, I tried to think of the fastest way for me to find Riley. I had no idea where Devon had taken her, and trying to find her in a city with over a million people in it would be like searching for a needle in a haystack. If there was anyone on the planet who could come up with a way for me to find her, it would be Riggs. Praying that he would have the answer, I reached for my phone and called him.

16

RILEY

I'd never realized how powerful fear could be until I was trapped in that car with Devon and his friends. With each second that passed, I could feel the terror in the pit of my stomach growing with every beat of my racing heart. Like a wild animal, it clawed at me, demanding to be freed. I tried to fight it, tried to focus on something other than the men next to me with their guns sticking out of their waistbands, but no matter how hard I tried, the fear was still there. I could feel it pressing against my organs, digging into my ribs as it swelled inside of me. When it finally made its way to my throat, I looked up in order to open the passageway for some air to enter my lungs, and then I inhaled a shallow breath. It felt like I was suffocating when my mind drifted back to the moment Devon killed my sweet Anna Belle. A wave of nausea washed over me and I could taste the bile at the back of my throat, but I forced it down. Inhaling a slow cleansing breath, I tried to concentrate on steadying my heart rate, hoping that it would be enough to calm me down. I had to keep my wits about me and focus on the hatred I felt towards these men for kidnapping me and killing Anna Belle. I needed to use that anger to keep myself in control. It was the only way I was going to survive this.

I looked out the window, and even though it was getting dark outside, I knew we were entering Frayser, one of the roughest parts of Memphis. It was gang territory, known for its violence and endless illegal activities, and people who had any sense at all about them did everything they could to steer clear of the area. More than eighty percent of the people there lived below the poverty line, and it showed. Gang graffiti marked every street corner. The homes were so dilapidated that it was hard to believe anyone actually inhabited them, and the businesses were often dirty with old, dingy storefront signs that hadn't been updated in years. The streets were lined with various hoodlums searching for their next score, and prostitutes looking for their night's companion. I didn't know which was worse—the danger that was looming in the car with me or the danger that lurked in the dark alleys of the 'hood. I assumed I was safer in the car, thinking they wouldn't hurt me as long as my father got them their weapons, but then one of the men turned to me and said, "You sure are a pretty thing."

I didn't want to respond, thinking it would only open the door for more conversation, but he wouldn't stop looking at me. Feeling like I had no other choice, I replied, "Thank you."

"Ah, look at that. She's not only a looker. She's shy,

too." His eyes skirted over me, and a creepy grin spread across his face as he said, "You know ... there's just something about the quiet girls that gets to me."

"I think you're on to something, Leon." Marcus chuckled from the front seat. "It's the quiet ones who can surprise ya. Hell, some of 'em get downright freaky when they want to."

"What about you, cowgirl? Are you a lady in the streets and a freak in the sheets?" The conversation was going south fast, and I was scared that anything I said would just provoke him to take things further. When I didn't answer, Leon snickered, "That's all right. I'll find out for myself soon enough."

I knew exactly what he was insinuating and was horrified by the thought of him or any of the others raping me. I could feel the tears burning my eyes as I turned my focus back to the side window. I thought he would continue harassing me, but thankfully, the man sitting to my right leaned forward and said, "Give it a rest, Leon."

"What's wrong, Zeek? You don't want a piece of the prissy, little cowgirl?"

"What I want is for you to shut the fuck up for a minute and remember why she's even with us right now," Zeek growled. "You got any idea how pissed Malik is gonna be if we don't get that shipment to him?"

Devon cleared his throat as he looked up at the rearview mirror and glared at Zeek. "That's enough out of both of you."

The car grew quiet as we continued down Crump Boulevard. We'd been in that damn car for hours. Other than a few random stops, we'd just been driving around, and I was in desperate need of a break. I needed to stretch my legs and go to the bathroom, but I was too afraid to ask, fearing they might use the stop as an opportunity to do vile things to me. I shifted in my seat, doing what I could to relieve the pressure on my bladder as I studied the men who had kidnapped me. They were each dressed similarly in their puffy winter coats, loose-fitting jeans, and bright white sneakers, but they each had their subtle differences. Even though Devon appeared to be the youngest, it was clear that he was in command of the group. He wore a thick gold chain around his neck and a fancy watch on his wrist, and whenever he spoke, the others listened. Marcus was tall and lanky with narrow, dark eyes and dreadlocks that went down his back. While the look of him made me uneasy, it was Leon who worried me the most. He was muscled up like a linebacker with tattoos covering his hands and neck. There was a large diamond earring in his left ear, and his teeth were too big for his mouth, making him look even more threatening. I would've been even more terrified of him if it hadn't been for Zeek. Of all the men in that car, he was the only one who didn't seem completely evil. While it wasn't easy to see with his burly build and rounded jaws, there was a kindness in his eyes that the others didn't have, but I knew better than to count on him to keep me out of harm's way. He was one of them, and in the end, I was nothing but a pawn and none of them would think twice about putting a bullet in my head.

Just as another hour was passing by, Marcus looked

over to Devon and announced, "I need to take a piss and get some more smokes."

"You ain't the only one," Leon told him. "I need a cold one, too."

"I'll stop up here at the Little General," Devon told them as he put on his blinker. Once he pulled into the parking lot, he reached into his pocket and took out some cash. "Grab us a twelve pack, and I need some smokes, too."

Once Marcus took the money from his hand, he and Leon got out of the car and headed inside. Several minutes went by, and I was considering asking Zeek if he would let me go to the bathroom when Devon shouted, "What the fuck is taking them so long?"

After seeing that Devon was losing his patience, I decided to keep my mouth shut. I glanced over at the empty seat beside me and the door handle that was just a few feet away. For a split second, I actually considered trying to escape, but knew that Zeek would just grab me, preventing me from making it very far. Feeling hopeless, I sank back into my seat and sighed as I waited for Marcus and Leon to return. When I looked through the store's front window, I could see them standing at the cash register, and they were both busy flirting with a young woman behind the counter. My attention was on them when a red and black Camaro pulled up beside us. I wouldn't have thought anything about it if Devon hadn't muttered, "Damn. Looks like we might have trouble."

Zeek peered out his window as he asked, "How many does he have with him?"

"Can't tell. Looks like it's just three of them."

About that time, another car drove up behind us and parked, blocking us in. When Devon noticed what the driver had done, he growled, "Motherfucker."

I had no idea who these men were, but it was clear that Devon was shaken by their arrival. At first, neither Devon or Zeek moved. I could feel the tension radiating off of them as they sat there waiting for Marcus and Leon to return. I could hear Devon mumbling, "Come on. Come on."

Just as Marcus stepped outside, the Camaro's doors opened and three Hispanic men got out. Marcus's eyes grew wide as the men started towards him, but his confidence quickly returned when Leon stepped up behind him. Leon puffed up his chest, trying to make himself look more intimidating as he nudged Marcus in the side with his elbow. "Well, look what the cat dragged in."

One of the Hispanic men stepped forward, closing the gap between them as he snarled, "My brother, Carlos, was on his way home last night when a bullet found a way into his heart. You or your boys know anything about that?"

"I don't know shit about your brother." Leon's eyes narrowed as he said, "So, get the fuck out of my face before a bullet finds its way into your fucking head."

"Watch your tongue, amigo, or I'll cut it right out of your fucking mouth."

"You know better than to threaten a Hurricane, Mateo." Leon gave him a shove. "Now, back the fuck off, *cholo!*"

I had no idea what Leon had just called him, but it was obviously not a compliment. The Hispanic man cocked his head as he told Leon, "You just made a big fucking mistake, cabron."

I thought they were just spouting off until the guy pulled a knife out of his back pocket and aimed it towards Marcus. Marcus shook his head as he warned, "You don't want to do that, man."

Mateo ignored him and lunged forward, doing his best to stab Leon in the gut, and when he missed, a fight ensued. From there, everything moved in slow motion— their body movements, their facial expressions, and even their words. From what I could tell, Leon and Marcus were holding their own, but it didn't last for long. As soon as the men in the second car got out and joined in the action, Leon and Marcus were no longer able to fight them on their own. Knowing he had to do something, Devon shouted, "Come on, Zeek. Let's end this shit now."

And just like that, they opened their doors and jumped out, leaving me completely alone in the car. I had my chance for freedom, but I had to muster the courage to take it. My heart raced with apprehension as I took a quick glance around me, gazing for a brief moment at the door handle, and back to the front of the store. Customers were scattering as fists flew through the air, and it was at the moment that I convinced myself that Devon and his friends had forgotten about me. It was doubtful that I would get another opportunity like this, so I decided to go for it.

My hands were trembling as I eased over to the empty seat beside the door and lifted my hand up to the door handle. I inhaled a deep breath as I slowly pulled it towards me, opening the door with just a small crack. I looked back over to the fight once more, making sure they hadn't noticed what I was doing, and when I saw they were still fighting, I opened the door and slipped out. The cool night air hit me with a rush as I crouched down and carefully closed the door. On my hands and knees, I crawled towards the trunk, hoping that I could stay hidden long enough to put some distance between me and their car. I could feel the adrenaline pulsing through me as I made my way over to the next vehicle in the lot. It was amping me up, making me want to just make a run for it, but I couldn't take the chance on them noticing me. I inched a little further and managed to make my way behind a third car. I glanced back over to the others, and I could no longer see what was going on. Worried that my time was running out, I took a deep breath and took off running. I dug my feet into the pavement and ran harder, faster than I'd ever run before. I had no idea where the hell I was going, but I never checked up. I just kept moving forward, hoping against all hope that they weren't coming after me. And then it happened.

I was just about to skirt behind one of the local businesses when I heard a gunshot. Before I had a chance to think, I felt a searing, burning sensation in my side. I'd been shot. I had no idea how bad, but I didn't stop. Even though I could hear them calling out to me, I didn't look back. I just kept running, praying that they wouldn't shoot me a second time and darted behind a thicket of trees. It wasn't long until their voices grew faint, but I wasn't taking any chances. I kept moving, remaining in the shadows as I raced from one street corner to the next.

My lungs burned and my legs were growing numb, but I kept pressing forward. When I felt certain that I'd finally lost them, I slowed my pace, and for the first time since I took off running, I looked to see where I was. I didn't need a map to know that I was in the heart of Orange Mound—a place where a young, white female should never be alone, especially at night. Damn. I'd just jumped from the frying pan into the fire.

17

MURPHY

he club always comes first. Always have your brother's back. Don't make promises you can't keep. Don't buy into other people's bullshit. Never let your emotions rule you. Those were the rules I'd lived by for years. They'd gotten me through some tough spots, in and out of the club, so it didn't make sense why I'd ignored them when it came to Riley. But I had. To make matters worse, I knew I was doing it, and now, Murphy's Law had come back to bite me in the ass, and I had no one to blame but myself. I'm the one who'd let my guard down. I'd let her draw me in, making me want again —*need again*, and I couldn't deny that I liked the feeling. I liked it so much that I never thought about the possibility of something going wrong. I knew what was at stake. I knew I'd let my emotions rule me. I hadn't pushed harder. I hadn't stayed on Nichols until I'd persuaded him to do something about his lack of security, because I let my focus get blurred. Now, the time had come for me to pay the consequences for my actions. Only it wouldn't just be me who had to pay the consequences—my brothers would be there right by my side, putting their lives on the line to help me get Riley back. My chest tightened at the thought, and I eased my foot down on the accelerator, increasing my speed as we turned out of the Nichols' driveway.

Knowing time wasn't on my side, I called Riggs and quickly explained the situation with Riley and the motherfuckers who'd taken her. Just as I had hoped, he had an idea for tracking them down. "I need you to call Nichols. See if he'll give you the number he used to get in contact with Devon."

"You gonna try to track him with his cell?"

"Yeah, maybe, but there's no guarantees it'll work. If the guy is using a burner, I won't be able to pick up his location ... at least not with any real accuracy. But if the number we have is from a regular cell, then I can track him in a matter of minutes."

This wasn't exactly news to me. Hell, all the brothers used burners so no one could trace our calls or monitor our location. We weren't the only ones who took such precautions. Anyone who wanted to keep their identity a secret used burners—at least, anyone with half a brain would use one. If my gut was right, Devon wasn't thinking anyone would be checking up on him. "I'd guess a guy like him would think he was fucking invincible."

"Only one way to find out," Riggs replied. "Call me as soon as you get the number."

"Give me two minutes."

As soon as I got off the phone with Nichols, I called

Riggs back and gave him the number he'd given me for Devon. We were just leaving the city limits of Somerville when he finally returned my call. "You were right. The dumbass was using a regular cell."

"Does that mean you have his location?"

"Right now, he's on Park Street ... just a block or so down from the Little General. Looks like they're sitting in an empty lot."

"Damn. Right in the middle of Orange Mound," I grumbled.

"Yep. That'd be the place," Riggs confirmed.

"I'm headed that way now. See if you can find out anything about Devon and these fucking Hurricanes before we get there."

"I'm on it." Before he hung up, he said, "I'll let you know if his location changes."

"Thanks, brother."

As I soon as I hung up the phone, I shared Devon's location with the others, then glanced up at my rearview mirror to check on Shadow and Gauge. Just as I'd expected, they were right behind me and following my lead as I drove towards Park Avenue. The further we got into town, the more traffic I had to contend with. It seemed like everyone had forgotten how to fucking drive, and it was making me lose what was left of my patience. I whipped around several slow-moving vehicles, and by the time I got in front of them, my knuckles were completely white. The uneasiness building inside me was growing with such fervor and intensity that I was afraid I'd explode right there on the spot. It was almost too much to bear. I looked over to Blaze and wondered if he or Shadow would feel the same anxiety if it were their ol' ladies who'd been taken. Knowing them the way I did, I had no doubt that they'd be just as wound up as I was.

We were ten miles away from the location Riggs had given me when my burner started to ring. I put it on speaker so the others could hear as Riggs announced, "They're on the move ... They've left the empty lot and are headed east on Park. They're moving slow, like really slow. You'd think they were pushing the car instead of driving it, so you shouldn't have a problem catching up to them."

"Got it." As I gassed it, I told him, "We're getting close. Just now passing the Little General."

"By the way, I did some digging. The Hurricanes only have fifteen to twenty members, but they've made a name for themselves around the Mound. They have a habit of causing all kinds of mayhem over there." He paused for a moment, then said, "Hey ... they're just a few blocks ahead of you now. They've stopped at a red light on the corner of Park and Second. I still have no idea why they're moving so fucking slow."

"We'll find out soon enough." As I continued forward, I asked, "What else did you find out?"

"They've been in a turf war with Arañas, one of the local Hispanic gangs, for months. A guy named Malek Harrison seems to be running the show. He's a local. Folks were killed in a drive-by. He's got a rap-sheet, but nothing out of the norm there."

"We're coming up on First."

"Keep straight ahead. Looks like they're only a quarter of a mile or so ahead of you."

I was chomping at the bit as we grew closer. There was a nagging voice in the back of my mind that told me something wasn't right, and all I could think about was getting to Riley. The motherfuckers who had her better pray that she's okay, because if she wasn't—if they'd touched one hair on her head—I'd kill every last one of them. Just as we were coming up on the next stop sign, Riggs announced, "They're right in front of you."

"I see 'em."

The black BMW was in the middle of the fucking road with the back doors wide open. I stayed behind and watched as two guys came running out from the back alley. Paying us no mind, they hopped into the backseat and closed the doors. Blaze leaned forward and asked, "What the fuck are they doing?"

"Hell if I know."

When they started to move, I told Riggs, "I'll call you back."

I hung up the phone and slipped it in my pocket as I drove up on the BMW, just inches from their rear bumper. I put on my high beams and eased up even closer. It was difficult to see through their dark-tinted windows, but I was almost certain that Riley wasn't in the backseat. I turned to Blaze and asked, "Do you see Riley in there?"

"I don't know, brother. It's hard to tell for sure."

The BMW continued to creep forward ever so slowly, but they quickly caught on that we were tailing them when they started to pick up the pace. It wasn't long before we were in a high-speed chase. Hoping to lose us, they took several quick turns, but I hung tight. There was no way in hell I was letting them get away, not without knowing if Riley was in the car with them. When we came up on a side road, Blaze turned to me said, "We aren't getting anywhere with this bullshit."

"We gotta try something different." Gunner eased up from the backseat and said, "Hell, nobody uses this road anymore. Let's see if we can shoot out their back tires."

He was right. The road was practically abandoned with no one around for miles, but I wasn't sure that shooting the tires out was a good idea. "I don't know, brother. Riley might be in there, and if they wreck, she might get hurt."

"A few bumps and bruises are better than a bullet," Blaze replied flatly. "We need to end this thing, brother."

"Do it."

Blaze rolled down his window and a rush of cold air filled the truck. I took in a deep breath, hoping to slow the adrenaline that was surging through me as he leaned out the window and took his shot. The back end started to swerve back and forth as the driver appeared to lose control of the vehicle. They hit a loose patch of gravel, causing it to jar to the side, and seconds later the car took a nose dive into a ditch. As we pulled up next to them, I could see that the front end had crumpled like a fucking can when it hit the embankment, and smoke was billowing out from under the hood, making it clear that the car was done. I parked on the side of the road and killed the engine. As Gunner started to open his door, he warned, "Take it slow. You know these guys are packing."

I didn't want to take it slow. I wanted to run straight for that damn car and open every fucking door to see if

Riley was inside, but there was no way in hell that was going to happen. None of us knew what was waiting for us in that car, so we had to play it safe. I took a deep breath and let my instincts kick in. "I'll take the front with Blaze. You and Shadow cover the back with Gauge and Rider."

"You got it."

My heart was beating a mile a minute as we eased out of the truck with our weapons drawn. We all quickly realized that those dark-tinted fucking windows weren't going to work in our favor as we proceeded towards the car, but that didn't stop us from advancing forward. With every step we took, they were watching us. I could feel it. Their eyes were making the hairs prickle across my skin. Blaze slowly came around me. He was just a few steps away from the front passenger side door when it flew open. My breath caught when one of the men shot several rounds in his directions, but as I expected, Blaze was sitting on go. As soon as the asshole pulled the trigger, Blaze returned fire, killing him instantly. He kept his weapon trained on the vehicle as he growled, "Fuck!"

Tension crackled around us as the driver's door slowly started to open. With my gun aimed at the driver, I shouted, "Don't even think about it, asshole."

"Hold up!" He held his hands in the air like he was being arrested and pleaded, "Don't shoot!"

"Get out of the car!"

"All right, man. Just go easy on that fucking trigger!"

I kept my gun aimed at his head as he stepped out of the car and closed the door behind him. "Who's in there with you?"

"My boys ... Leon and Zeek." The rear doors eased opened, giving us a clear view of the two men in the back-seat. "Your fella done killed Marcus."

"Marcus should've known better. No one shoots at a brother from Satan's Fury and lives to tell about it."

"What the hell is all this about? We ain't got no riff with the Fury," he grumbled as he wiped the blood from his brow.

"You do now." I looked him dead in the eyes as I asked, "Where the fuck is she?"

"Who?"

I was done wasting time. I stepped towards him and placed the barrel of my gun under his chin. "The Nichols girl. Where the hell is she?"

"What the fuck is it to you?" he snapped.

And with that, the dam broke. I moved my gun from his chin to his thigh and pulled the trigger. Curses were streaming from his mouth as I growled, "I'm not going to ask you again!"

His eyes widened and his breath was ragged as he answered, "I got no idea, man."

"You seriously want to go down that road?"

His hands clung to his wound as he said, "I ain't lying, man. She took off running when we stopped to get some smokes."

"Running? There's one of her and four of you. How the hell did she get away from you?" Blaze asked.

"We had a run-in with a few of the Arañas."

"What kind of run-in?" Gunner pushed.

"The kind where we kicked their ass in front of the fucking Little General where ever'body could see. We showed those assholes who's running shit around here," he boasted.

"Um-hmm. I'm sure you did," I scoffed. "And the girl ran off when you were fighting with this Arañas gang?"

"Yeah. That's how it played out," he admitted. "We've been looking for her, but the bitch ain't nowhere to be found."

"How long have you been looking for her?" Blaze asked.

"An hour or so ... maybe more." His voice was strained as he said, "You ain't gotta worry though. White girl out running in these streets is as good as dead."

I knew how bad things could be, and my mind was suddenly bombarded with all the possible dangers Riley might have to face while running through the dark streets of the 'hood. It would be a fucking miracle if she managed to survive. I looked at the man before me, and rage rushed over me when I thought about everything he'd put her through—killing her horse, kidnapping her, and exposing her to this kind of danger. Thinking about it infuriated me. Riley should've been home. She should've been sleeping soundly in her bed, but instead, she was out there in the streets alone, fighting to survive. And it was all because of him. He was the reason that she was in harm's way. He was the reason I might never see her again, and he'd pay the ultimate price for doing so. I looked him in the eyes as I brought my gun up to his head, and his dark eyes widened in horror when he heard the familiar click of my finger engaging the trigger. When his lifeless body dropped to the ground with a hallowed *thud*, one of the men in the backseat started cursing and shouting like a wild man. "What the fuck? He fucking killed him. Goddamn it! He really killed him."

I didn't move. I didn't speak. I just stood there staring at Devon's body sprawled out on the ground, wishing I could kill him all over again. Seemingly concerned, Shadow stepped up beside me and asked, "You okay, brother?"

"I'm better now," I grumbled. The truth was, I'd been hanging by a thread, and the thread just broke. I had no idea where Riley was and it was fucking with my head. "We've gotta find her."

"What do you want us to do?"

Before I could answer, my burner started ringing. When I answered, I heard Nichols' voice say, "She just called me."

"What?"

"Riley just called me," Nichols repeated.

Relief washed over me. "Is she okay? Where is she?"

"Not sure. Somewhere in Memphis." He was talking fast, making it difficult to understand. "She gave me the address, but I got no idea where it is."

"Give me the address."

He paused a moment, then replied, "It's ... uh ... 1329 South Park Street."

"Got it. I'm headed that way now."

"Good. And Murphy. You need to hurry." I could hear the urgency in his voice as he went on, "Riley said she was okay, but the lady that was with her mentioned something about her being shot."

"Shot?"

"Yeah. Apparently, one of Devon's guys shot her when

she was running away from them. I have no idea how bad it is, so you …"

I didn't wait for him to continue. "I'm leaving now."

When I hung up the phone, Shadow looked over to me and said, "We've got this. You and Blaze go find Riley."

I glanced back over at Devon and his mangled car. "But we've gotta figure out something to do with …"

"Don't worry about that." Shadow cocked his eyebrow and gave me one of his looks as he assured me, "I've got a plan."

I didn't argue. I knew I could trust Shadow to handle it, so I gave him a quick nod and headed for the truck. Despite knowing she was alive, I couldn't get to her fast enough. I needed to see for myself that she was truly okay, and even that wouldn't be enough to extinguish the rage that was still burning deep inside of me.

18

RILEY

I'd always heard that you shouldn't judge a book by its cover, and it was only after running for my life and finding refuge in the most unlikely of places when I fully understood the truth of that statement. I'd always assumed that the people who settled in areas like Orange Mound were shady at best. From the rumors I'd heard and the things I'd seen on TV, I thought they were all criminals who had no pride in the way they lived. All those assumptions were proven wrong when I was trying to find a place to hide and found myself in Ms. Claudine's backyard. I'd been on the run for hours—first, from Devon, and then from various derelicts I'd encountered on the streets—and I was beyond exhausted. I had no phone, no money, and no one to turn to for help. I was screwed.

Thankfully, I was wearing my hoodie and used its hood to cover my head and my face. I'd hoped that it would help me blend in and not attract any unwanted attention as I wandered from one bad area to the next. My side was aching, my feet were throbbing, and my head was pounding. I was in desperate need of a place to just sit and rest for a few minutes when I came up on a row of small shotgun-style homes. Like most in the area, the paint was peeling off the exterior, the roofs were completely worn-out, and the small front porches were caving in. It didn't look like the safest place, but it was quiet, really quiet. I hoped that was a good sign and started towards the house on the end. With its pale blue color and the ivy on the metal columns, it seemed to be the most inviting. When I reached the driveway, I slipped through the fence and inched my way to the back of the house.

I was about to step into the backyard when I heard someone say, "Hey, you!" I quickly turned and looked up onto the porch only to find a woman standing there in the dark. She was clutching her little pink bathrobe as she tried to protect herself from the cold night air. "What you doing back there?"

"Umm ... I'm sorry for trespassing, ma'am." My voice trembled as I removed my hood and said, "I wouldn't have come through your yard like this, but I'm lost. I don't have my phone or any money ..."

Before I could finish my sentence, she interrupted me, "Of course, you's lost, child" She chuckled under her breath. "Pretty young white girl like yourself ... Hmph. No way you'd be in this neighborhood if you wasn't lost as a goose." She motioned her hand over to the front steps. "Come on in here, child, and let's get you warmed up."

Tears of relief filled my eyes as I started towards her. "Thank you."

"You don't have to thank me for doing what's right." She waved me forward as she fussed, "Now, come on. You'll catch yourself a chill."

"Yes, ma'am." As I walked up the old wooden steps, I was worried that they wouldn't be able to withstand my weight, but thankfully they held up until I reached the top step. When I got closer, I could finally see she was older than I realized. Her hair was short and completely gray, and she had these kind dark eyes and a welcoming smile that immediately put me at ease. I smiled as I introduced myself, "I'm Riley Nichols."

"It's good to meet you, Riley. I'm Claudine Brown." She opened her front door and placed her hand on the small of my back as she led me inside. "Make yourself at home."

As soon as stepped inside, I was engulfed in a feeling of warmth and comfort like I'd never felt before. I thought it had something to do with the house, but as I looked around, I had my doubts. There was an old tan sofa sitting under the front window and a small, round coffee table, with various magazines stacked neatly on the edge, positioned in front of it. A leather recliner was nestled close to a potbelly stove, and her oversized Bible was laying wide open on the small TV tray next to it. As I stood there looking around the small, quaint living room, I quickly realized that that feeling of comfort had little to do with the actual house or the furnishings inside. The feeling was all her. It was her kindness, her compassion and faith that loomed in the air, and you could tell that she was a special lady simply by the way she took care of her little house. While her belongings were far from new, most of them were very worn, it was impeccably clean and everything was carefully put in its place. I was standing there, soaking it all in when Ms. Claudine came up beside me and asked, "Can I get you something to drink?"

I nodded. "Yes, ma'am. That would be wonderful."

"I have some sweet tea"—she padded towards the kitchen with another offer—"or would you like something warmer like coffee?"

"Tea would be fine."

When she returned with a glass of iced tea, she asked, "You look like you've had quite a night. Are you in trouble or something?"

"Yes, ma'am." I took a sip of my tea before I continued, "I had some bad men chasing me, but I'm pretty sure I lost them."

"Bless your heart. You're lucky you were able to get away from them." Concern filled her eyes as she asked, "Should we call the police or something?"

Knowing I could never tell the police the real reason why Devon and his gang were after me, I quickly answered, "No. That's not necessary, but it would be great if I could call my father."

"Of course." She pointed to the wall by the kitchen as she said, "The phone is right over there."

"Thank you so much." I rushed over and lifted the receiver. I couldn't remember Dad's cell phone number, so I called the home line. It rang over and over, and I was beginning to think no one was going to answer when I heard my father's voice say, "Hello? Nichols residence."

"Daddy?"

"Riley!" His voice cracked with emotion as he asked, "Is that you?"

"Yes, Dad. It's me."

"Thank God," he gasped. "Are you okay? Did they hurt you?"

"I'm fine, but I need you to come get me."

"Of course. Just tell me where you are."

I turned to Claudine and asked, "What's your address?"

"Oh, goodness, child." Her eyes were wide with worry as she stood there staring at my hip. "Did you know that you're bleeding?"

I glanced down at my side and grimaced when I saw the blood stains on my hoodie. With the excitement of getting off the streets, I'd all but forgotten about it. I studied the hole where the bullet had ripped the fabric, but I was too scared to look at my actual wound. "Yes, but I don't think it's bad. It's not hurting like it was."

"You sure 'bout that?" She stepped towards me, trying to get a better look, and then gasped, "Oh, sweet Lord. It looks like you've been shot."

"Wait ... Did she just say that you've been shot?" my father shouted through the phone.

"I'm fine, Daddy. Really." I looked at Claudine and asked her again, "I need your address."

Without seeking my permission, she lifted my shirt so she could get a better look, and as she inspected my wound, she answered, "It's 1329 South Park Street. Tell him it's the fourth house on the left."

I repeated what she'd told me to my father, and just before I hung up the phone, he asked, "Are you sure you're okay?"

"Yes, I'm sure."

"I'll be there as soon as I can, sweetheart."

As I hung up the phone, Ms. Claudine asked, "Did those men do this to you?"

"Yes, ma'am. They did."

"Well, it looks like you got lucky. It looks like it just grazed you." When she started down the hall, I got curious and lifted my hoodie. I was relieved to see that she was right. The graze was two to three inches long, and with its dark edges, it looked more like a burn that an actual bullet wound. I was still studying it when she came back into the room with her hands full of Band-Aids, gauze, and hydrogen peroxide. She motioned me into the kitchen as she said, "Come on over here and let's get that cleaned up."

I walked over and watched as she laid everything out on the table. When she was ready, I lifted my shirt and said, "Thank you, Claudine."

"What did I tell you about thanking me, child." She poured some hydrogen peroxide on a rag. Before she pressed it against my skin, she said, "This is going to sting a little."

Boy did it ever—and I gasped. "Dang. That hurts worse than I thought."

"Why don't you tell me how this happened?"

"It's a long story."

"I got nothing but time, dear."

I didn't go into exact detail, but as she went back to cleaning my wound, I told her about Devon and his friends kidnapping me. I told her how we'd stopped at the gas station and the men who appeared shortly after. She seemed surprised that they hadn't succumbed to shooting each other, but didn't interrupt as I told her about my escape. When I started telling her about how I'd hidden from them, I found myself thinking how odd it was that I used to love playing hide and seek when I was a kid. When I was hiding from Devon, I couldn't have been more terrified, but when I was younger, it wasn't like that. I used to love that tingly feeling you'd get whenever you were waiting for someone to find you, and the way your breath would catch whenever they were drawing near.

As I told her about all the different places I'd hidden and the moment when I thought they were going to find me. I'd done just like I had when Hunter and I were kids. Whenever he got close, I would remain perfectly still and hold my breath. I didn't care how long it took. I wouldn't budge until he'd admitted defeat. I'd done the exact same thing with Devon, and it actually worked. They eventually left the alley, and I was finally able to get out of the dumpster. By the time I got to the part where I showed up in her backyard, she had finished cleaning my wound. As she put on the last Band-Aid, she said, "It sounds like you gave those boys a run for their money."

"Yes, ma'am, I did."

"Well, I'm glad you did." She looked down at my

blood-stained hoodie and said, "Let me see if I've got something else you can put on."

"That would be great."

She went back down the hall, and moments later, she returned with a heather-gray sweatshirt. As she offered it to me, she said, "I think this should fit you."

"I'm sure it will be fine." I slipped it over my head and smiled when I saw the Memphis Tigers logo. "Are you a fan?"

"Not really. I have a hard time keeping up with all the teams. My grandson left this the last time he was here."

"Well, thank you for letting me borrow it."

After I helped her clean up, I followed her back into the living room. We were just about to sit down when there was a knock at the door. Claudine looked over to me and said, "I imagine that's your father, but just to be safe, you stay put."

I nodded. "Okay."

She made her way over to the door, and when she opened it, I heard her ask, "Who are you?"

"I'm a friend of Riley Nichols. Is she here?"

At the sound of his voice, I eased over to the door. Lincoln and one of his brothers were standing on the front porch, and I rushed towards him. "Lincoln! What are you doing here?"

"Your father called." He wrapped his arms around me, hugging me tightly as he asked, "Are you okay? Did they hurt you?"

"I'm fine."

"Your father was worried that you had been shot or something."

"Yes, but it wasn't bad ... just a scratch. Claudine bandaged me up."

With a look of apprehension, he replied, "Okay, but you're going to need to see a doctor to be sure."

"I'm really okay. I promise. Right now, I just want to go home."

He lowered his mouth to mine, kissing me briefly before he looked down and said, "Then, let's get you home."

I gave him one more quick squeeze before I turned back to Claudine and said, "Thank you for everything, Ms. Claudine. I don't know what I would've done if you hadn't helped me like you did."

"You are welcome, sweet child." Concern filled her voice as she warned, "Now, get on home and get you some rest."

"Yes, ma'am. I will."

Before we left, Murphy handed her a slip of paper and said, "Thank you for taking care of her like you did. If you ever need anything, help is just a phone call away."

"I know there's more to the story I heard, but a sweet girl like her has no business running around these streets." She took the paper from Murphy's hand and slipped it in her pocket, then she said, "I sure hope you'll see that it doesn't happen again."

"It won't happen again. You have my word on that."

Lincoln reached for my hand and led me outside. As soon as we reached the truck his friend got in the back-seat, and when he closed the door behind him, Lincoln pulled me towards him and wrapped his arms around me once more. He didn't say a word as he buried his head in the side of my neck. He just stood there and held me close, and with every second that passed, I could feel the weight of my fear and heartache starting to fade. That's when it hit me. I couldn't believe that I hadn't realized it sooner. The signs were all there, but I hadn't let myself see them. Maybe I was just too scared to believe it, but as I stood there in his arms, I could feel it with every beat of my heart. I was in love with Lincoln, and in his arms was exactly where I was meant to be.

19

MURPHY

I never would've dreamed that the sound of someone's voice could get to me the way hers did. I didn't think it was possible for anyone to have that kind of power over me, but the second I heard my name from her lips, everything around me came to a screeching halt. The panic, the anger, and the fear that had been raging inside of me stopped all at once, and I was finally able to breathe again. There was no one else on the planet that could make me feel the way she did, and I was going to do whatever it took to protect her. When we started driving towards the club-house, Riley looked over to me and asked, "Where are we going?"

"To the clubhouse." I looked over to her and added, "You'll be safe there."

"What about my dad and Hunter?"

"You can call them when we get there." As I looked back towards the road, I told her, "But you might want to prepare yourself. He isn't going to be happy that I didn't bring you home."

"Honestly, I don't really care if he's mad. None of this would've happened if ... It doesn't matter."

"I know you're upset with him and you have good reason, but he was really worried about you tonight. There's no doubt that he loves you."

"I know he loves me, and I love him, that doesn't change anything. I still don't want to go back there, at least not yet." She turned and looked out the side window as she said, "It's never going to be the same ... not after what they did to Anna Belle."

Before I could respond, Blaze said, "It'll take some time, but eventually it'll get better."

When Riley turned to face him, I said, "I don't believe you've met Blaze."

"No, I haven't ... at least, not officially. I remember seeing you on the day you came out to the farm to see my father."

"I remember that day all too well." He chuckled as he told her, "You left quite an impression on my brother that morning."

"He left one on me too." She looked over to me and smiled. "And it wasn't necessarily a good one."

"Yeah, well, I'm pretty sure I redeemed myself."

"That, you did." When we finally pulled up to the gate with one of our prospects keeping guard, she asked, "Is this your clubhouse?"

"It is."

She leaned forward to get a better look while she mumbled, "Man, it's really something."

Riley's eyes were wide with wonder as we got out of the truck and started inside, making me wish I'd brought her by sooner. I knew meeting the guys and seeing how we lived would be a lot for her to take in, especially considering everything she'd been through, but I didn't have a choice. Under the circumstances, it was the safest place for her to be, and it would give me a chance to speak with Gus. She was silently checking everything out as we walked down the hall towards his office. It was late, but I'd texted him when we left Claudine's to let him know we were on our way. When we walked in, he was at his desk with Moose, our VP, sitting across the room on the leather sofa. He stood up and smiled then said, "So, this is her?"

"Yes, sir. This is Riley." I looked over to her as I explained, "This is our club president, Gus."

Gus extended his hand as he told her, "It's nice to finally meet you, Riley. I've heard a lot about you."

"It's nice to meet you too." As she shook his hand, she told him, "I wanted to apologize for that night I called your cell. I wasn't thinking very clearly that night."

"Yeah, I might've heard about that." He chuckled. "From what I hear, you had another rough night tonight."

"I've definitely had better," she scoffed. She looked down at her dirty, tattered clothes and said, "I'm kind of a mess."

"Don't give that a second thought. We're just glad to see that you're okay, especially Murphy." Then, Gus turned to Blaze. "Why don't you take her out into the hall so I can have a minute with Murphy?"

"You got it."

As they started toward the door, Gus told Riley, "If you need anything, anything at all, you just let one of us know."

She nodded. "Thank you."

Once they were outside, I closed the door behind them and said, "I know I fucked up. As soon as that asshole opened his mouth, I just lost it."

"I heard."

"I've got no excuse for letting that asshole get in my head like that. I was just wound up and he said the wrong-fucking-thing at the wrong-fucking-time." I shook my head in disgust as I told him, "I let you down, I let the club down, and I let myself down."

"You're being too hard on yourself. The guy had it coming, Murphy." His brows furrowed as he threw his hands up in the air. "There's not a brother in this club who wouldn't have done the same thing if they were in your shoes."

"Maybe so, but that doesn't change the fact that I put the club in a bind." I ran my hands through my hair as I continued, "To make matters worse, Shadow's out there cleaning up the mess I made! And we all know, I left one hell of a mess."

"We've talked to Shadow. He's handling it, Murphy," Moose interjected.

"But, he ..."

"You need to take a breath, son, and remember what this club is all about," Moose interrupted. "Shadow isn't doing anything you wouldn't have done for him."

"Moose is right." He looked me in the eye as he said, "This isn't a one-way street, Murphy. Your brothers have your back, just like you've always had theirs."

Knowing they were right, I nodded as I told them, "Understood."

"Good. Now, go tend to your girl," he ordered. "She's going to need you after what she's been through."

"I know, but what are we going to do about her father and ..."

"We'll go over everything in the morning when we meet for church," he answered.

"Okay. I'll see you both then."

I walked out of the office, and when I got into the hall, I found Blaze and Riley standing there waiting for me. Riley had a concerned look on her face as she asked, "Is everything okay?"

"Yeah. Everything's fine."

Blaze looked over to me as he said, "She called her father to let him know she was okay."

"Good. How did that go?"

"You were right about him not being happy that I wasn't coming home." She shrugged. "But overall, I think he understood my reasons for not wanting to be there."

Blaze put his hand on my shoulder and said, "If we're good, I'm going to head out."

"Yeah, we're good."

"Good deal." As he started for the door, he said, "I'll see you two in the morning."

Once he was gone, I took Riley's hand in mine and led her down the hall. We hadn't gotten far when she asked, "Where are you taking me?"

"To my room."

Surprised, she asked, "You have a room here?"

"All the brothers do."

When we got down to my room, I opened the door and she followed me inside. We walked past the king-sized bed and her cheeks reddened when I led her into the bathroom. She waited silently as I reached into the shower and turned on the hot water before facing her. "I thought a hot shower might do you some good."

"I would love a shower, but I don't have any clean clothes."

"I'll find you something." I lowered my hand to the hem of her hoodie and carefully lifted it along with her t-shirt over her head. Just as I had dropped it to the floor, I noticed a large, make-shift bandage of gauze and Band-aids situated just above her hip. "This looks like it's more than just a graze."

"It's really not. Claudine just got carried away with the bandages." She looked up at me with those gorgeous eyes and tried to assure me, "So, don't freak out about this. I'm fine."

I'm fine. She kept saying those words over and over, and each time she said them, I found them harder to believe. There was no way she could be fine after all she'd been through. I slowly peeled the bandage back and grimaced at the sight of the wound. While it could've been much worse, it gutted me to see that she'd been hurt. "You don't have to put up a brave front for me. You can talk to me."

"I know I can talk to you and I will, but I just can't right now." Riley reached for my hand as she said, "I just

L. WILDER

want to put it all out of my head ... even if it's just for a little while. Is that okay?"

"It's more than okay." I grabbed Riley and pulled her towards me, and once she was close, I lowered my head and whispered, "Just know that I'm here for you. Now or whenever you need me."

She lifted up on her tiptoes as she briefly pressed her lips to mine. As she dropped her hands to the waistband of my jeans, she replied, "I need you now. Take a shower with me."

I wasn't sure that it was a good idea, especially with her wound, but there was no way in hell I could refuse her, not when she was looking at me like that. Once we were both undressed, I removed the rest of her bandage then led her into the shower, pulling her close as the warm water cascaded down our bodies. After several moments, I turned her around, flattening her back against my chest as I reached for the bottle of body wash. I poured some onto the sponge before lowering it to her shoulder, carefully washing her back then slowly making my way down her arms. Taking extra care around her wound, I washed her abdomen, then inched my way up to her breasts. Needing more, Riley reached for the sponge I was using and tossed it, then she took my hands and placed them on her breasts.

A low moan vibrated through her chest as I spread the soapy bubbles all over her, my palms gliding over her smooth, soft skin. I plumped her breasts in my hands, and as I ran my thumbs over her nipples, she ground her ass against my growing erection. My hands moved with a mind of their own, roaming and exploring Riley's flesh, sliding effortlessly across her body as she moaned her approval. While trailing kisses along her shoulder, my fingertips slid lower and lower along her belly, and I was careful not to hurt her as I eased my hand between her legs. When the tips of my fingers raked across her center, her head eased back against my shoulder as she widened her stance, urging me on. I placed my mouth close to her ear as I whispered, "You like my hands on you, don't you?"

"God, yes!" she hissed as she rocked her hips forward against my hand.

"Good. Get used to it." I moved my fingers in slow, methodical circles against her clit, increasing the pressure with each turn of my hand as I told her, "Because I like having my hands on you."

I eased my fingers deep inside her, massaging the spot that drove her wild, and a pleasured moan escaped her sexy mouth as I started to move my fingers faster and harder. Riley's body grew tense as the sounds of her soft whimpers started echoing through the room. I removed my hand from between her legs and held her close as her breathing slowed. Moments later, she turned to face me, and with her eyes sparkling with mischief, she said, "My turn."

I watched with fascination as she lathered the body-wash between her palms. Riley was so damn beautiful. It was hard to believe that she was mine. "You do know, you're mine, Riley."

Looking at me through eyes filled with desire, she

placed her hands on my chest and worked in painstakingly slow strokes to soap my skin. I could tell from the gleam in her eyes that she was enjoying having free rein to savor the moment. Her hands dropped to my stomach, and I thought I would lose all control. Repeating my words back to me, she looked up at me as she whispered, "I hope you know that ... you're mine, too."

My cock twitched as her hands trailed up my legs. I was trying my damnedest to let her wander and enjoy, but she wasn't making it easy, especially when her greedy eyes dropped to my growing erection. Her soapy fingers gently wrapped around me, moving ever so slowly up and down my thick shaft. Trying to keep from coming unglued, I pressed my hand against the cold tile and growled, "Fuck!"

I never knew that a woman's touch could turn me on as much as hers did. After several long, firm strokes, she stepped to the side, letting the water rinse the soap from my body. Her hands slid along my skin, taking the rest of the suds with them ... and the last of my patience. As she finished, she ran her fingertips once again over my chest, looking up invitingly into my eyes, she said, "You have no idea how much I want you right now."

And at that moment, the dam broke. I turned off the water as I looked down at her and said, "You've got me."

I took her hand and led her out of the shower and handed her a towel. Once we were dried off, I lifted her into my arms, carried her to my room, and lowered her onto the bed. Then reaching into my bedside drawer, I took out a condom, and she watched with anticipation as I rolled it down my thick, throbbing shaft. Her flushed body squirmed against the mattress as she pleaded, "Hurry."

I had no intention of making her wait. Hell, I wanted her just as much as she wanted me. I lowered myself down on the mattress and settled between her legs as I dropped my mouth to hers. I felt her tremble beneath me as I slid deep inside her. I stilled, not because I wanted to, but because I had to. She felt so fucking good, so wet and tight, that I had to fight the urge to come right then and there.

"You feel so damn good," I growled as I finally started to move. Her nails dug into my lower back as her hips rocked against mine, meeting my every thrust. I began to drive deeper and harder until I found the pace that we were both desperate for. I could feel the pressure building, forcing a deep, needful growl from my chest. She tilted her ass towards me, grinding harder against my cock as the sounds of my body pounding against hers filled the room.

Her head reared back as she moaned, "Oh, Lincoln, don't stop!"

Her body began to tremble as her orgasm took hold, her muscles contracting around me and pulling me deeper. I continued to drive into her, and a sense of satisfaction washed over me when I finally heard the sound of air gushing from her lungs and felt her body fall limp beneath me. My growl echoed around us and my entire body tensed as I came deep inside her. After several moments, I managed to collect myself, discard the condom in the small basket next to the table, and lay down on the bed next to her. Instinctively, she curled into my side with her head on my shoulder and her leg resting on top of mine. Once our breathing slowed, I looked down at her and said, "There have been times in my life when I've been afraid, but I've never been as scared as I was tonight. I don't know what I would've done if something had happened to you."

"I'm here now, Lincoln, and I'm not going anywhere." She placed her hand on my chest as she asked, "Do you know why?"

"Tell me."

"Because I love you." Her eyes locked on mine as she added, "And right here with you is the only place I want to be."

"I love you, too, Riley Nichols. More than I ever thought possible." I leaned down, and just before I kissed her, I said, "I've made mistakes, plenty of them, but taking this chance with you wasn't one of them."

We shared a kiss that was long and tender, then I got up and gave Riley some clothes to put on. Once she was dressed, I called Mack to come down to the room. After he checked her wound, he bandaged her back up and gave us some ointment that would help with the healing. As soon as he was gone, we both got back in bed. Riley settled back into the crook of my arm and it wasn't long before she drifted off to sleep. For hours, I just lay there watching her sleep until I finally gave in to my own exhaustion. The next morning, she was still sleeping soundly next to me, and it pained me that I had to leave her. I could have spent the entire day with her wrapped in my arms, but I had club business that had to be tended to before that could happen. Careful not to wake her, I eased out of bed, threw on my clothes, did my business in the bathroom, and slipped out the door. When I got down to the conference room, Gus was already there with Riggs, Blaze, and Shadow. "Where is everybody?"

"They'll be here soon. We wanted to go over everything with you before they got here." Gus waited for me to be seated before he turned to Shadow and said, "Why don't you start things by telling him what happened last night with Devon and his crew."

Shadow looked to me as he asked, "Do you remember what Devon told us about how Riley got away from them at the gas station?"

"Yeah. They were in some fight with some gang."

"That's right. This gang apparently thought they had something to do with the death of one of their members." Shadow handed me a slip of paper. "Riggs told us last night that they'd been in a turf war with the Arañas for months."

"Yeah, I remember."

"I figured we might as well use their war to our advantage." He leaned back in his chair and crossed his arms then said, "After we took care of the two assholes in the backseat, we put Devon back in the car and torched it. Then we waited until the flames died down and tagged the side door with the Hurricane's gang sign. After we crossed it out, we wrote over it with the one Arañas uses, making it look like a retaliation strike."

"Damn. That was good thinking, brother."

"Maybe. I'm just worried about Nichols getting blowback from it. Malek was expecting a shipment from him, and now, he's got four of his members dead and no guns. He's not going to be happy about that."

"Who's to say that Nichols didn't already give them the weapons?" Blaze turned to Riggs and asked, "Can you check Devon's phone records and see if he made any calls after he left the farm?"

"I already did. There were no calls coming in or out."

"Then, there we go." Blaze sounded pleased as he continued, "Nichols gave them the shipment and it was stolen when they got hit."

"None of that matters anyway," Gus interjected. "I talked to Nichols this morning. I've put the family and their farm under club protection. He's given me a list of his buyers, and I'll see to it that they know he's no longer in business."

"Seems rather generous of you," Moose told him as he walked into the room. "Is this because of his daughter and Murphy, or is there another reason?"

"He got me in contact with his supplier. We'll be able to buy direct and save a shit-ton of money. Is that reason enough for ya?" Gus grumbled.

"Yeah, that'll do just fine."

"Glad you think so. Before the others get here, I wanted to make sure we were all on the same page with Rider. He's been prospecting for just over a year, and I think he's more than proven himself to be an asset to the club."

"Agreed," we all replied.

"Then, we'll put it to a vote."

With that, the others started rolling in, and church was set into motion. As I sat there listening to my brothers talking back and forth, I felt like all the pieces of the puzzle were finally falling into place. I had my brothers, my family, and against all odds, I had my girl, so I guess the saying is true—"In the end, we only regret the chances we didn't take."

I had always loved being at the farm. It was my home. Full of precious memories and feelings of warmth and happiness, it was a place of childhood dreams and fantasies. Whenever I was there, I felt safe and loved, free from judgement and disparagement. It used to be my happy place, but that all changed the day Devon kidnapped me.

It had been three weeks, and I was still haunted by the memories of everything that had happened, especially the moment when he killed Anna Belle. I could still see the cold look in his eye when he lifted his gun in the air and pulled the trigger. I hadn't even realized what he'd done until her lifeless body fell to the ground. There's no way to describe the heart-wrenching pain I'd felt when I realized she was gone. Even back when my father gave her to me, I never thought of her as just a horse. She was my gate to freedom. Whenever I was riding her, it was like magic. I could hear the thuds of her hoofs hitting the ground, and as they grew faster, the wind would start to whip around me. Seconds later, she would hit that perfect stride, and I would feel like I was soaring through the air, looking down at all the splendors of nature. After that, it wouldn't take long until all my troubles seemed to just slip away.

I didn't think I could bear to go back to the farm, knowing that Anna Belle was no longer there—that Devon had stolen that magic from me—but Murphy encouraged me to try, telling me I shouldn't let him steal any more of my joy. So I followed his advice, and each time I returned, it became a little easier. I was standing by the training ring, watching Travis adjust Requiem's saddle, when my father walked over to me. He put his arm around me and said, "I know there'll never be a horse that could ever replace your Anna Belle, but I wanted you to know ... when Requiem has his first filly, she's yours."

"That's very sweet, but you don't have to do that, Dad."

"I know I don't have to, sweetheart, but I want to." His eyes were filled with remorse as he continued, "I want you to have a reason to keep coming back here."

"I don't need a horse for that. I have you." The past few weeks had been really hard on him as well. He was riddled with guilt over what had happened, and he wanted desperately to make things right. I reached up and gave him a hug. "You're all the reason I need."

"I'm glad to hear you say that." Then he glanced over at Lincoln. "I'm not always the best at admitting when I was wrong, but I have to say, I was wrong about him."

"Yes, you were. I tried to tell you." I turned and watched as Lincoln hovered over the grill as Moose and T-Bone tended to the ribs. Rider was standing next to them, proudly sporting his new Satan's Fury cut, and they were all drooling over Moose's BBQ. Since Dad and his property were now under club protection, the brothers had been spending a lot of time at the farm. Gus wanted to make sure that my dad didn't have any trouble like he'd had with Devon, so there were always a couple of prospects keeping watch and Riggs had installed an unbelievable security system. Dad had been looking for a way to thank them for everything they'd done, so he used Requiem's arrival as an excuse to invite them all out for a BBQ. The guys jumped at the chance to have some of Moose's famous cooking. It also gave them a chance to celebrate the fact that Rider had been patched into the club, so they all came out with their families and they brought enough food to feed an army. When Lincoln saw that I was watching him, he smiled at me with one of those smiles that made my heart leap in my chest. "I'm just glad you finally figured it out."

"What can I say? I'm a protective father. You can't really blame me for that." Before I had a chance to respond, he asked, "So, how are you liking it over at his place?"

My new living arrangement was a touchy subject. Dad had made it clear from the start that he wasn't happy about me moving in with Lincoln, but like Lincoln, he was concerned about my safety and didn't put up much of a fuss. Having me gone hadn't been easy for him, but he was trying. "It's good, Dad ... really good. I'm happy there with him."

I could hear the sincerity in his voice as he said, "I'm glad you are. Really I am. You deserve all the happiness in the world, Riley, and if you don't find it there with him, you're always welcome to come back home."

"I know, but I love him, Daddy. My future is with him," I explained.

"I'm hoping this farm is a part of your future, too."

"Of course, it is, and you and Hunter are, too." I looked over at my brother and smiled as I watched him ride Requiem around the training ring. He was dressed in his best Wrangler jeans and ropers and his favorite cowboy hat, so there was no doubt that he was trying his best to impress Gigi, one of girls from the night he was arrested for stripping. I could see why he would be interested in her. Not only was she really sweet, but she was stunning with long blonde hair and beautiful green eyes. Unfortunately for him, he wasn't the only one who'd noticed. She was leaning against the fence, watching Hunter do all his fancy riding tricks, when Gunner came up and stood beside her. I knew right away there was going to be trouble. Gunner was a handsome thing, and if he took a liking to Gigi, she'd know it. When Hunter noticed that they were talking, he led Requiem over to the fence and asked her, "You doing okay?"

"I'm doing great." She smiled brightly as she ran her hand down Requiem's forehead. "He's really beautiful."

"Isn't he though?" Gunner winked at Hunter as he said, "He's almost as purty as you, Hunter."

Hunter's neck grew red with embarrassment. Trying

his best to rebound, he quickly replied, "Is that right? I didn't think you were the type to notice."

"Hard not to when you're all gussied up like that, but don't worry. You're not my type." Gunner looked over at Gigi and let his eyes slowly skirt over her as he said, "I have a thing for beautiful blondes."

Knowing he needed to get Gigi away from Gunner as quickly as possible, he looked over to her and said, "I'm going to put him back in the stables. I'll be right back."

"Okay." She smiled brightly, making me wonder if she'd been effected by Gunner's flirting. "I'll be here waiting."

I watched my sweet, frustrated brother as he rode Requiem out of the ring and into the stables. Hoping I might be able to help him out, I looked over to Gunner and said, "I'm sure Hunter could use some help with Requiem. Do you mind giving him a hand?"

"I'm sure he can handle it." I just stood there staring at him and eventually he got the hint. With a defeated sigh, he said, "But I'll go make sure."

"Thank you, Gunner. I appreciate it." I turned and gave Dad another quick hug, then said, "I better go see if I can help out in the kitchen."

As I started towards the house, he told me, "Let me know if there is anything I can do to help."

"You know I will."

Over the past couple of weeks, I'd gotten a chance to meet all of the brothers and their ol' ladies, and it was easy to see why Murphy loved them the way he did. Each of them had their own strong personality traits, especially the men. Blaze was very personable, but he clearly liked things done his way. Shadow was quiet and protective, especially of Alex. And Riggs was unquestionably smart and could do things with computers that would blow your mind. It was hard to believe that so many alpha-males could live under one roof without killing one another, but I think it helped that they had such awesome counterparts. When I walked into the kitchen, Kenadee was taking a pie out of the oven, and it smelled like heaven. "Oh, my. That smells incredible."

"I wish I could take the credit, but this one is Reece's." As she placed it on the counter, she looked over to Reece and asked, "Did you just bring the one?"

"No. There's another one in the fridge if we need it."

"You know we're going to need it, especially with T-Bone around."

She giggled as she replied, "You're not kidding. The man's like a garbage disposal!"

Alex came up beside me and said, "This place is incredible, Riley. I would've loved growing up on a farm like this."

"I love it, too, but it does have its downsides."

"Oh, really? Like what?"

"Like getting up at the crack of dawn to feed the horses. Cleaning out the stalls. Taking care of a sick mare in the middle of an ice storm. Rounding up horses in the rain." I shrugged. "It's just part of being out on the farm."

"I'd be okay with everything except getting up at the crack of dawn," Alex replied with a grimace.

"That would be bad, but I think cleaning out the horse stalls might be worse." Reece looked down at her son sitting in his high chair as she continued, "I've changed enough diapers to know that wouldn't be any fun."

"So, what about living with Murphy? How's that going?" Kenadee asked. "I'm sure it's been an adjustment."

"It'd definitely been an adjustment. I didn't realize how loud it was in the city until I moved there, but it's nice to be so close to school and Murphy ..." my mind drifted back to the night before when we'd made love by the fire, and I couldn't help but smile, "... he's been wonderful."

"You're lucky. Murphy is one of the good ones." Reece looked down at her son as she said, "He looks out for the people he cares about, almost to a fault, and he's absolutely wonderful with Tate. You should've seen them together at the cabin. It was a sight to see."

"I hate that I missed that."

Before I could continue, Alex moved over to the window and said, "Hey, y'all might wanna take a look at this."

Reece, Kenadee, and I rushed over to see what she was talking about, and I was surprised to see that Hunter was with Gunner, and they were leading Starlight out to the training ring. "What are they doing?"

"I'm not sure, but it looks like Gunner might be planning to take his first ride," Reece replied with a giggle. "He's been talking about giving it a try all week."

"Oh, man. I've gotta see this," Alex announced as she raced to the door.

Reece quickly grabbed Tate before we all followed Alex outside, and by the time we made it out to the training ring, all of the brothers had gathered around to watch the show. Hunter brought Starlight to the middle of the ring, and he was talking to Gunner when I rushed over to them. "Hunter, what do you think you are doing?"

"Nothing," he answered innocently. "Gunner said he wanted to take a ride, so I'm just helping him out."

Knowing he was just trying to get back at Gunner for flirting with his girl, I gave him a warning look and said, "I don't think this is a good idea."

"The man wants to ride. Who am I to stop him?" Hunter pushed.

"Don't worry, Riley. I've been watching Travis and your brother for weeks now." Sounding way too confident, he looked up at Starlight and said, "I'm good."

"Maybe so, but I don't think Starlight is the right horse for you to ride your first time, Gunner. She has a habit of—"

"Don't worry, Riley. I know what I'm doing." As he started to put his foot, in the stirrup, he looked to me and said, "I just put my foot in this stirrup thing, pull myself up, give her a little nudge, and use the strap things to steer. Nothing to it."

"It's a little more complicated than that, Gunner." I liked Gunner. He was sweet with a boyish charm, but at times he thought he was invincible. Hoping that I could change his mind before he did something he'd regret, I suggested, "Maybe you should try one of the older horses first ... one that's a little easier to ride."

With that, Gunner placed his foot in one of the stirrups and lifted himself up onto the saddle. It was clear from his expression that he felt quite pleased with himself. "See, I didn't do so bad, now did I?"

"You did great." As I reached for the reins, I asked, "How about I lead you around the ring a couple of times ... just until you feel comfortable?"

He glanced back at his brothers, and when he saw that they were all watching, he shook his head. "Thanks, Riley, but I've got this. You'll see."

"Okay, but don't say I didn't warn you."

He gave her a little nudge with his heel, and to my surprise, she started around the ring without any issue. In fact, she seemed perfectly content as Gunner took hold of the reins and led her around the ring. When they went by me, he looked over and smiled. "I think I was meant to be a cowboy."

"Give her a little gas," T-Bone goaded from the fence.

Taking the bait, Gunner nudged Starlight in the side with his heel, and as instructed, she started to pick up the pace. I couldn't believe it. Starlight must have taken a liking to Gunner. I'd thought that Hunter's plan was backfiring, when all of the sudden, Gunner nudged her again, only harder this time. At first she complied, but just as he was making it around the ring for the third time, she let out a grunt, letting me know that she'd had enough. I started towards them, hoping to stop her before she reacted, but it was too late. She lifted up on her hind legs and sent Gunner sailing. His arms flailed through the air until he hit the dirt with a hard thud. He fell back with his body sprawled out, making me worry that he'd really been hurt. We were all completely silent as we stood there waiting for a sign that he was okay, and thankfully, after several seconds of uncertainty, we finally got one. Gunner sat up, shook his head in utter disgust, and then pulled himself up off the ground and dusted himself off. Once the guys were certain that he was okay, they started heckling him. "Way to go, cowboy!"

Hunter went over to him and took a hold of Starlight's reins. As he led her out of the ring, Gunner shouted, "You knew she was going to do that shit, didn't you?"

"Yep!"

"Um-hmm. You got one coming, Nichols."

Hunter smiled as he replied, "I'm sure I do, but it was totally worth it."

The guys were razzing Gunner pretty hard, but their teasing quickly stopped when Moose announced that the food was ready. The girls and I put all the food out on the picnic tables, and everyone sat down to eat. My heart fluttered when Murphy settled in next to me and slipped his arm around me, kissing me on the temple. I leaned into him and smiled as Gus stood up to say the blessing. As soon as he was done, everyone started to fill their plates. We sat there for hours, eating and talking, and as I looked around at all of Lincoln's brothers and their families, I realized that Murphy's family was quickly becoming an important part of my life. With their help, I was making new memories at the farm, good ones too, and I looked forward to all the memories yet to come.

EPILOGUE

*S*ix Years Later...

OVER THE YEARS, Riley and I had gone horseback riding a hundred times. While she loved riding the bike, it could never replace the feeling she had when she was on the back of a horse. I understood why she loved it like she did. There was something remarkable about being on the back of such a massive creature—feeling his power beneath you as he pounds his hooves into the dirt, and being so close to nature with the birds singing in the trees and the rush of water passing by in the stream. It was an incredible feeling, and the only thing that could make it better was being able to share it with Emma Grace, my beautiful, inquisitive three-year-old daughter. We'd only been riding for a few minutes, when she looked up at me and asked, "Why can't Momma come?"

"You know why."

"It's not fair." A pout fell upon her adorable face as she said, "I want Momma to come wit' us."

"I know you do, but it won't be long until she can ride with us again."

"And she can ride Belle?" she asked hopefully.

"Yes, sweetheart." Belle was Requiem's first mare, and she was by far the most beautiful horse I'd ever laid my eyes on. Riley was hesitant to accept the horse as a gift from her father, thinking it would be too hard after what had happened to Anna Belle, but inevitably, Riley fell in love with her and decided to keep her. I looked down at Emma as I told her, "We're almost to the bridge."

"Are we going to da' water?" Excitement filled her voice as she told me, "I want to see the fishes."

"Yeah. We're going to the water, but we can't stay long. We need to get back and help Grandpa with the gate."

"Okay." When we got up to the edge of the river, I led Belle a little farther up so Emma could have a good view of the water. "Closer, Daddy."

"We're close enough." I held on to her as she leaned closer, trying her best to spot a fish. Thankfully, it wasn't long before a school of minnows came swimming up to the edge. I pointed towards the water as I asked her, "Do you see them?"

"Yes! I see 'dem, Daddy!"

I gave her a few minutes to watch the fish, before telling her, "We gotta go, but I'll bring you back soon."

"Wit' Momma?"

"Yes, Emma." I chuckled, "With Momma."

We rode back to the farm, and when we got to the

stables, Riley was checking in on one of the two newest foals. She slowly waddled over to us and asked, "How was the ride?"

"It was good." I lifted Emma Grace and carefully lowered her down to the ground. As Riley reached for her hand, I got down off of Belle and started leading her into one of the empty stalls. "Emma Grace wasn't happy about you not being there with us."

Riley looked down at her daughter as she said, "You know I would've come if I could."

"I know." Emma Grace placed her hands on Riley's full belly as she said, "My broder' is coming soon."

"Yes, he is, and until he gets here, it isn't safe for Momma to ride," Riley explained.

"Okay." When she noticed Riley's father sitting on the front porch, she shouted, "Pawpaw!"

We both watched as she ran over and jumped into his arms. He gave her a big hug as he twirled her around in a circle, making her squeal with laughter. Riley's lips curled into a smile, and just like the first time I laid eyes on her, she looked absolutely breathtaking. Unable to resist, I took a step towards her and placed my hands on her hips, pulling her to me. Her eyes locked on mine as I lowered my mouth to hers, kissing her long and hard, and when we finally came up for air, she gasped, "What was that for?"

"Couldn't help myself." I placed my hand on her stomach as I asked, "How you feeling?"

"Like I'm about to deliver a basketball," she joked. "But I'm making it okay."

"Just a few more days."

"I know." With love in her eyes, she looked down at my hand on her belly and said, "He'll be here before we know it, and then we'll really be in trouble."

"Nah, together we can make it through anything," I assured her. "Even two toddlers."

"I hope you're right."

"If I'm not, at least we'll have each other."

"You know what?" Riley wound her arms around my neck. "I love you."

"And I love you too." I lowered my mouth to hers and kissed her once more. "More than I ever imagined."

THE END

MORE TO COME FROM SATAN'S FURY MC- MEMPHIS!

For information about upcoming releases and chances to win giveaways, be sure to sign up for my newsletter. Just click on the following link- http://eepurl.com/dvSpW5

ACKNOWLEDGMENTS

I am blessed to have so many wonderful people who are willing to give their time and effort to making my books the best they can be. Without them, I wouldn't be able to breathe life into my characters and share their stories with you. To the people I've listed below and so many others, I want to say thank you for taking this journey with me. Your support means the world to me, and I truly mean it when I say appreciate everything you do. I love you all!

PA: Natalie Weston

    Editing/Proofing: Lisa Cullinan- editor, Rose Holub- Proofer, Jenn Allen- Proofer

    Promoting: Amy Jones, Veronica Ines Garcia, Neringa Neringiukas, Whynter M. Raven

    BETAS/Early Readers: Kaci Stewart, Tanya Skaggs, Charolette Smith, Neringa Neringiukas

Street Team: All the wonderful members of Wilder's Women (You rock!)

Best Friend and biggest supporter: My mother (Love you to the moon and back.)

A short excerpt of Riggs: Satan's Fury MC-Memphis Book 3 is included in the following pages. Blaze and Shadow are also included in this Memphis series, and you can find all three on Amazon. They are all free with KU.

EXCERPT FROM RIGGS: SATAN'S FURY MC

PROLOGUE

Riggs

I WAS NEVER one of those guys who bought into all that love at first sight bullshit. Hell, it's not like it's hard to get shit mixed up when your hormones get to talking. A raging hard-on over a smoking hot chick can do things to a man's head and make him think he's feeling something he's not. The next thing he knows, he's convinced he's met *the one*. I'd been worked up over my fair share of gorgeous women, but never once had love ever crossed my mind, especially over some chick I didn't even know. The notion seemed completely absurd *until her*.

Some of my brothers and I had taken Blaze down to Sullivan's to celebrate his birthday. We hadn't been there long when I noticed her sitting at one of the back tables with several of her friends. They were all beautiful women, dolled up in their Saturday-night-best, but none of them held a candle to her.

With just one glance, she had me completely captivated, making me oblivious to everyone else in the room, including my brothers who were sitting right next to me at the bar. I couldn't explain it. There was something different about her—something that drew me to her like nothing I'd ever felt before. No matter how hard I tried, I couldn't take my eyes off her. For almost an hour, I sat there just watching her, studying the way her mouth moved when she spoke, how her head fell back every time she laughed, and the way those crystal blue eyes of hers sparkled with desire every time they locked on mine. *Fuck.* Just seeing that glimmer of interest made me want to throw her over my shoulder and carry her right out of that bar, claiming her as mine in the most carnal way.

I got my window of opportunity when I noticed an empty seat right beside her. A couple of her friends got up to go to the restroom, so I grabbed two beers and walked over to her table. When she noticed me coming in her direction, she quickly turned and whispered something to her friend, which made me wonder if I'd misread her look of interest, until she glanced back over to me with a nervous smile. Damn. That smile got me right to the core. I tried to keep my cool as I casually sat down next to her and asked, "Is this seat taken?"

"It is now," she answered in a playful voice.

The blonde sitting next to her leaned forward and her words were slurred as she mumbled, "Damn, Reece. You were right. He is *hot*."

Her eyes widened as she scolded, "Danielle!"

"What? You were just saying how good-looking you thought—"

"*Danielle!*"

Ignoring her friend's protest, Danielle pointed her finger at me as she said, "Girl, you need to get you some of that."

"Oh, good Lord. Will you stop?"

"What? Take a look at him ... those pretty green eyes and a hot bod to match." The chick was practically drooling as she just kept at it, "Hell, I'd bang him in a heartbeat."

Reece turned to me with a mortified expression and said, "Please, ignore her. She's normally not so *obnoxious*. It's just the alcohol talking."

"It has a way of doing that." I motioned my hand towards their collection of empty beer bottles and shot glasses. "Looks like you ladies are having a big time."

"One of my sorority sisters just got engaged, so we're out celebrating with her. It's been fun, but I'm the backup DD. I'm just biding my time until I can get out of here."

"Backup DD?"

"Yeah." She shrugged. "We've had a few mishaps with designated drivers over the years. My girls aren't exactly reliable when it comes to hot guys and booze."

"I can see where that could be a problem." I chuckled as I lifted the beer I'd brought over for her. "I guess you won't be needing this."

Before she could respond, one of her friends said, "Go for it, Reece. I'm good. I haven't had a drop all night. I can make it another hour or two."

"Okay, but I'm holding you to that." Reece took the beer from my hand and said, "Thank you."

Remembering that she mentioned her sorority sister, I asked, "You go to school around here?"

"Yes and no. I've been going to U of M, but I'm about to transfer to Vanderbilt University in a couple of weeks. I'm hoping to get my law degree there."

I couldn't imagine why someone so sweet and innocent would want to become a lawyer, but I could hear the passion in her voice when she talked about getting her degree. For one reason or another, it clearly meant something to her. She'd just started to say something else when she stopped and glanced down at my hand. I was fidgeting with my old Zippo lighter, causing it to cast a flicker of sparks every time I raked my thumb over the flint wheel. It was something I'd started doing after I'd quit smoking. When I realized it had caught her attention, I smiled and said, "Sorry. Nervous habit."

"Nervous habit, huh? Are you saying I make you nervous?"

"I have a feeling I'm not the first guy you've made feel that way."

She smiled brightly as she replied, "I don't know about that, but if it makes you feel any better, you make me pretty nervous, too."

"I'll take that as a good sign."

"Yes. I'd say that's a very good sign."

I twirled the lighter in my hand, and just as I was shoving it into my back pocket, the intro to "Faithfully" started to play. She let out a deep breath and smiled as she said, "I just love Journey. They have to be my all-time favorite band."

"Can't disagree with you there."

Danielle leaned across the table and mumbled, "Hey ... you. Mr. Tough Guy with the hot bod. You need to get out there and dance with my girl ... show her a *good time*."

Before she had a chance to argue, I extended my hand. "You heard the lady."

"But ..."

"Girl, if you don't dance with him, then I will." Danielle snickered.

I chuckled as Reece took my hand in hers and said, "I'm going. *I'm going.*"

"Good ... and don't forget to do a little smooching and ass grabbing while you're out there," Danielle ordered.

Reece looked over to the group's designated driver and laughed as she announced, "No more booze for Danielle!"

"Why you gotta be like that?" Danielle protested. "I'm just trying to help a sista out!"

Without responding, Reece followed me out to the dance floor, and like we'd done it a hundred times before, she slipped her arms around my neck while mine wrapped around her waist. It was at that very moment I knew I was in trouble—the kind of trouble that makes a man rethink his very existence. I'd never thought of myself as one of those guys who'd settle down and spend the rest of their life glued to one chick. I liked things to be easy. Get in. Get out. No feelings. No expectations. No complications. But after just one touch, she had me thinking of white picket fences and fucking station wagons. I couldn't explain it, but there was something about the way her body was so in sync with mine. It felt so right, like a void that I didn't know existed had suddenly been filled, and I was desperate to hold on to that feeling. When she rested her head on my shoulder, an odd sensation of comfort and ease washed over me. Then, she looked up at me and pressed her full, perfect lips against mine, and I was done. I had an over-whelming desire to claim every inch of her body, and there was no way in hell that I was going to let her leave that bar with anyone else but me. I was thankful that after a few more dances, some heavy flirting, and several long, seduc-tive kisses, I'd managed to persuade her to go somewhere quiet. Seconds later, Reece was on the back of my bike, and we were pulling out of the parking lot.

While that bike ride to my apartment and the nights that followed were unbelievable, they'd both come to haunt me in ways I could never have imagined. The sex was incredible, nothing else compared, but that wasn't even the best part of our weekend together. It was the conversations we shared that left the biggest impression on me. Wrapped up in each other's arms, we told stories that filled my small bedroom with laughter and unex-pected emotion. I felt a connection with her—the kind of connection you'd expect from someone you'd known a lifetime—making me wish the moment could last longer. Unfortunately, all good things come to an end.

As Reece stood there in my doorway, looking up at me with those gorgeous blue eyes, stammering through her heartfelt goodbye, I'd never seen a more beautiful sight. I leaned against the doorframe, staring at the faint blush that still lingered on the crook of her neck, and when she handed me a slip of paper with her number and address, I wanted to reach for her, do whatever it took to persuade her to stay. Sadly, another night just wasn't in the cards. While I thought I'd found the girl I'd been looking for, that all my dreams had come true, I would soon discover that she didn't feel the same. She walked out that door, got in her cab, and never looked back.

1

RIGGS

*W*hen I was kid, I never would have imagined that I'd become a hacker for one of the most notorious MCs in the South. Back then, I didn't even own a motorcycle, much less know how to ride one. I'd been too busy screwing around with video games. It was a way for me to escape my mundane existence and pretend that I was in another world, fighting battles that would alter my imaginary universe. In my small town, I'd been known as the best around. I'd win every popular game, conquering all the levels, and there wasn't a kid around who could touch me—until Tommy Demarco. I thought he was lying when he started boasting about the secret levels and cheats he'd uncovered, so I went to his house to see it for myself.

He showed me how he'd managed to circumvent the manufacturer's restrictions on the gaming system, enabling him to hack into all of my favorite games. I was blown away. Seeing what he'd been able to do set a spark

inside of me, and I became obsessed with learning everything there was to know about hacking. It wasn't easy. I
didn't have someone there to teach me, so I had to figure
it out on my own. Thankfully, I had a knack for it, and
with each new challenge, I became even more driven to
succeed. In a matter of months, I had learned all the ins
and outs of coding: with just a few manipulations, I'd
uncovered a whole lot more than the same secret levels
and cheats that Demarco had bragged about.

There was something about cheating the system that
intrigued me, and I found myself wanting to know just
how far I could go. I had altered the settings on my
phone, my cable box, and my parents' computer, and that
was just the beginning. It wasn't long before I was
hacking into anything and everything, discovering a
world that surpassed my wildest imagination—a world
most people didn't know existed. While my folks had no
idea what I was really up to, they could see I had a gift;
although, they'd hoped that I would use it to go to college
and find myself an acceptable career. I gave it a try but
quickly learned that I already knew more than most of
my professors. After just three semesters, I became bored
with the whole college thing and ended up dropping out.
While my mother wasn't happy about my decision, my
father seemed to understand and trusted that I'd find my
way. It took some time. I'd spent those next few months
bouncing around the city, working odd jobs here and
there, but eventually, I'd proven my father right and
found the place I was meant to be.

I had been bartending at one of the pubs downtown
when Gus, the president of Satan's Fury, came in for a

drink. I was surprised to see him at my bar—and was even more surprised when I found out that he'd actually come there looking for me. After hearing about a job I'd done for one of his associates, he decided to offer me a chance to prospect for the club. Even though I'd worked with some pretty dangerous folks over the years, I'd never been approached by someone with his kind of notoriety. While there'd never been any witnesses to any of their crimes, or a mention of their names on the news, everyone in Memphis knew you didn't fuck with the members of Satan's Fury. Maybe it was all speculation, but these men had made quite a name for themselves, instilling a sense of fear throughout the city. Assuming the rumors were true, I'd always done my best to keep my distance, and being so close to their president had put me on edge. I couldn't help but wonder if I truly had what it took to prospect for men like them, but my curiosity outweighed my doubt and I'd decided to take him up on his offer.

Over the past ten years, there hasn't been a day that has gone by that I've regretted that decision. The ties I'd forged with my brothers were stronger than blood, and there was nothing I wouldn't do for them, including hacking into the FBI's data base to find information on our latest threat. It was something I'd done many times before, but on this particular morning, I was experiencing some difficulty getting past one of their security walls. I'd just come up on an unexpected end-to-end encryption, when Big asked, "Have you thought about trying a DDoS?"

Big was a member from our chapter out in Washington State and a fellow hacker. He'd come to Memphis with several of his brothers to help us track down Josue Navarro, a cartel boss who'd recently become a threat to our pipeline. Like the rest of us, he was eager to get the information we'd need to locate him by any means necessary. His suggestion to use a DDoS didn't come as a surprise, but unfortunately, the method meant using multiple computers to simultaneously flood their system with data. Knowing it wasn't a feasible option, I replied, "I considered it, but setting that up would take time and equipment that we just don't have."

"Damn." He let out an exasperated sigh, then turned his attention back to his computer. Since he was considered to be a high stakes criminal, we both knew that the FBI would have the most updated information on our guy, but time wasn't on our side. It wouldn't be long before the FBI picked up on our presence, and then we'd be fucked. "What about using a RAT? We just need the right agent to take the bait, and then we'd have full control of his computer. We could use it—"

Before he could finish his thought, I told him, "I know how a RAT works, Big."

"Sorry, brother. I'm just thinking out loud."

"No problem." I knew he was only trying to help, but this wasn't my first rodeo. "Besides, I think I've got it. Just give me a second."

The last time I'd hacked into their system, I'd left a type of malware that would be secured deep within their data base, and as soon as I activated it, I'd have access to all the data it had saved on the main frame. Big leaned towards me, and once he'd seen what I'd done, he smiled and said, "A root-kit? Fuck, I hadn't thought about that."

Seconds later, I'd gotten in and started searching for Josue Navarro's file—an infamous cartel boss who had the kind of power to take down anyone who got in his way. None of us considered him a potential threat until Shadow's ol' lady, Alex, mentioned his connection with her father's business. As soon as Gus discovered that he was her uncle, he put the entire club on high alert. Alex's father, Rodrigo Navarro, was one of the largest drug traders in California, and when he decided to expand his business, he set his sights on Memphis. Not only was this our territory, it was also the city where his daughter had been hiding for over eight years. Alex had done her best to keep her real identity, Alejandra Navarro, and her location a secret. She hadn't even told Shadow the truth, hoping that her father wouldn't be able to find her. Unfortunately, her efforts were in vain, and three days ago, he came after her. The club tried to step in, but Rodrigo was taken out before we ever had a chance to get our hands on him. Regardless of who'd killed Rodrigo, Gus knew that his brother would be looking for someone to hold accountable, and he wanted the club to be prepared if the blame fell on us.

As soon as I got the information we needed, Big turned to me and asked, "What do you need me to do?"

I handed him a sheet of paper. "Here's a list of their latest stakeouts. See if you can figure out what's what, so we know where to focus our search."

We spent the next few hours collecting everything we could find on Navarro, and once we had it all sorted, we took what we'd found to Gus. When we made it down to his office, he was sitting behind his desk talking to Cotton, the president of the Washington chapter. Gus looked over to me and asked, "Were you able to find him?"

"Yes and no. I already knew that his cartel, the Parcas, was based out of Colima, Mexico, but I didn't realize how powerful he'd become. He's been shipping his product all over the world, and his distribution to the US has nearly tripled over the past year. The FBI has been trying to shut him down. From what we could tell, Robert Hamilton, the agent who's been investigating him, was getting close to taking him down—*too close*."

"And?"

"Navarro has gone underground. There's been no sign of him in months."

Big handed Gus the file as he said, "Looks like the agent was able to catch a break when he connected Navarro to the murder of six men in Cancun. They were competitors of his, and this motherfucker not only had them tortured and killed, he hung their bodies from local bridges for everyone to see."

"That's one way to make an impression," Cotton grumbled. Over the years, Cotton had made his own impression with the brothers in our charter. He was one of the youngest presidents, but he'd proven himself to be a strong, unwavering leader. I wasn't surprised when he came up with the idea for several of our clubs to join hands and create a pipeline for our gun distribution. It has been a profitable venture for all those involved, and I had no doubt that Cotton wasn't happy that the last run had been put on hold. He leaned back in his chair with a blank expression and grumbled, "If he's smart, he'll cut his losses with his brother and move on."

Gus cocked his eyebrow as he replied, "I highly doubt that's going to happen."

"The Parcas are at war with a neighboring cartel, the Mortales." Big shook his head as he continued, "Hell, the entire city of Colima has turned into a battle-ground with bodies turning up left and right. It's only been a couple of days, so maybe there's a chance that he's been too distracted to even know that his brother is missing."

"Maybe, but it won't be long before he gets suspicious." Gus reached into his pocket for a cigarette, but just before he went to light it, he said, "We know Josue is the lead man. Hell, I bet Rodrigo never made a move without consulting him first."

"Have to agree with you there. There's no doubt Josue knew his brother was in Memphis, and I'd go so far as to say that he knew he'd found out that Alex was here and was planning to bring her home."

Gus took a long drag off his cigarette as he replied, "You're probably right about that."

"Which means, he'll come looking for her when he can't contact her father," Big added.

"Fuck. We don't have time for this shit," Gus barked. "Our buyers are waiting on their shipment, and we can't keep putting them off."

"We can't put the pipeline in jeopardy. It's too important," Cotton replied.

Big glanced over to me and suggested, "Maybe we can

come up with a way to distract him ... just long enough for us to get this run carried out."

"I was thinking about that myself." Cotton looked over to Gus as he continued, "You know, you told me everything that happened with Rodrigo and how he was killed, but you never told me what you did with his remains."

Confusion crossed Gus's face as he answered, "Didn't think that was important ... but you don't have to concern yourself with that. My boys are careful about that shit. It would take some fucking miracle for anyone to ever find his body, including Josue. For all anyone around here knows, he's still alive and well. You have my guarantee on that."

"That's just it. Maybe it would be better if Josue actually knew he was dead."

"What are you getting at, brother?" Gus asked.

"If we moved Rodrigo and his men to some remote location and staged the scene to look like someone else had killed him, then there would be an investigation. It would only be a matter of time before the news hit the papers, and Josue would be all over it. He'd want to find out for himself who'd killed his brother, and—"

Before he could finish, Gus said, "He'll go looking there instead of searching for him here."

"Exactly. I'm not saying that it'd take heat away completely, but it might buy us some time to pull off the run. Once we get that out of the way, then we can figure out the best way to take this motherfucker down."

I was skeptical at best and didn't hesitate in asking, "You really think that could work?"

"No idea." Gus stood up, and he sounded optimistic as he continued, "But it's worth a shot. Let's go discuss it with the others."

We all followed Gus out of his office and down the hall to the bar. When we walked in, Shadow, T-Bone, and Murphy were at one of the tables drinking a beer with Stitch and Clutch. After each of us grabbed a beer of our own, we went over and joined them. Murphy, our sergeant-at-arms, had an amused look on his face when he asked Clutch, "So, you're saying you've got yourself a weak stomach?"

Clutch reached for his beer as he said, "Poke fun all you want, but you didn't hear the conversation I just heard. I've always known Stitch could do some fucked up shit when he had to, but listening to him talk about it with Shadow shed a whole new light on the situation. There's no way in hell I'd ever want to be on the other end of what they were dishing out."

Shadow hadn't been our club's enforcer for very long, and he'd taken Stitch, the Washington chapter's longtime enforcer, down to his holding rooms to see if he had any suggestions. Against Clutch's better judgement, he went along for the ride and ended up getting more than he bargained for. "I never knew all the things that you could do with a simple set of pliers. Damn. That shit is gonna give me nightmares," he said with his face contorted into a grimace.

I'd met Clutch just over a year ago when he was establishing the route for our pipeline. At the time, our lead mechanic was laid up after a motorcycle accident, and Clutch ended up staying several weeks to help out in the garage. While he was here, we all learned that he had a great sense of humor, so I had no problem busting his chops. "Too bad your girl, Liv, isn't here to hold your hand."

"I wish she was ... I don't think I'm gonna sleep a wink tonight."

"Don't worry. Stitch will be there to keep you safe." I chuckled.

"Is that supposed to make me feel better? Because it doesn't."

I was just about to respond when Gus interrupted me. "I hate to break up this riveting conversation, but we have an important matter that needs to be discussed."

The group fell silent as they listened to Gus share Cotton's plan. It was clear from their expressions that Shadow and T-Bone were intrigued by the idea, but Murphy was a little skeptical. "You do realize that these guys have been buried for days."

"Yeah, but it might not be as bad as you think," T-Bone argued. "We wrapped and bound each of them in plastic. That, along with the lime we poured over the ground, should make it easier to move them."

Shadow turned to Murphy and said, "Really, it doesn't matter the shape they're in. We'll torch the place and burn whatever is left of them."

"You've got a point there." Murphy chuckled. "We'll need to leave the cops a few clues to help them identify Navarro, otherwise it could take weeks to sort through the ashes."

"No doubt about that."

Murphy looked over to Gus and asked, "So, when you wanna do this?"

"The sooner the better."

We spent the next half hour making arrangements to relocate Navarro's remains. While none of us believed that it would keep Navarro's brother at bay forever, we all agreed that it would buy us some time—time that we would use to prepare for the day he came knocking at our door.

YOU CAN FIND the rest of the story on Amazon under Riggs: Satan's Fury MC- Memphis, along with Blaze and Shadow.

Made in the USA
Monee, IL
19 February 2020